W9-BUC-991

dream queen

also by

betsy thornton

A SONG FOR YOU

A WHOLE NEW LIFE

DEAD FOR THE WINTER

GHOST TOWNS

HIGH LONESOME ROAD

THE COWBOY RIDES AWAY

dream queen

BETSY THORNTON

MINOTAUR BOOKS
A THOMAS DUNNE BOOK
 NEW YORK

This is a work of fiction. All of the characters, organizations, and events portrayed in this novel are either products of the author's imagination or are used fictitiously.

A THOMAS DUNNE BOOK FOR MINOTAUR BOOKS.
An imprint of St. Martin's Publishing Group.

Printed in the United States of America. For information, address St. Martin's Press, 175 Fifth Avenue, New York, N.Y. 10010.

www.thomasdunnebooks.com
www.minotaurbooks.com

Library of Congress Cataloging-in-Publication Data

Thornton, Betsy.
Dream queen / Betsy Thornton. — 1st ed.
p. cm.
ISBN 978-0-312-60205-5
1. Newcombe, Chloe (Fictitious character)—Fiction. 2. Brothers and sisters—Fiction. 3. Missing persons—Fiction. 4. Women detectives—Arizona—Fiction. 5. Arizona—Fiction. I. Title.
PS3570.H6645D74 2010
813'.54—dc22

2009047480

First Edition: August 2010

10 9 8 7 6 5 4 3 2 1

TO MY LITTLE SISTER SALLI,

FAR AWAY

acknowledgments

Thanks again to Tom Glass, my trusty weapons expert; and to Radianne Porter for some long-ago medical advice; to Elizabeth Atwood Taylor for expert editing; to Harold Heck aka Hogan for the car stuff; and to my agent, Vicky Bijur, for sticking by me when I really needed her.

dream queen

chapter one

IT SEEMS LIKE SO VERY LONG AGO THAT I boarded the plane from New York City to Arizona, on my way to the small town of Dudley, to see my little brother Danny and to see Hal, and, in fact, it *was* long ago—before cell phones came along and BlackBerrys and computers you could Google on. *Hal.* I am haunted by him still—I think of time and how elusive it is, how yesterday is no further away than tomorrow. As if by an act of will we might silence our ambitions, our desires, so that we no longer go forward but slip backward over that barrier of time into the past, changing things at will.

But I had been able to change nothing, and what happened first with my older brother James, then with Hal and with Danny, set me on the course of a life I never could have imagined before I boarded that plane.

"The future is fixed," Hal, the perfect man, said to me once. "The past is always changing."

This was back before Arizona, when I was visiting the sunny house in Topanga Canyon where my brother James lay dying.

So why is it, with the future so close, on the next breath we take, it gives us no warning? I had no premonition, no feelings at all really, wrapped in a cocoon of travel fatigue as the plane began its initial descent into Tucson. The woman seated next to me who'd boarded in Albuquerque leaned across to look out the window. She was dark-skinned, Hispanic or Indian, with odd eyes, one brown and one blue. Her fat brown hand, embedded with silver and turquoise rings, rested on the back of the seat in front.

"There's the Pinaleño Mountains," she said with a sigh of satisfaction.

The jagged humps of mountain lay below like a dinosaur resting, the terrain unbelievably empty. Later I learned they call these mountain ranges in the middle of the desert sky islands. Had we already flown over Dudley? Back in New York I'd had to look closely before I found it on the map, just a dot in the southeast corner of Arizona, close to the Mexican border.

It was early fall, but the pilot had said it was ninety-five degrees in Tucson, ninety-five degrees and clear. The plane sped through a sky that seemed as if it would always be clear, too blue to have even heard of clouds. In the bright light, my black leggings and black top looked rusty, the skin of my arms and my hands clasped in front of me city-pale.

"Do you live in Tucson?" The woman gave me one of those sideways looks that take in everything.

"No," I said, and hesitated. A few years earlier I'd taken a bus from New York City to Barnet, Vermont, to visit my brother James at Karmê Chöling, where he was studying Buddhism. I'd sat next to a woman who'd tried to convince me hour after hour that she was the real Duchess of Windsor, usurped, banished. Since then I've been leery of conversations with fellow passengers, but this woman, her life laid out in the map of wrinkles on her face, held me with her strange eyes.

"I'm going to Dudley, actually," I said.

"Dudley," she said. "That's that mining town. But the mines closed down. It must be like a ghost town now."

I smiled, conjuring up an image out of a cowboy movie: a long dusty street fronted with boarded-up buildings. Pale wraiths slipped through the boards, suddenly becoming ghosts of former boyfriends and then of Logan, whom I'd loved for nearly a year.

Giving up a man is like giving up cigarettes. You know he's not good for you and you don't even really like him anymore, but just one more time can hardly make a difference. I was flying away from Logan and the chaos of separation, reunion, separation; vertigo.

Maybe I'd find a new life out here, better—just thinking that made me want to spruce up, get ready. Was there still time, I wondered, before the final descent? Yes.

"Excuse me." I stood up, squeezed past the woman, and went down the aisle to the restroom.

In the bright cramped space, miles above earth, I applied blusher and eyeliner. Maybe someday in the future when things were different between men and women, I would give up my eyeliner, the little line I apply along the lower lashes that makes all the difference. *Damn Logan anyway,* I thought, as I used my little finger to smudge the line.

Trying to get my bearings, to find a mythology for the place where I was going, I remembered a movie set in Arizona I'd seen years ago, *Alice Doesn't Live Here Anymore,* and the kind, vulnerable rancher, played by kind, blue-eyed Kris Kristofferson. Alice hadn't appreciated him; she was bent on a singing career and freedom. *Freedom.* Heady with the word, in the springtime of the women's movement, women had met and talked in little groups in empty lofts and stuffy apartments, myself included.

I'd departed from a marriage as a result of it: what was a kind and vulnerable man compared to that magic word?

I think of long ago, of James, Danny, myself, and our parents at the country club after church. Out the enormous picture window was a pond with ducks, and my professor father was expounding on their migratory patterns. Beyond was the golf course. We sat at a round table, the Newcombe family, neatly dressed but unchic, except for James, who adorned everything he wore with his presence. He was already in high school, winning class elections, making straight-A's. I was in eighth grade, uninterested in ducks and squirming to be free of my dull family, whose idea of fun was a wild night *en famille* playing card games or Scrabble.

Thinking of my professor parents at that country club table, I see them differently now, but then I saw my father, wearing the same awful Harris tweed jacket he'd worn for years, and my mother, youthful and unsophisticated in a sweater and plaid skirt, and I knew there were enormous mysteries in life involving pain and uncontrollable passions, mysteries I was prepared to dedicate my life to understanding, but I could find no clues there with my innocent parents at the country club.

And I also see Danny, who sat across from me, his hair newly cut, too short, wearing a blue suit, which was a little small. Those things made him seem vulnerable. He had not yet given up trying to live up to the impossible model of James, so on the lapel of his suit he was proudly sporting his perfect attendance button from Sunday school.

* * *

A male and a female flight attendant flanked the door of the plane as the passengers filed out. "Thank you for flying US Air," they chimed. "Have a good day."

"You too," I said politely, but their smiles were closed off, their eyes unseeing, as if only their voices belonged to US Air.

Inside the airport a cluster of tanned healthy people stood waiting, dressed as though they were on their way to the beach, their bright shorts and halter tops making me feel like a drab alien. They waved and spoke excitedly: met and embraced. I walked through the crowd alone, searching for a glimpse of my brother.

So many years had passed since that day at the country club. James, so brilliant, talented, and kind, had died of AIDS in California two years before my flight to Dudley. Danny, of the perfect attendance button, was a renegade who'd gone to prison in Michigan for a year when he was eighteen for dealing marijuana; a good-looking bad boy and not always reliable. Would he even be there at the airport?

Then there he was, standing by one of the windows, hands in the pockets of his black jeans, looking out at a big plane. His dark hair was slicked straight back and he needed a shave, giving him the scruffy elegance of a pop star. He wore beat-up ostrich-skin boots and a white dress shirt, buttoned at the throat pseudo-nerd-style. I thought he looked wonderful, romantic.

A rush of love made a lump in my throat, and I held back, looking at him. A young woman carrying a baby walked in front of me, blocking my view for a moment, and when she passed on, I saw that Danny was talking to someone, a man in a pale blue linen sports jacket. The man looked prosperous: hair was well cut, the jacket too. A friend? But Danny's face was angry—they seemed to be arguing.

Then Danny looked over and saw me. At least I thought he did, but his face showed no sign of recognition. He said something to the man, who turned away, toward me—round apple cheeks, boyish—then he was gone, swallowed up in the crowd.

Danny smiled and waved. "Chloe, hey!"

We reached each other and hugged, his beard scratching my face. I rested my head on his chest for a second, reassured by his physical solidity.

"Who was that man?" I asked.

"What man?"

"The one you were just talking to, in the blue sports jacket."

"No one." He stepped back, his eyes crinkling with charm, that con man charm that he had learned in prison. I worried about his time in prison clinging to him forever, an albatross. "Look at you, little Chloe, all dressed in black like a poet manqué."

He took my carry-on.

"And what's a poet manqué?" I asked.

He grinned, ducked his head. "I'm not sure."

We walked together down the long hall toward the main terminal.

"Hal," I said. "How is he?"

Danny shrugged. "Dunno."

"But you're staying at his house?"

"He's hardly ever there," he said flatly. "I mean, every now and then he'll show up for a day or two, but mostly he's gone—working with AIDS patients in Tucson, some kind of group-living thing. He's got a place in there where he sleeps. You know he moved out here right after after Ja-Ja-Ja—"

Danny had stuttered for a while in grade school. He'd conquered it, but it came back every now and then under stress. I finished his sentence: "After James died."

"Yeah. After the funeral." He paused. "I bet you really came to see Hal, not me." His voice was strained. "You've always been in love with Hal."

"That's not true!" I felt my face flushing. "I came to see *you*, Danny"—I touched his arm to reassure him—"*and* Hal."

Hal had been James's lover, and the last time I'd seen him was at the funeral. It wasn't a good sign that after two years Danny could hardly say James's name.

By now we had reached the main terminal. We walked across the industrial carpeting and Danny stopped at a bench.

"Let's wait here for Kristi," he said. "She went to the restroom."

"Kristi?"

"My—my girlfriend Kristi Marsh. Didn't I mention—"

"It's okay," I said.

"Chloe, I'm really glad you're here. You don't know how glad." There was an urgency in his voice that alarmed me. "How are the parentials?" It was Danny's term for our parents, a way of deflecting feeling.

"They're in Italy right now," I said. "On sabbatical. Oh, Danny, you're so bad the way you don't write. They worry."

But I understood. Danny was waiting for something to happen first, something that would turn his life into a success story. I thought of the letter I'd mailed them back in New York, written by a cheery upbeat person who didn't exist. Like the letters Sylvia Plath wrote her mother, before she turned on the gas. Well, I didn't want to extend the comparison too far.

I sat down on the bench, but Danny stood leaning against the wall, his face closed off.

I watched people go by—a thin tired woman in Birkenstocks with a baby on her back and a little girl holding each hand; a hurrying businessman in a pale linen suit, meant to impress, but now sadly rumpled; a tall young woman, pale blond hair short, walking in that self-conscious way very pretty women do, knowing everyone is watching.

Danny straightened up, put his fingers to his lips, and gave a sharp whistle. "There she is." His voice was proud.

The blond woman, a bright flashy creature, came toward us, smiling, radiant. On three-inch heels, she walked like a gazelle. Kristi.

Gorgeous, I thought, and with looks like that, quite a handful, and I was willing to bet she had problems. Danny was a crusader where women were concerned. He liked them with problems, shady pasts, abusive former boyfriends. He liked to nurture them, protect them, bring them back to a better life.

I was introduced, the sister meeting the girlfriend. The three of us: ordinary, even banal—safe.

Danny and I walked out of the terminal while Kristi seemed to run circles around us like a puppy.

"I've been looking forward to meeting you so much, Chloe," she said. Her voice was much younger than her sophisticated looks. "I could hardly wait. Danny told me all about the mink poodle pin he bought you for Christmas when you were ten and how much you hated it and about the time you chased him around the yard with a knife."

"It was rubber," I protested laughingly, startled by the memories.

"But he didn't know that!" said Kristi gleefully.

I smiled at Danny, our eyes meeting. It felt good that he'd talked to Kristi about those silly things so full of meaning in close families. I was glad he could still tell the stories about our childhood, the times before disaster had struck—the death of James, Danny's time in prison.

Above us was that clear blue sky, palm trees everywhere, and in the distance were mountains. I had a sense of emptiness, of space to breathe. We walked through the parking lot and reached a van, maroon with portholes, old and dented. Kristi got in back so I could be up front with Danny. Inside, it was equipped with swivel seats, a refrigerator, and a large pair of tacky foam dice hanging from the rearview mirror.

"What kind of van is this?" I asked Danny.

"A Dodge, I think," he said. "Pray it starts."

"Danny," said Kristi. "Of course it's a Dodge. He doesn't know anything about cars," she added proudly.

"Neither does Chloe." Danny closed his eyes and turned the key. The engine turned over. "Thank God. Had to jump-start her to get out of Dudley."

"It's so great, great, great you're here." Kristi's high excited voice filled the car with energy. I turned sideways to look at her. Her color was high, her eyes glittery. "We'll have to go to Mexico, Chloe. It's only ten miles from Dudley. We can buy curios. I bought a painted dragon there with fire coming out of his mouth. They make them down in Oaxaca. If Danny ever gets his act together, I'd like to take a trip—"

"Kristi," said Danny protectively, "calm down a little, okay?"

The atmosphere changed, filled with an enforced silence that was palpable. We left the airport and drove down a street, stopped at a red light.

"It's neat," Kristi bubbled up again, glancing at Danny but unable to contain herself. "You guys being a family and all. I never had anyone but me. My mom just had one kid. Maybe my dad had more. Maybe I've got a bunch of half-brothers and -sisters. I don't know my dad. I have a stepfather."

Danny turned in his seat to look back at her significantly. "Otto's a nice man." There was pain in his voice, but I didn't know why.

"He's a nice man," Kristi agreed dutifully. "There's a Circle K just ahead. Don't we need gas?"

The light changed and we turned into a quick-stop place, a big circular sign with a K in the middle. Danny pulled up to the gas pumps.

Kristi jumped out the back. "I'll go pay."

"Ten dollars' gas and get some Thirst Busters too," Danny called after her.

I got out and stood beside Danny as he clicked the gas pump to on. "Lots of energy," I said.

"Too much today," he said. "She's wonderful and I love her, but she's got this bipolar mood disorder. When she's up she gets crazy. She goes up and down all the time unless she takes these pills, but she thinks they're bad for her. I got busy with something and she stopped taking them, but I got her back on. She should be leveling out soon."

The gas nozzle clicked off.

Kristi came out, balancing three enormous paper cups. A man in a cowboy hat stood holding the door for her. As she went through, he bowed and tipped his hat.

"What kind of pills does she take?"

Danny stood holding the gas nozzle, looking down at it.

"Danny?"

He replaced the nozzle.

I hit him gently on the arm. "Danny? Earth to starship, come on in."

He looked at me unseeingly for a second, then shook his head. "Sorry. I've got a lot on my mind right now."

We drove out of Tucson on Interstate 10, a long straight stretch that gently climbed. Kristi sat quietly, calm at last, looking out the window. Danny was silent, preoccupied.

Lulled by the van's motion, gingerly I checked my mind for memories of pain like a person testing scar tissue not quite healed. I thought his name—Logan—and felt nothing; remembered my first sight of him, out the kitchen window of my friend Giddie's house, the sleeves of his blue shirt rolled up, playing croquet. He aimed a shot carefully, and the ball rolled gently through the wicket. He looked up, smiling smugly, glancing around to make sure everyone had seen the shot. Maybe not a really good sport.

I blinked, and came out of a trance to a landscape of what I now know was golden grass, desert willow, scrub oak, mesquite, and dirt, dirt, dirt. Hardly a sign of human beings at all except a large billboard advertising RV City.

The van chugged along, engine working too hard, until we peaked on a hill. A long valley lay before us, striped in mauve and purple and rimmed with mountains. Behind us to the west the sun was setting and black storm clouds were massing, bathing the whole scene in an eerie unreal light that film crews might wait days to capture.

What had happened to my cloudless skies? "Rain?" I said. "I thought we were in the desert."

Danny laughed. "It rains in the desert. Not so much maybe this late in the season. Don't worry. Wait till you see Dudley. Just to get there you go through a time tunnel."

"Dudley's full of crazy people," said Kristi. "One of them even shot a bullet through Hal's front window."

"What?" I said.

"Nothing," said Danny. "It was all a mistake."

"How can you—" Kristi began.

"Cut it out, Kristi," Danny interrupted. "Chloe's here to have a good time."

For a moment extreme fatigue swept over me. For this I left New York City?

It was almost dark when we turned off the freeway at a town called Benson. Signs for Chief Four Feathers KOA, Quarter Horse RV Park, Sunshine RV, a motel cluster, and the one main street, four lanes wide, going straight through the center of town. Low stores and another Circle K, a Dairy Queen, and then an off-the-road shopping center anchored by Revco and Safeway. You could see where the town ended and the desert began.

"Forty miles to go," said Danny.

At the first light the van stalled.

"Well, shit." Danny put it out of gear and turned the key over and over.

"Don't. You're just going to flood it," Kristi said. "We can coast over to that gas station."

We just made it. A young good-looking Hispanic boy in jeans and an oil-stained purple T-shirt came out of the garage, wiping his hands on a greasy rag, as we got out of the van. "You folks got a problem?" His eyes veered appreciatively to Kristi.

"I think it's maybe the battery," Danny said. "If you could take a look." He rammed his hands in his pockets. "Goddamn it." He exhaled a long breath, looked at me and Kristi. "Why don't you two go over to the Wagon Wheel Café, it's just across the street? Order me some chili."

"Let me help out here a little," I said. "I have my Visa card. I can cover this."

"No, it's okay," Danny said.

Kristi and I headed across the wide street to the restaurant, its name spelled out on the front window in blinking red neon. Halfway across I looked back. Danny stood by the ugly maroon van, hands still in his pockets, looking tired and discouraged; then he glanced up, caught me looking.

"You're sure?" I called back.

He grinned, shrugged. "I'm sure," he shouted, and waved a long parody of a wave, like a passenger on an ocean liner waving to the onlookers on shore, as the big boat moves slowly out of the harbor.

chapter two

THE WAGON WHEEL CAFÉ WAS FULL OF MEN in plaid shirts and jeans, women with permed hair, and their blond children. They watched Kristi and me as we walked by.

"On their way to yo-yo land," I heard a woman say.

"Yo-yo land?" I asked Kristi.

She giggled. "Dudley has kind of a reputation."

We sat in a wooden booth near the back on cracked red vinyl seats, patched here and there with shiny gray duct tape.

"Honestly," Kristi said, "I just don't know where Danny's at these days."

I looked at her across the scarred wood table. "What do you mean, you don't know where Danny's at?"

Kristi flipped rapidly through the jukebox selector. "You didn't notice anything weird? Like maybe he's decided to live on some other planet?"

I had to smile, thinking what I'd said to Danny at the gas station. "It's true," I admitted. "I did notice."

Kristi paused at a selection. "'Drop Kick Me, Jesus (Through the Goalposts of Life),'" she read out loud. "Should we play it? No, we shouldn't." She dropped her hand from the jukebox selector.

Even in the glary unflattering lights of the Wagon Wheel her skin bloomed. Her round, blue-gray eyes, set far apart, gave her a childlike look. In that half-envious way that women will, I searched her face for flaws and found none. What was Danny doing that preoccupied him so much he was neglecting her, while time passed and everything it touched faded?

"He was talking to some man at the airport," I said.

"Oh," said Kristi without interest.

"They seemed to be arguing. The man was well dressed, kind of middle-class—wearing a pale blue sports coat."

Kristi shook her head from side to side. "You'd have to ask Danny."

"I did ask him," I told her. "He said it was no one."

The waitress came over. We hadn't even looked at the menus. "Get the green chili," Kristi told me. "That's what Danny and I always get."

We ordered three bowls. When the waitress went away, Kristi looked at me expectantly. "Danny says you're a private eye."

I laughed. "Technically I guess I am—really I'm more like a financial investigator. I check out potential husbands, their debits and assets, that kind of thing."

"I still can't figure out what I want to be." She looked discouraged. "It must be nice to have it all settled."

It had been an accident, really, a profession by default for someone who'd majored in literature. After being a wanderer, a holder of odd jobs, briefly and unhappily a housewife, a social worker, I'd seen the ad for Friendly Investigations, Friendly being the name of the owner and not the tone of the investigation. I applied there, was hired, and worked for two years as an investigator. The work satisfied my morbid curiosity about people's secret lives, just as literature had.

"'All settled.'" The phrase reminded me of what one was after death. "I don't know about that."

"But who do you investigate?"

"Mostly I work for women wanting to know about their boyfriends or their fiancés."

"You mean they won't marry them unless they're rich?" Kristi looked indignant.

"More like they won't marry them if they've been lied to."

"Oh." She nodded, looking satisfied, but I wasn't sure I was. It was a good line, but lately I'd been feeling as though I were working for a bunch of greedy females whose hearts were stamped with dollar signs. But love comes and goes, is it any more reliable than money?

In the front window the neon lights blinked on and off, the red and green smeary. It had started to rain.

Kristi persisted flatteringly. "Do you carry a gun?"

"Actually, I do own a gun. With a permit and all. It's back in New York City in a dresser drawer. A snub-nosed .38." And I remembered Logan again, showing me the gun. *Blued steel,* he'd said. *That's what accounts for the bluish cast to the metal.*

Kristi wouldn't want to hear all that. "But I haven't shot a boyfriend or a fiancé yet," I added.

The waitress brought the chili. It looked rich and tasty, but we were waiting for Danny. Over the cash register was a big white clock with black hands. I glanced at it surreptitiously. Where was he?

We sat in silence while steam came off the bowls.

"You know something?" Kristi's voice was dead serious. "Maybe I shouldn't say this, but you're Danny's sister. I think about this a lot. I think Danny feels he should have died, not James."

It was like a stab in the heart, shocking, coming from a stranger. But she was his girlfriend, loved him. I hoped.

I wanted to be straight with her, to acknowledge things, but not now. "We'll sit down sometime, maybe talk about that at length. Okay?"

She bit her thumbnail and looked embarrassed. "Sorry," she said in a stricken voice. "Danny's always saying I'm not tactful. I wish he'd get here. I'm hungry."

"Why don't you go ahead and start? I can check." I was glad for an excuse to get away, ease her embarrassment. "I'll just run over there and see what's happening."

Outside, it wasn't raining hard, just drizzling. It was getting dark and the neon lights made red and green stains on the sidewalk and the black asphalt of the street. I crossed over to the garage. Inside, some spirited Mexican music was playing and the attendant was whistling and keeping time to the radio by beating his fist on the fender of the van.

He grinned when he saw me. "Love those mariachis," he said. The hood was up. There was no sign of Danny. "Almost finished. 'Bout time that guy invested in a new battery. I told him I could charge the old one up and he could get a new one cheaper at Pep Boys, install it himself, but he said go ahead and put one in. He said he didn't want to spend his life in auto parts stores."

"Where is he?"

"He ran out. Took off just like that." The kid snapped his fingers.

"Did he say where he was going?"

"Naw." The kid shrugged. "Here one minute, gone the next."

"Oh," I said. "Which way did he go?"

"Dunno. I was under the hood, enjoying the scenery. You could use an oil change. It makes a big difference to the life of your vehicle."

"Well, when he comes back," I said as I turned to go, "tell him his chili is waiting for him."

"Wait. He forgot his wallet. I guess he must have had it out on the seat looking for his credit card before he took off. It'd fallen on the floor, so I grabbed it."

"Thanks." I took the wallet, leather embossed with western scenes, the kind you could buy cheap in Mexico, and put it in my purse.

Outside, there wasn't much else on that side of the street: a vacant lot, a Sonic Burger fast-food place, closed down for a long time, from the look of the weeds growing in the drive-thru. I went back across. Next door to the Wagon Wheel was a Laundromat called the Iron Chinaman, and beyond that a western clothing store for women, then the Gospel Book Nook, the Rock Shop, and a video store.

I peered into the Laundromat, as if Danny might have suddenly decided to do a wash. It was an all-nighter and looked unattended and empty. The clothing store, the Gospel Book Nook, and the Rock Shop were closed. A poster in the window of the video store featured *Black Rain.* A cop movie that I'd seen with my very own cop, Logan. They'd killed off Andy Garcia too soon—he'd been the only living thing in the movie. A sign on the door said GRAND RE-OPENING, SAFEWAY PLAZA. There was no sign of Danny anywhere, up or down the street.

Stymied, I stood in the rain, feeling that curious déjà vu you get in places that are so typical you feel you've been there forever. The rain was warm, almost balmy, the night streaked with lights. In *The Big Sleep* Humphrey Bogart had waited in rain like this, outside the bookstore of Arthur Gwynn Geiger. A kind of peace came on me in spite of everything, as if this place were enchanted, seedily entrapped in some timeless film noir.

A woman came up behind me, fast, her heels loud on the pavement. I hadn't realized what a trance I was in until she touched me on the shoulder and I jumped. It was Kristi.

"He's gone, isn't he?" Her voice rose. "I knew it would happen one day. It always does, they're crazy about you and then they're gone."

"Kristi," I said reasonably, "this isn't like you've just been stood up. I'm here too. His sister all the way from New York, remember?"

Her face was strained, her eyes somewhere else. "I was his daughter and he left, I was a tiny, tiny baby just born. He didn't even want to look at me." Rain glinted on her face like tears. "Oh, Chloe."

I hoped she wasn't about to lose it right here on a rainy street in a strange town. What was it Danny had said? Bipolar mood disorder.

"Danny wouldn't go off for no reason," I said sensibly, though I had no idea if this was true or not. "The attendant said he took off just like that. Maybe he saw someone he knew? Does he know anyone here?"

"I don't think so." She wiped her eyes with the sleeve of her blouse and sniffed. "And I guess I would know. Of course, everyone on earth drives through here on their way to Saint David and Tombstone and Dudley and Mexico too if you want to cross the border quietly."

"Let's go back to the Wagon Wheel," I said, "and finish our chili. Then if he still hasn't shown up we'll go back to the gas station. But probably he'll come back while we're eating. There could be lots of reasons why he took off without telling us."

I couldn't think of one.

In the restaurant, we tried to enjoy our chili, but worry made it difficult to swallow. I stirred mine, while Kristi hid hers with crackers. Over the cash register the second hand of the big clock swept around and around, wiping Danny off the face of the earth. Another half an hour later, as we still dawdled over the chili, the waitress came over.

I pointed to the bowl we'd ordered for Danny. "Could you put this in a take-out container? And bring us the bill."

"He can eat it in the van," said Kristi forlornly as we left the restaurant.

Back at the gas station the attendant came over.

"Did he come back?" I asked.

"You mean he still hasn't shown?" He looked amused. It was man's nature to leave women waiting.

"It doesn't make sense." Irrationally, I wanted him to share my worry. "It's been more than an hour."

His eyes veered off mine noncommittally. "Well, you got yourself a good-running van now," he said, as if lost men were nothing compared to a vehicle that ran. "But don't forget about the oil change."

I paid with my Visa card. "Could you tell me where the police station is?"

He looked surprised. "Hey, you're really taking this seriously." But he directed us to the station.

"If he shows up, tell him to wait here, okay?" I said.

We got in the van. Automatically I took the driver's seat and Kristi got in back. She lay down on the seat and closed her eyes tight. I had a thought, remembering all my friends in New York, struggling with life and their own psyches.

"Is it Prozac you take?"

"Lithium," she said.

Behind the window at the police station was an alert-looking redhead with hard lines around her mouth.

"My brother's vanished," I told her. "We had car trouble, so we waited for him in the Wagon Wheel while he was at the Texaco station, but he never showed up. Then we went back to the station and he wasn't there. It's been an hour or more. I know something's wrong."

"You call home?"

"He lives in Dudley—we're on our way there. How could he be home? He left his van here. Even his wallet."

"Hitchhiked? I don't know the guy," she said, "his habits. Or what's going on with him and the two of you." She cocked her head. "If you know what I mean."

"Nothing," I said. "Nothing was going on."

"I'll get someone out here to talk to you. In the meantime, do me a favor and call home. You said an hour or so he's been missing?"

"Yes."

"Okay. It's about forty-five minutes to Dudley. Guy might be just walking in the door. Make that call just in case. Here." She pushed a phone across the counter.

I punched in the number; I knew it by heart, I'd called so many times from New York, setting up this visit. The phone rang and rang until an answering machine kicked in.

"This is 555-2110," said Hal's voice. It unhinged me; the sound equivalent of a snapshot, and like a snapshot the person was there yet out of reach. "If you have a message for Hal, Danny, or Kristi, leave it after the sound of the beep and we'll get back to you."

Memories came back: the three of us, me and Hal and James, in the pretty, airy house in Topanga. James enshrined on a large couch in the living room, looking ethereal, the only blond in our family. He'd lost a lot of weight, revealing the polished beauty of the bones beneath his skin.

I'd imagined all of him as beautiful, his liver, his pancreas, the blood in his veins—the disease that was killing him some miniature biblical monster that Hal and I were fighting with our love.

Hal had busied himself around the house, cooking, creating an atmosphere with new art, flowers, even weeds he'd gathered in the hills and arranged in pots or vases or mason jars. We watched movies, crazy for the films of Gloria Grahame, the suicide blonde—*In a Lonely Place, The Big Heat*; played games as though we were children again, back home with the family. James loved games, and when he won and looked happy, Hal and I felt we were the ones winning.

Then the beep of the answering machine brought me back.

"Danny," I said to the machine in the strange and unbelievable present. "I'm calling from the police station in Benson. If you're there, pick up. We're worried."

A cop came out from a door by the big glass window. His hair was graying, his blue eyes obscured by pouches. He walked toward me, hand out. I shook it.

"Detective Rick Seed," he said.

I introduced myself and told him all the relevant information and gave him Danny's description.

"You getting along with your brother?" he asked. "Not in the middle of a big fight, were you?"

"No," I protested. "I flew here from New York City and he'd just picked me up at the Tucson airport. We were glad to see each other. I know when something's not right. I'm very worried about him. I'm an investigator myself, back in New York, Officer."

"That so?" He rubbed his chin. "You with law enforcement there?"

"No."

He looked away as if losing interest. "Tell you the truth, when it's an adult like your brother we don't put out an APB for forty-eight hours, but I'll have our guys keep a lookout. And I'll talk to DPS too—that's your highway patrol. Meanwhile, best thing you can do is go on to Dudley—probably your brother'll show up there. I mean . . ." He shrugged. "Where else is he going to go?"

"We can't just leave."

"Why not? You guys could run all over town missing each other. If you're home, at least he can get in touch." Rick Seed scratched his head. "It's a whole lot peacefuller here than it must be in New York—we got hitchhikers getting killed, bar fights, some sexual assaults, a few armed robberies, that's about it. Unless you're talking drugs, then that's a different story."

"We're not talking drugs."

"Look," he said, his voice sympathetic. "Ninety percent of missing person cases get found. Okay? We'll be looking, you go on home."

"Okay," I said reluctantly. I turned to go.

"Give us a call when he shows," Rick Seed called after me.

When, not if.

Out in the van, Kristi was still lying on the backseat, eyes closed, but she sat up when she saw me. I shook my head. She got out and got in the front.

"It could be worse," she said in a trembly voice. "At least they didn't find any body." Her voice went upward on the word body, verging on hysteria.

"Look." I made my voice calm, controlled, fighting the contagion of her emotions. "We'll go back to the gas station one more time. If he's not there, we'll drive to Dudley. That's what the police recommended. Just try to think clearly and help me out. On the way we're going to discuss all the rational explanations for this."

"What rational explanations?"

"We'll think of something." A giggle rose in my throat. I squelched it.

We drove back to the gas station, but the attendant shook his head, giving us the thumbs-down sign.

"If he does show," I said, "tell him we went on to Dudley. Tell him to call."

And then there was nothing left to do but drive to Dudley in the rain and the dark, those ridiculous foam dice, Danny's little joke, dangling off the rearview mirror.

chapter three

I DROVE SLOWLY OUT OF BENSON ON A narrow country road, headlights shining a path through the darkness. It was still drizzling. The window was down a couple of inches and the air smelled fragrant, newly washed, blending with the mysterious smells of the desert. There were no other cars ahead or behind. *Danny,* I thought, *Oh, Danny.*

A lot on his mind, he'd said. Like *what*?

The tires hissed on the asphalt, like ink on the old-fashioned printing press an ex-boyfriend of mine had used to print his unsalable poems. Clunk, clunk went the wipers, back and forth, lulling me into a false calm, but underneath was urgency.

"How did you and Danny meet, anyway?" I asked Kristi.

"Through Hal."

"Really," I said.

"My stepdad Otto's a therapist like Hal. They met at some conference. I guess they got to talking and Otto mentioned he had a stepdaughter, so Hal invited me and Danny to dinner. Hal used to like to cook for people, back in L.A. but here he's all wrapped up in this job in Tucson so he hardly ever comes to his house in Dudley." She sighed. "Danny and I hit it off right away."

"You said Danny's been . . ."—I hesitated, decided on her word—"weird for a while?"

Kristi took off her high heels and put her feet up on the dashboard. Her toenails were painted bright blue. "I guess he started to get weird about six months ago. Maybe it was my job. That's what I thought at the time."

"Your job?"

Behind us headlights appeared and approached rapidly.

"I got a job at the Play Room. I had to wear this uniform that was just a couple of strings. I was making good tips, but Danny wasn't happy about it. It wasn't any worse than a bikini. I mean, anyway, so what?" She wiggled her toes, the blue nails glittering in the bright lights from a car behind.

Then lights came up in the rearview mirror and a pickup passed us, going maybe eighty miles an hour, red taillights receding fast. "And?" I said.

"I'd come home from work and he'd be gone. He'd leave me a note—like when he'd be back?—but he'd never tell me where he was going. I thought he was pissed about my job. He wanted me to go to college. He said he was always sorry he'd dropped out his sophomore year."

Talk about euphemisms. Actually he'd been busted in his off-campus apartment at the University of Michigan with two kilos of marijuana and twenty hits of blotter acid. It sounded like he hadn't told Kristi he was a convicted felon; never found the right romantic moment.

She went on. "He said he wanted things to be better for me than they'd turned out for him. Anyway, I'd ask him where he'd been and he wouldn't tell me. I found out, though. He doesn't like to carry cash. I checked his Visa bills and his check stubs."

"That was smart."

She tossed her head. "Yeah. Well. One time he went to Portland, Oregon. Another time San Diego, some little place outside the city in the mountains. He'd never talked about knowing anybody in those places."

We were approaching a town. My headlights hit a sign, ST. DAVID. Then another, APACHE MOBILE HOME PARK. I downshifted to thirty miles an hour. The streetlights shone on Kristi's face, exaggerating dark circles of fatigue under her eyes. Behind the streetlights were small white houses set back from the road. We passed a church, Jesus Christ of Latter-Day Saints. Alder, mulberry, and massive cottonwood trees lined the road. For the first time since I'd arrived in Arizona there was the cool nostalgic smell of green.

"Mormons," Kristi said. "They're all Mormons here. Farmers."

St. David went by quickly, the farmers, Barrows Trailer Park, Fish Hook RVs, Twin Lakes Recreation Ranch. Had all the retirees in the whole United States come here to southern Arizona? Outside of town, I asked, "What do you think Danny was doing?"

"At first," said Kristi, considering, "I thought he was de—doing something he shouldn't."

Oh, God. I asked neutrally, "Dealing, is that what you were going to say?"

"But if that was it, he wouldn't have had to leave L.A. I mean, he had this job cleaning out swimming pools. He could have just sold to his customers."

"And did he?" There were things that had always bothered me about Danny, other times, other places that I'd visited him. Armani jackets one time I saw him, no money for his electricity bill the next.

"Oh, shit. It doesn't matter. He was never what you'd call a real dealer anyway." She sat bolt upright. "It really, really doesn't matter. Danny's going to be home anyway," she said longingly. "And he wouldn't want me telling you this kind of thing."

"And if he isn't there?"

"All that was in L.A.," she said, ignoring my question. "We came here once to visit Hal. Then three weeks later Danny decided we were going to move here, just like that. Out of the blue. Now, that was really weird."

"Now that you're here, does he still take those trips, like to San Diego and Portland?"

"No. All he does now is go up to Tucson a lot."

"Why does he go there?"

"I don't know." Her voice was petulant, tired.

The road was straight now, on and on into the night. Clunk, clunk went the wipers soothingly. I wanted to rest my head on the steering wheel, close my eyes; hear cars, sirens, people arguing passionately down on the street below my apartment. Wanted to lie in my bed in New York City, sick only with the common sorrow I'd come here to get away from.

Kristi was so silent beside me it was like being alone as I drove. Ahead was another town, defined by dots of light.

After a while Kristi said, "Danny was kind of mad at me 'cause we went to the mall before we picked you up. He dropped me off 'cause he had to go someplace else."

"Someplace else?" I said. "Where?"

Kristi shrugged. "Dunno. But anyway I didn't have much to do at the mall, so I bought a dress."

"Oh?"

"It was expensive—almost a hundred dollars. When I showed it to him, he said, 'Where did you get the money?' and I said, 'I just *had* it.'"

"Oh," I said again.

"I bought it to wear for my father." Her voice was defiant.

But her father, I remembered her saying earlier, was someone she didn't know, hadn't she said that? I looked over at her. Her eyes were closed.

She began to talk in a dreamlike voice, the voice she'd used back in the rain, in front of the video store.

"It was so different. I had to try it on. Social Dresses was the name of the department in Foley's. It was real short, and cut like an evening dress, but it was brown tweed. Different. I put it on and went out to look at myself in the big mirrors. Then the saleswoman came up and told me how good it looked, like they always do, but it was true. So I got this vision. Of my father, calling me up on the phone. *Kristi,* he'd say. *Please forgive me for leaving like I did. I want to meet you. I've been thinking about you from the day I left. I want you to go with me to Las Vegas. We'll stay at the Mirage.*"

We had reached another town: Tombstone. Signs for the Round Up Trailer Ranch, Tombstone KOA, Wells Fargo RV Park, as if the residents needed to be ready anytime to pack up and drive on to the next town, the next RV City; seeking something new just out of reach over the next mountain. Boot Hill went by.

"I could see us together at the Mirage," Kristi went on, "so clearly. Arm in arm under the bright lights, the fountains sparkling, me in the dress. . . . Mom says he was very handsome. She doesn't talk about him when Otto's there—but sometimes when Otto's gone she does." She paused. "Danny acted mad, but I knew he wasn't really. He never gets mad about my father stuff. Just sad."

I could see how he might be sad, doomed to be number two forever. I thought of how we often choose our lovers for their surface, thought of Logan's black, black hair, his arrogance.

We drove out of town; it had stopped raining.

Danny would be at the house where we were going, Hal's house in Dudley. Hal would be there too. He would have spent the afternoon cooking up something southwestern, with local ingredients. He'd just stepped out when I called. Danny and Hal would be there and later on Hal and I would discuss Danny and his new, beautiful, and charming but definitely crazy girlfriend; discuss them judiciously and think of ways to help them out.

chapter four

IT WAS TEN O'CLOCK, ONE A.M. NEW YORK daylight saving time, when we climbed a long steep hill, over the top, and down into a tunnel cut through the mountain. MULE PASS TUNNEL, it said at the entrance, but over the words someone from an alternative Chamber of Commerce had scrawled in black spray paint: TIME TUNNEL.

The van roared noisily through a long tiled barrel of space, garishly lit with bright lights on both sides, then emerged back out into darkness.

"You take the first turn," Kristi said, "at the Tombstone Canyon sign."

I saw it almost immediately, coming up at me out of the dark. I made the turn and drove almost full circle to a stop sign. Here we paused, the van heaving like an exhausted animal. Hills blocked any view of where I was going: me, a woman who knew without a second thought which subway would take me anywhere in Manhattan. Tension grabbed me by the neck. What the hell was I doing here?

"Turn right," Kristi told me.

The street ahead wound downward through the canyon,

curving, so you could never see very far ahead. Vaguely I was aware of frame houses with porches, lining the streets and clinging to the hillside. The town was a riddle; without Kristi I would have been completely lost.

Goddamn it, Danny, I thought, *you'd better be at the house. You just better.*

Then the street widened and to my left was a statue of a miner, done in the streamlined proletariat style of the thirties, wide shoulders. I kept going, through a slide show of a quaint western town from the nineteenth century, two- and three-story brick buildings full of arts-and-crafts stores and little galleries and rock shops, all closed, no people. Then it widened into an intersection, dominated by a three-story art deco building.

"That used to be the company store," said Kristi dutifully, like a tour guide weary of her job. "Turn left. That's Brewery Gulch over to your right."

On the Gulch the town came to life. People out on the shabby street, a street not yet renovated or stuffed and preserved, but living firmly in the present and lined with brightly lit bars.

"It's kind of drunk city here," Kristi said, "if you make the bar scene. Which Danny and I do sometimes because, like he said, there's not even a movie theater."

Bars. Ah, Logan's kind of town.

We drove up past the Copper Queen Hotel, then up a steep hill that got steeper. Following Kristi's directions, I made another sharp turn near the top, into a driveway.

An empty driveway, no lights on in the house, no Danny waiting for us, why would he be? No Hal either. The engine hummed softly. I hadn't really believed they would be there, but the hope had nourished me for a while.

* * *

Inside, Kristi turned on a light and I stood there blinking in a daze, the road remembered under my feet. We were standing in a big kitchen. We were standing in Hal's house. Kristi dropped her shoes on the floor and they made a little clunk that echoed in the emptiness as she stood barefoot, vulnerable, in the kitchen.

"Home, sweet home," she said in a brittle voice.

I put down my carry-on.

Kristi went to the refrigerator and took out an apple. "Want one?" she said.

"No."

On a long shelf at one end of the kitchen was Hal's Lu-Ray Pastels china collection that I remembered from Topanga. He had everything: plates, cups and saucers, soup bowls, vegetable bowls, pitchers, creamer, sugar bowl with lid, all the delicate colors, blue, pink, and green, dulled by dust. Past a long counter was the dining room with a ladder on a drop cloth in the middle of the floor.

I pointed to it. "What's this?" I asked.

"It's Wally's."

"Who?"

"Hal hired him to work on the remodeling."

Kristi showed me around—a living room with bare wood floors, a large white couch with pillows, familiar—all of them covered in faded tropical flower prints cut from what your grandma in the thirties would have called drapes. On days when James was feeling well, he and Hal went to thrift stores and yard sales, hunting out the china and the prints.

Now the pillows looked older, even more faded, shabby. There were no plants, unlike the house Hal had shared with James, no rugs. Things seemed plunked down, hung quickly. One wall seemed to be made of some shiny substance: insulation. No ambience had been created, no sign of an inner life. Not a house where someone might spend the afternoon cooking for expected guests.

There was an office, with bare Sheetrock for walls, a little bedroom where Kristi and Danny slept, and a big bedroom with a futon in it already made up into a bed. The big bedroom was otherwise empty except for cardboard boxes piled high in one corner.

"This is Hal's," said Kristi. "You get it."

I thought it might be a good idea to lie down on the futon right now and sleep forever, but instead I found the phone, pushed the rewind button on the answering machine, and played it back. There were several beeps and then my own voice, strained and urgent. "Danny, I'm calling from the police station in Benson. If you're there, pick up. We're worried."

"Jeez," said Kristi.

"I should call Hal," I said. "Do you have his number?"

"No!" Kristi's voice was too quick, too emphatic. "I don't have it. Besides, Danny wouldn't want you calling him."

"Why not?" I demanded.

"It's late to call. I mean," said Kristi, "if Hal knew where Danny was, he'd have him call us right away."

This was true, I knew it.

There was a silence, then, "There's something else," she said.

"What?"

"Remember I mentioned the window getting shot out?"

"*No.* I mean yes." I sat down suddenly on the white couch. "Shit." I didn't even want to know. "What about it?"

"There was this guy Danny knew, Chip? Chip O'Leary? I don't

see how it could be connected, but I guess I should mention it anyway." She paused.

"Go on," I said.

"He got murdered."

I was confused, then angry. Wonderful, I thought, just wonderful. Hal lets Danny stay at his house and he turns it into a crime zone. "What does that have to do with the window getting shot out?" I heard my voice, impatient, irritable.

"I don't know. It was after he was killed. I just thought I'd mention it, is all." She was still holding the apple, half eaten, and looked like she was about to cry.

"Sorry." I sighed. "We both need to sleep. Go to bed," I said. "Okay? We'll talk in the morning."

"I'm going to take a shower," she said.

I was exhausted, but I wanted to sit for a few minutes in Hal's living room. Sit on the white couch I knew so well and think of Hal the last time I'd seen him—two years ago after James's funeral, when he'd taken me out to dinner, alone.

"We're different from other people, you and me, Chloe," he'd said. "We need to understand things too much, experience things directly. We need to take chances, but the more we learn from our risks, the more awful the world becomes. But it's always too late to turn back, so we have to go forward."

I was flattered to have him include me in his world. It took away the sting of my dreadful early marriage, divorce, and ensuing flaky relationships with men and turned it all into a search for visceral knowledge, a crusade for truth. This was before I'd met Logan, when truth became something more complicated and ultimately irrelevant.

Sitting in the restaurant with Hal, I'd picked at the steak I'd foolishly ordered, feeling we were in a kind of bubble together, that the two of us had understood James better than anyone else. Who could eat? Distraught and needing calm after the funeral, I paid Hal the kind of rapt attention you pay when you are first in love and it's all new. I knew nothing could come of it, but that in itself was restful.

The sound of the shower stopped and the sudden silence brought me back. To give us both some space, I retrieved my carry-on, took it into the bedroom, and closed the door. I unpacked my nightgown, undressed, put it on, and lay down. The streetlight shone through the trees outside and made patterns on the curtains. I tried very hard not to think about Danny at all. In the silence of my not thinking, the roar of the van and the clunk of the wipers echoed in my ears as if I were still driving, like a Southwest version of the Flying Dutchman, on and on through a vast and empty desert.

Then at some point a door opened, closed, somewhere in the house. I sat up in bed, listening. Danny? Nothing. It took a long time for sleep to come, my body tense, rigid, waiting for Danny.

chapter five

IT WAS MORNING. HALF DREAMING, HALF remembering, I lay in bed beside Logan, that first time, and traced my finger on his thigh, down the long scar, red and puckered. Wasn't there some phrase in the I Ching, wounded in the thigh? One of the changing lines maybe. But what did it mean? I forgot.

"How . . . ," I'd begun.

"Knife wound," he'd said. "Domestic violence call. They're the most dangerous kind. All cops hate them. A kitchen knife. There were bits of pizza sauce mixed in with my blood and tissue." He laughed without meaning it. "A little bitty girl, maybe thirteen."

I drew in a breath. "Why?"

"Ah, she was going for her stepfather." His voice was husky with regret. I covered the scar with my hand, but I couldn't cover it completely. "He'd been slapping her around."

Thirty-nine years old and retired on disability; you hardly noticed the limp. Banished from a world he loved, a world full of comradeship and danger, and drinking hard for oblivion. How much could a woman, any woman, do?

Sunlight poured through the curtains in the bedroom, pricking at my eyelids, enveloping me in a white foreign light, intense and insistent, forcing me back into the present, but the present had its dangers too. I struggled against waking, not wanting to face what had happened last night, and the not knowing.

Then I heard the sound of a key in a lock, a door opening, and someone walking into the house. Heavy footsteps, masculine.

Danny, I thought, *thank God.* I jumped out of bed and walked out to the dining room in my nightgown. But beyond the counter that separated the two rooms I saw a stranger standing in the kitchen. He grinned at me, a stocky man with a blond beard, a nose that looked permanently sunburned, glasses with masking tape wrapped around the nosepiece.

"Hey, there," he said. "You must be Danny's sister, Chloe."

I stepped back, closer to the bedroom door. The Mexican wedding dress I used as a nightgown was not revealing, but I felt vulnerable. "And you are . . . ?"

"Wally, Wally Ferguson, working on the remodel." He gestured at the ladder as if in explanation. "Chloe. Interesting name, it means green. Green as in verdant, did you know that?"

I blinked, dazed by this onslaught of too much information.

"Dudley used to be a mining town, did you know that?" he went on. "These remodels are fascinating. They built the walls in these old houses with flat boards and canvas stretched over them. The boards are all different shapes and sizes, scavenged from whatever was lying around. Very ingenious. You know, the Japanese were like that too, made gardens just out of rocks. Art out of poverty, but unfortunately the art is missing from these places. If there's a right angle anywhere in this house, I haven't found it yet. Then there's the wallpaper, a whole history of taste in every—"

Past him, I could see the room where Kristi had slept, door

wide open. "Wally," I broke in. He reminded me of my father, off on a topic. "Excuse me."

"Oops," he said apologetically. "Talking too much again, wasn't I?"

"Where's Kristi?"

His eyes shifted away from mine. "Went out for coffee? Where is she ever?" he added philosophically. "I was about to make some right here. The best thing about this job is the coffee. Hal orders it specially. As a New Yorker, I assume you're addicted to caffeine?"

"Yes . . . no." What exactly was he asking me? I had no idea.

"Kristi!" I called. "Excuse me."

I went to the room where she had slept and looked in just to make sure, but the room was empty. I came back to the kitchen. Wally was grinding coffee beans. I was so on edge, the noise cut through my head like a jackhammer.

"I'm sorry if I'm short with you," I said to Wally when the beans were ground. "We've been having a crisis." I told him the story of Danny's disappearance.

"Strange." For a second he looked bewildered.

"Do you know when is Hal coming back?" I asked. "Or maybe you have a number where I can reach him?"

"I can't answer either question. He keeps in touch because we can't always reach him, but Kristi would have a number."

"You're sure?" I asked.

"Sure I'm sure."

She'd told she didn't. She'd lied.

"She— My goodness." He stopped and peered through the front door, which he'd left wide open. "Here comes a man from law enforcement."

A man appeared at the door, wearing tight-fitting jeans,

expensive running shoes, and a brown plaid shirt over a high-necked T-shirt, a look I associate with cop modesty. My stomach lurched. Danny, he was here to tell me something bad about Danny.

"Well, good morning to you, Jack Nance," Wally said with a trace of discomfort. "Come on in. What's up?"

I wrapped my arms around my chest. My heart started beating faster, loud. I imagined they could both hear it, thudding in the kitchen, rattling the Lu-Ray china.

Jack Nance had white hair, but his face was unlined. The hair made his eyes seem bluer, his square pink jaw rosier. He nodded at Wally. "I'm looking for a Miss Chlo Newcombe," he said dropping the *e* at the end of my name.

"I'm Chlo*e*. Is this about Danny? Is everything okay?" I asked urgently.

He didn't answer.

Wally's bearing had changed subtly. There was something folksy yet unctuous in his stance. He walked to the stove to pour the boiling water over the coffee grounds, still keeping his eyes on the man.

"Would you care for a cup of coffee?" he offered. "I understand these beans come all the way from San Francisco." He began to whistle a little off-key about where he had left his heart.

"No, thanks." The cop turned to me. "Jack Nance, like Wally said. An investigator for the Dudley police. Could we talk somewhere privately?"

I stared at him. A phrase I'd learned from Logan came to my mind: *death notification.* My hands were cold, my head empty. "For heaven's sake," I said. "My brother's missing. If he's been found, I'd appreciate knowing that right away."

"He hasn't turned up," said Nance, "as far as I know."

Wally handed me a cup of coffee. "Well, at least he's not dead," he said kindly. My hands holding the cup were shaking and I set the cup down firmly on the counter. "I hope," he added. I searched Nance's face for sympathy, but the person behind his eyes was hidden.

"Just let me fill my cup," Wally said to Nance, "and I'll be in that room over there." He pointed toward the office. "I'll close the door. I won't be able to hear a thing over the slap of the Sheetrock mud and my undeleted expletives."

"Undeleted expletives," said Nance. "What are you doing, Wally, slapping Sheetrock mud on walls, when you could get a desk job?"

There was a strained silence as Wally poured himself coffee.

For the first time I noticed, taped to the side of the refrigerator, a page torn from a glossy arts magazine; a Mapplethorpe photograph, sensual and erotic, of a naked black man, his skin color deep and dense and glistening. This was a state where they'd elected a racist governor, even though they'd later gotten rid of him. Conservative to the max. I wasn't sure an Arizona cop would understand.

Abruptly I sat down on one of the high stools at the counter, blocking the photograph from Nance.

"Your brother went missing in Benson," Nance said, "so it would fall within the jurisdiction of the Benson police. But Rick and I work together on certain kinds of things. We got a computer network links us with the different police departments, the Border Patrol, sheriff, and the BAG guys."

"Bag?"

"Border Alliance Group. I'm a drug investigator. This is hot drug territory, Miss Newcombe, if our reputation hasn't reached you back where you come from in Crack City. Old Rick Seed tells me you're a private investigator. Divorce cases, that kind of thing?"

"Mostly just checkups on people's background." My voice was apologetic. "Their finances. I hardly even see the people I'm investigating." I took a sip of coffee. "What does all this have to do with Danny?"

"Well, Chlo, your brother does have a record." He'd shifted to my first name as if we were now buddy-buddy.

"It's Chlo*e*," I said coldly to put him in his place. I wished I weren't still wearing my nightgown. "You pronounce the *e*." The white hair and those blue eyes were pretty striking. That didn't make me like him, though. "Is that all? My brother's disappeared. What does his record have to do with that? It was a long time ago and he served his time."

"Well, we had something nasty happen here three months or so ago. A homicide, drug-related."

I looked into his cool blue eyes. "And . . . ?"

"Guy was beaten up bad then shot to death out in the Valley. Didn't find him for a couple of days. It's just desert out there. Coyotes had a time with him."

I flinched, swallowed. "Danny knew him? Or what?"

Nance hitched up his jeans and sat down on the stool by the counter, putting him more at eye level with me.

"Yeah, he knew him. Name of Charles O'Leary, but they called him Chip. Came from a nice Arizona family. They've been here a long time. Chip was premed at the U of A is my understanding, but something got screwed up. This isn't hippie-dippie dealing anymore like maybe Chip was thinking and maybe your brother too back then in Michigan, thought it was a kick. Drugs are in the hands of the bad guys now, the real bad guys. That's what Chip found out, when he tried to sell a little coke. You being a private investigator, I thought maybe your brother mentioned it to you."

"No, he didn't. Danny's only been here a couple of months."

"Course, everyone knew the guy," Nance went on. "You know people here whether you want to or not. Just that those other folks don't get their windows shot out."

"Oh."

"Oh," mimicked Nance. "You heard about it, then?"

"Very little. Did Danny report it?"

"Lady next door did. She's a nice Mexican lady. She doesn't want anyone shooting out the windows next door. Danny wasn't helpful."

Nance rubbed his face, clearly thinking so many people weren't. I wondered if he drank. Finished up his shift and went down to the bar where all the cops hung out and drank himself silly.

"All I want to say to you, young lady, is keep the private eye stuff out of this case. You don't know what you're messing with. Leave it in the hands of the professionals."

"If I'm curious about my brother's disappearance," I said angrily, "it's because I love him. You don't even know him, all the good kind things about him. You just see the bad in everyone. It's your job."

Nance coughed. He shifted uneasily on the stool and his face got just a little pinker.

"Coming through," said a loud voice, and Wally emerged from the room with a bucket.

"It's okay," said Nance. "Miss Newcombe here is just giving me a lecture. I've said my piece."

Wally put the bucket in the sink and ran water into it. "How's that ulcer holding up, Jack?"

"It's holding up better than me, you might say." Nance put his hand delicately on his middle.

"You should get out of the business," said Wally, "get a transfer, maybe into education, teach little kids the dangers of drugs, lecture at the high school. Become a role model. The local legend has it you were a pretty good ballplayer once."

"Naw, shit," said Nance, "I need the overtime."

After Nance left, I went into the room where I'd slept, closed the door, and lay down on the futon. I felt shaky. Unbelievable. Un-fucking-believable. I stared at the ceiling. If Danny led a normal life like everyone else, he wouldn't be around any drug killings. He wouldn't hang out with the kind of people who got themselves murdered. I needed to talk to Kristi some more, where the *hell* was she? And she'd lied about having Hal's number.

Yesterday, had Danny been engaged in some sort of drug deal? Dropped off a few grams in Benson while his sister and his girlfriend waited in the Wagon Wheel? Who was the man in the airport Danny had been talking to? No one? I decided I should drive back to Benson. Check it out in the daylight, see if I could find anyone who'd seen Danny. It would be nice, I thought, if Kristi were around to give me a hand.

For all I knew, she and Danny were in some kind of big trouble and planned an escape using me as cover. First Danny gets away, Kristi makes sure big sister gets safely to Hal's, then she vanishes too.

Here I was in this little old town where I knew no one and no one knew me. Would Hal show up soon? How could I get his number? Kristi had it, that little bi—

Anxiety pushed a burning needle into my chest.

I got up, took off my nightgown, and put on my black high-tops, my black T-shirt, my black jeans. I would get in the van and drive to Benson right now, talk to people, maybe someone there had seen something. Now that Danny had been branded as a convicted felon by law enforcement, they probably weren't even bothering to investigate.

chapter six

IN THE DAYLIGHT, THE TOWNS OF TWINKLING lights I'd driven through last night with Kristi were changed: diminished. The rains had gone and the sky was an unrelenting blue. I drove mile after mile of two-lane blacktop through mostly empty terrain: through desert, imagining I could drive backward through time, to the point just before Danny waved goodbye.

Stop, little brother, I would say, *stop, let me go with you.*

A wind had come up and the leaves of the big cottonwoods just outside Benson seemed to twinkle and glitter urgently. I slowed as I reached the center of town, hoping the odd noise when I braked meant nothing. Whatever had seemed mysterious in the dark was less intriguing in the light of day—Benson was just another down-at-the-heels town nestled against the freeway, feeding off the needs of travelers. Most of the storefronts needed a paint job, and trash scurried down the pavements at a faster clip than the few people out on the street.

I parked the van in front of the Wagon Wheel Café and got out. Across the street at the gas station I saw that a different man was pumping gas, older. The Dairy Queen still sported its CLOSED sign.

There were railroad tracks I hadn't noticed last night and a wooden booth next to them that must pass for a station. I had a little picture of Danny then—overwhelmed by the thought of two women, both needing attention—impulsively hopping a train for wherever it took him away, away, away.

The restaurant was almost deserted when I walked in, too late for breakfast, too early for lunch. I took a seat near the window and ordered coffee from a thin, wiry waitress maybe in her sixties, wearing elaborately framed, unbecoming glasses, not the same one who'd served Kristi and me last night.

When she came back, I asked her, "Where can you catch a train to from here?"

"Why, trains go all the way to New York, Boston, if that's where you want to go. Course, you have to change along the way. Stops in Albuquerque, New Orleans, Washington, D.C. People come from all over the county to catch a train here."

I took a sip of coffee. It tasted like the last of the breakfast batch left on the warmer too long. "No kidding? Where do you buy tickets?"

She pushed her glasses farther up on her nose. "Oh, you get them on the train. I took it myself to Albuquerque once. Had a real good time. I'd like to do it again. You know, nighttime when it stops you can see those lighted windows and the people sitting in there look so warm and cozy, not a care in the world." Suddenly she smiled, a wicked jaunty smile that lit up her face. "I tell my husband sometime when I get mad at him I'll just pack a suitcase, get on that train, and join the party."

She took a pencil from behind her ear and scribbled on my bill. "We got some pie, Danish."

"Just the coffee, thank you."

"I was here last night," I said as she set the bill in front of me.

"There didn't seem to be much happening in town at night. I guess everything closes up."

"I thought you looked familiar. You came in here with that striking blond girl. I bet you're the sister of the guy that disappeared. The cops were in here, asking questions."

"Really," I said. "So you were here last night?"

"Not working. Here for dinner. Me and my old man do that sometimes. Gee, it's awful about your brother, though. You haven't heard anything yet?"

"No," I said. "The cops, you said they were asking questions—did you or anyone here see anything?"

"Nothing that I know about. This is a little town, we talked about it some after the police left."

"Is there any—um—drug scene here?"

She straightened up and brushed at her apron. "You find me a place where there isn't," she said, "I'll move there right away. But maybe not as bad as the towns closer to the border. Douglas or Dudley."

There was a little silence.

"I can't stand just sitting around waiting to hear something," I said. "I looked around last night in case someone in one of the stores saw my brother, but nothing was open except the Laundromat and no one was in there."

She nodded. "Waiting'll kill you. That's what I tell my old man. You ever notice, it's women who always end up sitting around waiting? But Mrs. Booth should've been in the Laundromat. It used to be unattended, but they had vandals, you know, so she's usually in the back there with her TV. You wouldn't see her unless you went inside."

I took the last sip of coffee. "Maybe I'll go talk to her."

The waitress took the pencil from behind her ear then stuck it back again. "Can't hurt."

Inside the Iron Chinaman a young woman and three kids sat in a row on stuck-together yellow molded plastic chairs. The woman was reading a magazine and the kids, all with suckers plugging up their mouths, stared disinterestedly as I went past. Near the back a gray-haired stout woman in purple sweats and cowboy boots stood at a table, folding clothes. The smell in the Laundromat was hot and strong, compounded of detergent, bleach, and dryer lint.

"I'm looking for Mrs. Booth," I said.

"That's me." She shook out a ragged dish towel, holding it disdainfully with the tips of her fingers. Her broad face was red and sweaty. "Dollar seventy-five," she said, "for the wash and folding. Price has gone up for the labor."

"I don't have any wash. I'm here about my brother. We were coming through town last night and he disappeared. I was just wondering if you'd noticed anything, maybe saw him? I didn't realize anyone was here last night or I would have stopped in then."

Mrs. Booth began folding a stack of washcloths. "You mean they ain't found him yet? The cops were here, I'll tell you what I told them—I don't know what someone's doing vanishing like that, but I know how irresponsible men are. When I started staying here at night after we got vandalized, my husband offered to sleep here some of the nights, but then he's got suddenly a full schedule whenever I need him. He says, you decided to have a Laundromat, Iris, you got to be responsible. Like it was just some hobby and we didn't need the income." She snorted.

I made a sympathetic face. Maybe Mrs. Booth and the waitress should catch a train together. I could see them loosening up, their tired faces getting merry, maybe picking up a couple of old-timers in the bar car and getting them to buy the drinks.

"You didn't see me 'cause I like the place to look empty. That way I'm gonna catch those little buggers." She shook out a large-sized bra so vehemently the cups filled with air and briefly floated. "You wouldn't believe the filth they wrote on the dryers. Took me all of one morning to clean it off. I listen even when I'm watching TV, listen for those kids, so I heard this guy out front talking to someone in I don't know what, a truck maybe. . . ." She paused. "Not a car."

"Yes?" I prompted.

"The guy talking was on the wrong side, like he came from across the street."

"The garage?" I said. "Could he have come from the garage?"

She nodded. "Could of."

"Did you get a good look at him?"

"You can't see too good out the window. I'm like a fish in a fishbowl here, that's why I like to be in back. Think he had on a white shirt, though."

"Dark hair? Youngish?"

"Maybe. Anyway, I heard a door slam, so I guess he got in the whatever-it-was. It started up then and headed back towards the freeway."

"The freeway," I said blankly.

"Sounded like a truck, not a car."

"Did you see the color?"

"I told you I didn't see the truck that clear, if it was a truck. Come to think of it, maybe it was a car after all, one of those old gas guzzlers. Could of been a van too. I wouldn't swear to anything in court. It wasn't one of them Mack trucks or nothing, 'cause when they're here you can't see across the street and anyway they're louder. That Rick Seed who talked to me was the one investigated the vandalizing, and what did he come up with? Nothing."

"What time was all this?"

"I told Rick around seven 'cause *Personalities* was just coming on. I watch that, then *Current Affair*. But I been thinking maybe it was *Current Affair* just ending. That would be eight. They had the story about the girl with the multiple personalities where the guy's committing adultery with this flirty college girl, then halfway through she turns into a six-year-old so you got not a rape charge but a child molestation. I told Rick, I'm not here to keep track of everyone out on the street. That's a job for the cops, but they're so busy sitting on their butts at the Plaza One Truck Stop and filling their guts with pie and drinking coffee, they got to have the citizens doing their police work."

I scribbled my name and the phone number at Hal's on a piece of paper. "I'd really appreciate it," I said as I handed it to her, "if you'd call me if you remember anything else."

Then I thanked her and walked back through the Laundromat. One of the kids, a little girl, opened and shut her hand at me, an automatic wave reflex, not like she meant it.

At the police station I asked the man at the desk for Detective Rick Seed. "I filed a missing person report with him last night."

"Hey, Manny," he shouted. "You want to talk to this lady."

Manny came out of the back, chewing on a large sticky pecan roll. When he saw me he wiped his mouth.

"I was looking for Rick Seed," I said.

"What about?" Manny reached in his mouth gingerly with one finger and dislodged a nut. "These things'll tear out your fillings if you're not careful."

"I filed a missing person report last night," I repeated. "I haven't heard anything."

"Rick's off-duty right now," said Manny. "Guy name of Danny Newcombe, right? I bet you're the private investigator." He grinned at me, remnants of sticky bun on his teeth. His eyes were small and brown, set close together in a pear-shaped face, his body pear-shaped too, as if he might do well to cut down on pecan rolls.

"I just wondered—"

"Don't worry, we're on it."

"You haven't found out anything?"

"As far we could tell, he got in some kind of vehicle with someone and drove off somewhere. Voluntarily. Probably a friend. If it was a little kid missing, we'd get out with the search party and the helicopters, but this is a grown man."

"He was a kid once."

He gave a short bark of a laugh. "You said it, I didn't. You try calling friends? People he might be visiting and didn't bother to tell you?"

"I don't know who that would be."

"Tell you what. Go home, young lady, and wait for your brother to call. He shows up, make sure you let us know. Understand he might have a reason not to be found."

A reason not to be found? And then it occurred to me—the cops weren't really looking, they just figured it was some drug deal gone bad and Danny was either hiding out or dead. It wasn't like a search for a child or a Sunday school teacher or a lovable old coot who wandered off into the hills.

But it was Danny, my beautiful brother, in his black jeans and buttoned-to-the-neck white shirt—the only brother I had left.

Halfway between Benson and Tombstone, I had a picture, more like a vision than a memory, of Danny: how he'd looked when I'd gone to visit him in prison in Michigan. His hair shaved short, his pale skin. He'd looked remarkably buff, though, sporting muscles I'd never seen on him before. But his eyes were blank, looking inward, not out at me, his sister, who remembered him when he was small and innocent and honest.

I wanted my little brother back, where was he? All I'd learned in Benson was that Danny probably got into a truck or some kind of vehicle that took off in the direction of the freeway. He could be anywhere by now, anywhere, and nobody seemed to care that much but me.

I pulled over to the side of the road. There was nothing in particular to see. Some shrubby dry bushes and a lot of red dirt. I rested my head on the steering wheel and began to weep.

Go home, young lady, and wait for your brother to call.

Bullshit.

Logan was a jerk and I was glad I'd left town to get away from him, but he wouldn't have let those cops treat him like a helpless idiot. He would have known just what to do, I thought, as I wept. If Logan had been with me, he wouldn't have left Benson last night, he would have torn the town apart looking for Danny, would have had them put out an APB for any suspicious vehicles. I could go back to Hal's and call him right now.

When I was sure that I'd finished crying, I blew my nose. Probably I wasn't going to call Logan. At least I hoped not. I rummaged through my purse, found my makeup bag, and tilted the rear-view mirror down. Carefully I applied eyeliner, that little smudge under the eye that makes all the difference. Then I started up the van and headed back to Dudley.

chapter seven

I FELT AS OLD AND TIRED AS THE HILLS. FOR a little extra coverage I stopped at a Circle K in Tombstone and bought a pair of big cheap sunglasses. I kept them on when I got back to Hal's and went into the office to question Wally.

He was on the ladder, smearing gray pasty mud on the seams of the Sheetrock. He turned when I came in, mud in his hair and on his nose.

"Wally, do you know about the front window getting shot out?"

His eyes skittered off my sunglasses. "That glass was very old," he said. "I was sorry to see it go. It wasn't good quality, but it was history. I'd like to preserve as much of the old as possible, but of course these yuppie types want everything brand-new, tricked out to look old."

"Did Danny have enemies that you know of?" I asked, ignoring his obvious attempt to avoid any real communication.

Wally turned away and smoothed the mud carefully so I couldn't see his face when he answered. "It's hard to say." His voice was noncommittal.

I tried another tack. "Do you know the woman next door?"

"Lourdes Grijalva, of course I know her. Now, there's an interesting lady. The last of the miners' wives, and Hispanic to boot. Due to old prejudices Hispanics are hesitant to get involved in local politics, so they tend to get ignored, but her family's lived here a long time. Someone should sit down with her and videotape her family stories. I suggested that to—"

"Maybe I'll go talk to her," I broke in.

"Missing?" Lourdes Grijalva frowned. She had short styled dark hair, skin like apricots, and wore a brilliant blue sweatshirt that looked somehow too elegant to sweat in, and black knit pants. "For goodness' sake."

"I thought you could tell me something, anything, about Danny, what was going on in his life that you could see."

"Well . . ." She hesitated. "When I met him and Kristi I thought he was maybe a little old for just a little girl like her. So pretty, and nice clothes. Not sloppy like some people here. A little girl like that needs her youth."

I'd thought the same myself. Seeing as how Danny was my brother, I tried to look neutral.

She added apologetically, "I could see he was good to her, though. That's what really matters. I have a good man myself. He was with the mining company for twenty years before they closed down. Everyone in town worked there and now there's only two men left, him and one other." She sighed.

We sat in her living room. From the outside you could see French doors, but inside the doors were covered with heavy red velvet curtains and the place was wall-to-wall-carpeted in red. The furniture looked vaguely baronial. From every available horizontal surface photographs of the large extended family of Lourdes Grijalva smiled out from their frames.

"And, of course," Lourdes said, "there was the time someone shot out the window. You heard about that?"

I nodded, grateful she was the one to bring it up.

"I called the police. My goodness. Scared me to death. My husband was working that night. I worry a lot since all these new people came here."

"Did you see anything after you heard the shot?" I asked.

"No," she said, "and I didn't want to." She sniffed the air. "Oh, my chorizo. Come into the kitchen. I'll make you a little tortilla with chorizo and egg. You'll like it. Kristi loves my chorizo."

I followed her into the kitchen and sat down on a chrome and yellow vinyl chair at a yellow formica table. She went to the stove and began cracking eggs into a frying pan. "Chorizo's ready—and it's no time at all to cook eggs," she said. The smell in the kitchen was rich and spicy. Once again I was a little girl, sitting in my mother's kitchen, as safe then as I would ever be for the whole rest of my life. I watched her cook for a few minutes.

"So you don't have any idea at all who might have shot out the window," I said finally.

"I know he's your brother and all, but to tell you the truth, most of the bad stuff that happens around here is drugs." She flipped a tortilla in another frying pan. "I won't say names, but a boy grew up with my daughter Belen, got himself a brand-new Camaro. His family isn't rich. 'Where does it come from?' I asked Belen. 'Drugs,' she tells me. 'Everyone knows it.' His family, you tell me they don't notice? Belen says they take it up to Tucson, these kids, sell it. How come everyone knows but nobody tells? Here you are. A nice tortilla."

"Thank you." I took a bite. The chorizo was a kind of sausage, very hot and greasy. The eggs softened the fires of Mexico burning in the chorizo just enough.

Lourdes watched me. "Good, huh? You can't buy chorizo like that in the stores."

"Um," I said, my mouth full. "It's delicious."

"Before that gunshot, there wasn't even a car," Lourdes mused. "I listen for cars when my husband's working nights. When the police came they wanted to know, like you, if I saw anything. It was Reyes Carbojal and that Jack Nance. Jack was a big football hero in high school.

"He's not happy. He doesn't eat right, for one thing. His wife left him with the kids, two boys, and went off with a Border Patrol man. Imagine that. She was only in the eighth grade when I was just graduating, but even then she was something. Just a raving beauty. My husband tells me she won't look good for long if she goes around leaving her husbands. It'll start to show on her face."

Lourdes looked skeptical. "'You wish,' I said to him." She glanced at me. "I hope your brother's okay. That Kristi. Just a baby. If your brother's missing, who's looking out for her? That pretty little girl all alone. You look out for her. When I was young, we went out on dates. Went to parties. Danced. Oh, we thought we were wild, but we looked out for each other."

I remembered Kristi's vision of her father, a little girl with an older boyfriend, looking for Daddy. It was easy to see how Kristi would have come over here occasionally, to sit at Lourdes's yellow Formica table and be taken care of.

"Kristi!" I called, back at Hal's, but there was no one in the house except Wally, swearing at the Sheetrock.

I sat at the counter and went through Danny's wallet. He had a Visa and a MasterCard; a California driver's license; a very old condom purchased in Charlotte, North Carolina, brand name of Dixie Deluxe; a Social Security card; a card from the Circle K to rent videos; two twenties, a five, three ones; a New York City subway token; a picture of my parents, a photographic portrait they'd had done in which both their faces looked totally sanitized; a snapshot of Kristi in a bikini, with not one extra ounce of fat on her body; a business card that said, *Danny Newcombe: pool specialist*; a card from a mortuary in Tombstone saying, *Why walk around half dead when we can bury you?*

Then I went back inside to the room where Wally was working. "Who were Danny's friends around here?" I was so tired by now, my voice wobbled a little, but I carried on. "Someone I can talk to about him."

Slapped once again with the hot living reality of the present, Wally leaned over and added a little water to the Sheetrock mud. Then he took off his glasses and scraped them with his thumbnail. His eyes looked blind. "You might go and talk to Brody, I suppose. He was a pretty good friend of Danny's."

"Brody? Just Brody?"

"He owns a body shop in town. I don't know if that's his first or last name. I've never heard him called any other way." He brightened a little, reaching firmer ground. "It's not unusual around here. And many people go by descriptive names, a throwback to older times. That's where so many last names come from, Miller, Smith, those are good examples of occupational names. Let's see, there's Plumber Bill, Indian Joe, Sundance, the Black Widow, Pretty Michael, Ron the Rapist."

"Ron the Rapist?"

"Well, he never was *convicted.*"

chapter eight

OUR VEGGIES DON'T DO DRUGS, SAID THE sign in the window of the Natural Foods Co-op on Main Street. In front of the store was a table with a petition on it. No one was behind the table and the petition was held down by a large jagged rock. PROTECT THE NATURAL RESOURCES OF ANTARCTICA, it urged. Antarctica was far away, but the desert sun was not; it beat down, soaking into my black clothes, relentless and tiring as I walked down Main Street on my way to a body shop owned by someone called Brody.

At least I didn't have to drive the van, noisy, smelly, and gas-guzzling. You could walk just about everywhere in Dudley.

It was easy to tell the local stores from the tourist ones. The tourist stores sold earrings, two pairs for five dollars, also turquoise and postcards. There were a couple of art galleries, one that sold southwestern art of Indians and sunsets and one that sold local artists' work or at least showed it, called the Main Street Collective. In the window was a charcoal drawing from *The Last Supper*, all the disciples looking at television sets. *The Last TV Dinner*, it was titled.

I'd started at the post office, where a few old men sat on the benches in front, hailing other old men and watching the prettiest of the women. There were women with very short hair and boots and jeans, women dressed for work in high heels and short skirts or dresses, hippie-looking women in layers of bright clothing from Guatemala and South America. Men in cowboy boots, work boots, jeans, and khakis, men wearing old blankets like serapes, and preppy men in polo shirts, a few men in suits. Obvious tourists, polyester-clad retirees, gawked their way down the street, faces severely congenial.

Somehow it was all like a giant crafts fair, but I was an outsider, not there for the fun, as I searched the faces of everyone as if to find a clue as to what had happened to Danny. Farther up Main Street was a Baptist church, a large white structure, ponderous and maybe anachronistic now that the miners had left. I tasted a bitterness in my throat, compounded of fatigue and anxiety.

A block or so later Main Street changed its name to Tombstone Canyon and became residential: little frame houses with old-fashioned porches, surrounded with trees, chinaberry and those trees called variously ailanthus trees, cancer trees, trees of heaven—your basic New York City vacant lot tree. Around me the frame houses extended up the hillsides every which way, some all spruced up and painted in earth-tone multiple San Francisco colors, others with old cars and rusty bedsprings in the yard mingling with the marigolds.

In the drainage ditch that ran alongside the right side of the street, a trickle of water, perhaps once a stream, meandered through clumps of pink aster. Clouds of yellow butterflies fastened themselves to the last of the purple valerians, cicadas hummed busily, and I fell into a hazy dream of late summer early fall where people drank iced tea on their front porches and pondered on nothing much.

Brody's shop was a cement-block building between two small wooden houses, looking like a football player at an old ladies' tea party. Ailanthus trees yellowed gloriously around it. So the zoning was still loose here; the newer urbanized residents hadn't got a firm hold of the city council yet.

The door was open. I stepped inside. "Hello?"

"Howdy." A man stood in the back of the shop, wrench in hand. Tufts of red hair stuck out from under his NAPA Auto Parts cap. He had a large friendly nose and an expression of great goodwill.

"Brody?"

"None other. What can I do for you?"

"Wally sent me," I said. "I'm Danny Newcombe's sister, Chloe."

"No kidding." He grinned. "Well, hey, pleased to meet you."

"Wally said you and Danny were friends. I wanted to ask you some questions."

"Sure thing. Why don't you sit down while I give this wrench one more turn." He gestured to a car seat propped against the wall.

I sat and looked around. There was a little office in front of me and a bulletin board with a sign on it that read:

WANTED:
A GOOD WOMAN WHO
CAN CLEAN
AND COOK FISH, DIG
WORMS, SEW AND WHO
OWNS A GOOD FISHING
BOAT AND MOTOR.

PLEASE ENCLOSE PHOTO OF BOAT AND MOTOR.

Brody put down the wrench and walked over to a refrigerator in one corner of the shop.

"Pepsi?" he inquired. "Gatorade? Maybe you'd like a near beer. That's what I'm drinking these days."

"Diet Pepsi?" I asked.

"Nope."

"Then water," I said.

"You girls," he said, which was what you might expect from someone with a sign like that. I was too tired to be offended. It's hard work and life goes on the same as before. "Always on a diet whether you need it or not. Come on. Live a little."

A hit of caffeine might be useful. I accepted a Pepsi, sipped, then set it down on top of a milk crate piled with old copies of *Hemmings Motor News* and some car magazines, *Wild and Woody,* said the one on top over a picture of a wood-paneled station wagon accessorized with a healthy blonde in a polka-dot bikini.

In the middle of the floor was a very old car, maybe from the forties, dotted all over with silvery globs. "That's my Mercury," Brody said. "All Bondo'd to hell now, but she's going to be a beauty when I get done."

He opened the can of near beer and drank like he wished it were the real thing and there was the rest of the six-pack to follow. But it wasn't the real thing. I looked at him with interest: a real-man type and he didn't even drink. At least not at the present.

He set down the can. "Danny mentioned you were coming to town. What's up?"

"Danny and Kristi picked me up at the airport yesterday and we stopped in Benson. The van wasn't running too good, so Kristi and I went to the Wagon Wheel, and Danny—Danny—" I was starting to lose it. I took a deep breath. "Danny disappeared, vanished, just like that. I mean, he's gone, I don't know where."

"No shit." He looked at me. "I guess you know Danny's not exactly a flake, but he's pretty impulsive. You know what he reminds me of? Those guys shoot themselves out of a cannon into a net? He's the kind of guy, halfway out of the cannon is when he decides to check for the net."

"I wish I didn't keep thinking the net was me. Full of holes."

"Hey." Brody's voice was solicitous. "Don't rag yourself. I gotta admit the whole thing doesn't make sense." He scratched his chin. "I know for a fact Danny was looking forward to seeing you."

"I went to the cops," I said, "in Benson. Then, this morning—a detective came to the house. Jack Nance. He seemed to think there might be a connection between Danny's disappearance and some guy that got murdered. Chip O'Leary."

"That Nance," said Brody. "He's a workaholic. Nothing else to do with his time since Luann left him. That killing was out in the Valley. It's not even his territory. Sheriff's department investigated it. Nance had his eye on Chip for a while. Must have pissed him off, Chip getting killed out of his jurisdiction."

"But the connection," I said. "I don't see the connection with Danny."

"That's 'cause you're not Nance. Listen, okay? Danny and Kristi hung out here a lot. That damn van of his was just a piece of shit. He'd never fix it right, just wanted me to rig it up so it'd go a few more miles. Then we'd get stoned. Danny always had good shit."

"Danny was dealing?" My heart turned over. Dealing and

dead. Dead like O'Leary. No. God, how could I ever tell my parents; one child left, out of three?

Brody shook his head. "I never said that. To the best of my knowledge Danny wasn't dealing—not the whole time I knew him, okay?"

"But he knew Chip," I persisted. "Why was that?"

"So what?" Brody sighed. "Chip was a college-boy type, grew up comfortable, and thought that made him smarter than everybody: an amateur pretending to be big-time. First rule in dealing is keep your mouth shut."

"Jack Nance called him an amateur too."

"I don't have anything against Nance except his profession. He's kind of a car nut like myself, but it's got so you can't even go to the damn dentist for a root canal and get a decent painkiller—got to be something nonnarcotic. I'm not in favor of those big-time crack dealers or those gangs, but we got a lot of ex-hippies here smoking a quiet joint now and then don't need the aggravation. You notice how all of a sudden in the last few years nobody ever smoked dope in their whole lives? We got ourselves a nation of liars."

Abruptly he crumpled the empty near beer can as if that were what he wanted to do to a nation of liars and threw it neatly into an oil drum.

He rubbed his chin and went on. "Danny was a good guy—is, hell, he ain't buried yet—with a little problem 'cause of having been in the joint. I say use it, capitalize on it. I been incarcerated myself, not the joint, of course, but jail, up in Montana. Maybe Danny should have got a better lawyer. I plea-bargained, copped to a misdemeanor. All I had to do was pay a fine and leave the state. Looked good on their records, one more conviction, what with elections coming up. That time I spent in jail I read more books than the whole rest of my life."

"We should all be so lucky," I said sarcastically. In spite of the Pepsi, fatigue had started to numb my brain. Brody's face seemed to advance toward me, then recede.

"Anyway," he said, "I asked Danny one time how come he hung out with Chip, and he told me it was the photography."

"The photography?" I stared at him. "What photography?"

"I don't know what photography. Just photography in general. Wasn't Danny some kind of photography nut?"

"Not that I know of. He told you that?"

"I never asked. I just assumed it."

"It doesn't make sense," I said. "I mean, Danny *never* talked about photography."

"People change."

I looked at him skeptically.

"You know who you should ask about that? Guy who owns this Atelier Photography Studio over on the Gulch. Stan, his name is, Stan—aw, I forget. Chip and Danny hung out there sometimes. Course, you could just ask Kristi."

"I haven't seen Kristi since last night," I said. "We both crashed, then she wasn't around this morning when I got up."

"Ah." Brody's eyes shifted away from mine.

"What?" I asked "*What?*"

"Nothing." He looked at me speculatively. "You know what you need? A good night's sleep."

"Easy for you to say."

A horn honked and an old guy pulled up in a fancy pink convertible. He got out and advanced toward Brody, looking happy, you could tell he liked Brody a lot.

"Back to work." Brody stood up.

I stood too.

Photography? Danny had never expressed an interest in photography. I was hot and bone-tired: sick of strangers and still on New York time. Adrenaline had gotten me through the day so far, but even my supply of that was almost on empty. The little wooden houses in this strange town seemed made of cardboard, props from a movie whose script I'd forgotten to read. The winding street was full of potholes placed purposely by some malevolent person from Public Works to trip me up. I climbed a treadmill, watching my feet, my only goal the futon in Hal's bedroom.

"Kristi?" I called as I walked in the door. No answer. "Wally?" No Wally either.

I went to the door of the room where Kristi had slept last night and looked in, saw a mattress flush on the floor, unmade, a wicker end table with the core on it from the apple Kristi had eaten last night. I remembered now the door I'd heard opening and closing last night; it must have been Kristi, leaving.

I hadn't seen her since. Where had she gone? I closed the door on the room.

The phone rang. *Danny?*

"Hello?" I said.

"Chloe. It's good to hear your voice."

"*Hal.* Oh, Hal." I sat down at the kitchen counter, leaned my head on my hand, and wept once more. I wept and wept. When I had no more tears I told Hal everything that had happened. "This is your house," I added. "Aren't you going to come here soon?"

"I meant to use the house in Dudley more," he said, "but I work at the Windward House, it's for AIDS patients, and things are always so urgent here—right now we have a death. Listen, I'll come to Dudley tomorrow, okay, the soonest I can get away—sometime in the afternoon. Can you hang on?"

"Yes."

"Here's my number, just in case."

After I hung up I felt better. Hal was coming and he hadn't said things like, *Oh, he'll show up,* or *Don't worry.* I went into the bedroom and collapsed on the futon.

It was dark when I woke up. I looked at my watch. Three A.M. I got up and walked out of the bedroom. The door to the room where Kristi had gone last night was still closed. I opened it. Moonlight streamed in through a skylight, painting the empty room silver. It smelled like something sweet and rotten.

The apple core. I threw it away in the trash under the sink and fell back in bed.

chapter nine

I SLEPT TILL THE SUN FILLED THE BEDROOM, then I woke with a start, saw from my watch it was nearly eleven, and felt full of guilt that I'd slept late instead of looking for Danny. But at least Hal was coming, coming soon, this very afternoon. From the thumps and bumps coming from the other room, I gathered Wally had already arrived.

I got up, dressed, and went out into the main room.

"Wally?" I called

A white man appeared from the office, literally white, like a mime: his face and glasses and bandanna were white and only his nose seemed to have escaped powdering. He took off the bandanna and wiped off some of the dust and there was Wally. "Hi, there, Chloe. What's up?"

"I guess Danny didn't call or anything?" I asked without any hope.

Wally shook his head.

"And Kristi? Is she here?"

"No, ma'am."

"Where the hell is she?" I said.

I was annoyed with him, with this apparent inability to notice what was really going on, which, when I thought about it, had to be a big lie. Besides, I was worried sick about Danny, and Wally was the only person around to take it out on. My voice rose. "You must have *some* idea."

"Well . . ." Wally shook out the bandanna and shuffled his feet. "To be honest, when Danny was out of town Kristi didn't always sleep here."

"What do you mean?" My voice was relentless.

"That's all I know. It was just sort of talk around town."

"Great," I said. "Just great. So she had a boyfriend, is that what you're saying?"

Here Danny was missing, maybe in danger, maybe dead, and Kristi had gone off to see a boyfriend on the side—Danny sure knew how to pick them.

Wally took off his glasses and began to polish them. "I guess. But I don't know who, okay?" His voice sounded very tired. "I have a wife and a little girl. I would like to lead a life of quiet study. Academia is full of egos competing against each other, so I chose not to be there. I wanted to be in a small town where there are structures—kinships and loyalties. I don't know what's going on in this one. It passes beyond my understanding."

Suddenly I felt like a bitch. "Oh, Wally, I'm sorry. Hal's coming sometime this afternoon, by the way."

He nodded. "Thank God for that. I like working for him. He's a good person. We used to talk when he still spent time here. We talked about America. We live in violent times in a violent country. He's a well-read person." He smiled sadly. "Full of quotations. Here's one he gave me. It's beautiful, so I suppose there's some sustenance there." His voice slipped into another mode:

I am like the king of a rainy country,
Wealthy but helpless,
Young and ripe with death.

He put on his glasses, looking embarrassed. "Baudelaire. Excuse me for waxing poetic."

Photography. It made no sense and because it made no sense it seemed somehow promising.

Stan at the Atelier Studio on the Gulch was around sixty or so and had enough white beard to cover most of his face. He grinned at me and shoved some photographs of Chip O'Leary across the counter. I looked down at them.

"Oh!" I said.

There were three of them, one a head shot and the other two more casual, taken on the street, during what looked like some kind of crafts fair. Chip wore a cowboy hat in the head shot. He was dark-haired and looked so much like my Danny, for just a second I thought there'd been a mistake.

"Dead three weeks after that last photo—the head shot," said Stan. "Looked like he'd been burned all over with cigarettes, then shot in the head, least that's what they figured—coyotes got to him pretty good, I understand."

Chip stared at me with a know-it-all grin.

"I wonder if you know my brother," I said. "Danny Newcombe?"

"Sure, Danny." Stan scratched his beard. "Knew of him, but we never met. I'm not a socializer."

"Who did Chip hang out with?" I asked. "Who might be able to tell me more?"

"He had a girlfriend Darla, you could ask her. Got a studio over in Lowell."

"Where's that?"

"Just outside of Old Dudley, you go past the Pit."

"The Pit?"

"The Lavender Pit. It's what's left of the mining operation. You'll see."

I walked back to Hal's and got the van, then followed the highway out to Lowell, past a sign that said SCENIC VIEW—which apparently referred to the Lavender Pit on my right: a hole in the ground the size of a mountain in reverse, with terraced sides, now crumbling. The whole time I kept thinking about Kristi, what Wally had told me. I couldn't understand how she could be so thoughtless—leaving me to fend for myself.

I turned right, into Lowell.

It had once been part of Dudley proper, Stan had told me, until they dug the Pit, which cut off the connection between the two. Now most of the storefronts were empty, full of dust and spiderwebs where once there'd been a five-and-ten, a shoe store, a movie theater.

I parked the van in front of the theater and got out. In the display case was a poster advertising *Howard the Duck*. The choice of movie seemed to indicate one more reason why the theater had shut down. I couldn't resist peering in. There was the refreshment stand in a tiled lobby and those big old standing chrome ashtrays they filled with white sand where you put out your cigarettes when the lights dimmed. It looked like a good theater, probably had a wide screen and comfortable seats and a balcony, not broken up the way they broke up theaters nowadays, so you could hear the faint sound of the movie next door as you waited for yours to start.

Waited for Logan to come back with the Diet Coke, the popcorn, the Jordan almonds, the hand carelessly laid on the thigh. Further back in time, Danny and James and I hit the matinees almost every Saturday without fail, where we learned important things about life, things our parents hadn't taught us, splendid and seductive on the screen: greed, murder, revenge, and obsessive love. No one called it obsessive back then, we called it true. True love.

I walked away from the theater, around a corner to Darla's studio. In the big storefront window were displayed a series of cups, bowls, and pitchers in bizarre shapes, painted with bright intricate designs. A sign on the door said BACK IN with a clock underneath, hands pointing at ten o'clock. Except it was almost two o'clock now and the door had a padlock on it.

I drove back to Dudley.

As I drove up the steep hill back to Hal's, there seemed to be an inordinate number of cars parked along the sides of the street, including a police car. *What was a police car doing here?* My mind went blank and it took me a second to realize that the carport where I was heading was now occupied by a green camper. Hal? I hoped to God it was Hal. I backed up and managed to squeeze in a space halfway down the hill.

I got out and stood paralyzed for a moment, then hurriedly stumbled up the rest of the hill and into the carport. The door was open and the kitchen seemed full of people, including a cop and, thank goodness—finally Hal.

When he saw me, Hal came outside to the carport. He was

casually dressed in a blue polo shirt, khaki pants, his pale hair cropped close, not long as it had been at James's funeral, where people stared at him covertly. Our eyes met. There was a look in his that told me right away: something was wrong.

Fear can be a psychedelic drug, bringing everything into focus, imparting hidden meaning. The leaves of the cancer trees clustered by the carport glowed like a warning. Leaves once green, now gloriously dying. *Stop here and you're still safe.*

I ran to him, wanting to rest against him, to be comforted, to sleep. "Danny's dead," I whispered. "I know he's dead. Isn't he?"

"I don't know," Hal said. "But the police want to talk to you. This isn't about Danny, it's Kristi. Kristi's been killed."

chapter ten

"KILLED?" I SAID. "WHAT DO YOU MEAN? An accident?" I babbled.

Hal took my hand and led me to a far corner of the carport. "Shot in the head."

"Murdered? But how, why, where?"

"We'll talk about it later. You have to come inside, the police need to ask you some questions. They'll explain."

There seemed to be people everywhere. Wally on a kitchen stool, his face smeared with Sheetrock mud; two women, one in her fifties with a tight perm and glasses and another younger with a freckled country face. The younger woman brought me a glass of water, which I sipped.

"Chloe, I'm so sorry for your loss," she said. "I'm Ruth and this is Annie. We're with the Victim Witness Program."

My eyes skimmed off her. My mouth felt dry and the water seemed to make no difference. The Mapplethorpe photograph was gone from the refrigerator, bits of Scotch tape showing where it had been. Hal must have ripped it down as the police appeared and the Newcombe family destroyed the last shreds of his privacy.

And who were the two women? What was the Victim Witness Program anyway? Was polite conversation called for? I wasn't up to it. I folded my arms on the counter and rested my head on them, my eyes closed.

". . . alone?"

"Pretty upset . . ."

Then Wally's voice ". . . fresh pot of coffee?"

". . . not the best thing for people in shock," one of the women said. ". . . nice of you to offer."

Then Hal was beside me. "This officer needs to talk to you," he said, putting his hand on my arm. "Chloe. Can you handle it?" His voice urged me toward sanity, adulthood.

I raised my head. "Yes." I needed to get back in control.

A cop stood beside me, plainclothes, standard cop windbreaker, Logan had one just like it.

Hal was saying to the women, "I know Kristi's stepfather. Otto Marsh. He's a therapist in Los Angeles. Kristi's counselor here would have his number. I referred Kristi to her. Mary Ann Cunningham, over at Catholic Community Services. Maybe you could make the call. When you get her on the line, I'd like to talk to her when you're finished."

"Miss?" the cop said. He was approaching middle age, Hispanic, wearing aviator glasses tinted pale brown. "I'm Detective Bill Soto, miss. I'm sorry to intrude, but if you're more composed now I need to ask you a few questions. Maybe we could go outside."

I followed him out the door, Hal behind me.

"Sir," Soto said to him, "could I just have some time alone with her?"

Outside it was cooler than in the kitchen. We stood in the carport, where I leaned against the wall of the house, looking over at the green camper, at Hal's windshield covered with squashed bugs.

"Shot in the head?" I said disbelievingly to the officer.

"One shot, probably died instantly. No sign of a struggle, so it maybe wasn't a stranger."

"So you don't know who did it," I said. "Do you have the gun?"

"No. Miss—"

"Where did it happen," I cut in. "When?"

"When is hard to say right now, I think maybe you can help us there. They found her up at a house belonging to the gentleman inside. Hal. There was evidence of apparent drug use."

"But *this* is his house," I said stupidly.

"He owns more than one," said Soto patiently.

"Well, if there was drug use, it certainly had nothing to do with Hal," I said.

"Your brother's girlfriend, wasn't she? It's your brother I'm concerned about at the moment. He's missing. Want to tell me about that?"

Once again I told the story of Danny's disappearance. Each word was a bead, the story a string of them, smooth and hard and meaningless. When I finished, I asked, "But no one seemed very interested before. Why are you so interested in him now?"

"Maybe your brother showed up at the house where Kristi was shot."

Disbelief suddenly energized me. I stamped my foot on the carport floor like a spoiled child. "I just told you Danny wasn't here at all," I said vehemently.

"We'd like to question him. He could have arrived later. Met her at the house."

"That's pretty unlikely." I glared at him, furious. "Then where is he now? Why would—" But as soon as the words came out of my mouth I saw what he was getting at—Danny was a suspect—Danny, the convicted felon.

Soto looked out onto the street and patted his shirt pocket as if checking for cigarettes, then dropped his hand reluctantly. "These are things I need to ask you. I'd be remiss if I didn't investigate all the possibilities."

"It wasn't Danny," I said. "He really loved her."

"Maybe too much?" inquired Soto. He shrugged apologetically. "You know how it is."

I thought of what Wally had told me, Kristi spending the night elsewhere when Danny was out of town. I should tell Detective Soto that—it would give him a suspect. Or would it reinforce Danny as a suspect, give him a motive: revenge, jealousy?

Soto looked at me musingly. His face was battered, a tiny scar like a half-moon by his upper lip, his eyes behind the aviator glasses intelligent. A good man, maybe, concerned with the truth. Kristi had had a boyfriend on the side, maybe that was the truth, but how to convey the real truth to him? That Danny would not have hurt her.

Let someone else tell him about the boyfriend, I decided. Wally said it was all over town and I didn't have a name anyway.

"So you reported your brother's disappearance to law enforcement in Benson and drove back here. Then . . . ?"

"We went to bed. I was really tired and Kristi seemed tired too."

"Upset?"

"Of course," I said.

"Unusually so?"

"She wasn't in tears or hysterical. No more upset than me. Danny had disappeared. We were both upset. Is that so strange?"

"No, ma'am, it isn't. When did you see her last?"

A leaf detached itself from a cancer tree and floated to the ground. It seemed to take forever and no time at all. I was thinking of Kristi, her face tired and spent, dropping her high-heeled shoes onto the kitchen floor, sexy badges of adulthood, useless now.

"That night," I said. The night before last, and all that time after she'd probably been dead. Filled with an obscure guilt, a sense of failed responsibility, I covered my face with my hands.

Soto went back in the house, but I stayed outside for a few minutes, beyond tiredness to the point where I now believed I would never be able to sleep again. Irises grew in clumps behind the cancer trees. One of them bloomed, fall purple. I tried to forgive myself, but for what? I logically had no reason. I hardly knew Kristi and it was hard to mourn her. Full knowledge of death dawns slowly anyway, and hers was abstract and out of my sight.

She'd been shot; someone had pointed a gun at her and put a bullet through her brain. A pretty blond girl walking toward me at the airport. Giggling. I blocked the image.

They were already setting up Danny as a suspect and the only thing worse than that would be if Danny were already dead, and the more I searched for answers, the more in danger I would be too. *I need a gun,* I thought, *I need to find a way to get a gun.*

When I finally went back in, the two women hovered, clipboards in hand, looking bright-eyed and sympathetic. One of them handed me a card. "If you'd like to talk about this with someone, we can refer you to some counselors," she said.

"That's okay," I said politely. I looked at the card unseeingly and put it in my pocket.

Wally had vanished. Soto was talking to Hal at the counter. The house had that full yet abandoned feeling houses get in the aftermath of large noisy parties. I went into the living room area and lay down on the couch.

Soto was asking Hal, "You mentioned she was seeing a counselor here? Substance abuse, sir?"

"She had bipolar mood disorder. That means extremes of feeling—manic depression, it used to be called. She took lithium to control it. When she got here we talked about it and I referred her to Mary Ann. I'm a mental health professional myself."

"Mental problems, among them depression," said Soto, "the disappearance of the boyfriend. Not much of a support system in town, sir? Or was there? Anyone close to her here in Dudley we should know about?"

"I don't know," said Hal. He added, his voice sounding exhausted, "Please, won't you let us be alone?"

"Wait." I sat up. "How did they find Kristi anyway?"

"Anonymous phone call," said Soto.

"Are you checking that out?"

"Yes, ma'am, we check out everything."

Hal looked over at me. "Chloe, let the man do his job."

"Thank you, sir," said Soto. "That's all, sir. Call me, either of you, if anything relevant comes to mind. If Danny shows up we'll need to talk to him."

After Soto had gone I went over to Hal, who was standing by the front window. Outside there was a garden of sorts but neglected. Marigolds had taken over, leggy but still blooming stalwartly. In Topanga Hal had been proud of his garden with flowers blooming in every season.

"Kristi's counselor's going to contact the parents," Hal said. "She's a pro. I should do it myself—I know Kristi's father, Otto, Otto Marsh." His voice was so tired it frightened me. "But I don't have the psychic energy—this work in Tucson is draining me."

I took his hand. He was an easy man to touch. He let people near him. Sometimes you felt if he wasn't careful, all those needy people he let near would just swallow him up.

"It's okay, Hal. It's okay for her to do it."

"I have to get back tonight," Hal said. "I'd like to take a little nap, then I'll take you out to dinner. How does that sound?"

"Perfect," I said.

Hal crashed on the couch. I sat on the porch. It was getting on in the afternoon, a mellow day in the early fall, shadows just coming on. I closed my eyes, opened them. A barefoot blond girl, toenails painted blue, slipped away among the shadows, was there and then was not.

chapter eleven

IT WAS DARK WHEN HAL AND I LEFT THE house. Hal wore a khaki vest and I had on a light sweater against the evening cool. I'd gone into the bedroom and slept for an hour or two, then Hal woke me to go out to dinner. Lights shone from the houses that clung to the hills. The air was loamy and tinged with a whiff of marijuana as if all the residents were sitting inside in the evening quietly breaking the law. The curving streets were bisected by long flights of cement steps that went straight down.

Hal took the steps gracefully, lightly, head held high, hands in the pockets of his khaki vest. I held on to the iron railing, uncertain of the terrain. After a while, Hal paused to let me catch up.

He gestured with his head. "Up there. My house where they found Kristi, at the very top."

I looked up but couldn't see much except the top of the mountain where moonlight shone down. Vaguely I saw a dark shape above the rest, tiny.

"I call it the shack. It's where she went to meditate. When I moved to Dudley everything was incredibly cheap and it seemed like a place I wanted to be. People here, they aren't caught up in brand-name frenzies, careerism; there's not so much pressure to compete, to conform. I've got too much pressure in my life already. I got the shack for two thousand dollars. Such a deal, I thought. What's that expression—'dear at any price.'"

At the bottom of the steps we crossed the street and went down another flight. "They found drugs in the shack." Hal's voice was exasperated. "Danny swore there'd be no hard drugs in my house."

I didn't know what to say.

Down here the houses were set close to the steps. In the small yards a few roses still bloomed on straggly branches. A dog barked, another answered. Directly beside us, light streamed from an uncurtained kitchen window. Inside, a man and a woman sat at a table. The man was hunched over a plate of food while the woman, hands folded in front of her, stared at nothing.

"Cocaine and some other drug—they're not even sure what it is," said Hal. "They think maybe it's some street drug called Dream Queen, but they're going to do lab work on it."

"Where did she get it? Not from Danny," I said skeptically. "He was too concerned about her, worried about her taking her medicine." At the bottom of the second flight of stairs there was a streetlight. I looked up at Hal, wanting him to believe me.

His face looked drawn, ascetic. In the light there was a beauty about his eyes, his forehead, a natural serenity, as though God's hand had passed over his face, choosing him.

"I wish I knew where Danny was," he said. "I wish to hell I knew."

"I'm going to find him, Hal. I will." I had no ideas and no real leads. All my theories scared the hell out of me, but the last thing I wanted was to put more burdens on Hal.

He smiled at me wanly.

We walked together down the street in silence, up to a porch and into the Copper Queen Hotel. The spacious restaurant was nearly empty. There were white cloths on the tables and bored waiters hovering. We sat down at a table with a silver-colored vase crammed with sprays of fake freesia. It was ugly and Hal moved it aside impatiently. James had said once about Hal, "When he's lying in the grave he'll be figuring out how to redecorate the coffin."

He reached for the menus and handed me one.

"You can order for me," I said, as if we were an old-fashioned couple back in the 1950s and I was a frail woman unable to make decisions.

The waiter came over.

"Seafood pasta," Hal told him. He looked at me for approval and I nodded.

"Kristi," he said, circling back to the topic when the waiter was gone. "I didn't spend much time with them here—of course, I wasn't close to Danny the way I was with James. James had a center that Danny lacks, but sometimes I'd see James in Danny's eyes."

The waiter set a basket of rolls between us. I took one automatically and broke it apart, spread butter on it from a little foil wrapper.

"I introduced them," Hal said. "Had them both to dinner. Because I knew her stepfather."

I nodded.

Hal went on. "She was in a manic phase at that dinner. She shone like a star, I recognized the problem at once. After she and Danny got together, I talked to him, told him to monitor her pills. He was conscientious, but one time when I came to Dudley she was in a depressive phase full of sadness, darkness."

I put down the buttered piece of roll and waited.

"It was as if she'd been born with a terminal illness that was going to kill her sooner or later. It was very hard on Danny. I understand how hard it was, going through the days when it's all wonderful and you think everything's fine, then it reverses and you find yourself falling with them. No matter what you do, you're helpless." He paused as if he had run out of words.

In the silence, back in the kitchen, dishes clinked. Someone dropped something, swore. The waiter brought the pasta. He set the steaming plates down, hovering with a waiterly smile on his face.

"This is fine," said Hal. "Thank you. We don't need anything else."

The waiter left.

"Oh, Hal," I said desperately. "I want Danny back. I want him back." I blinked my eyes, afraid I would start to cry right there in the restaurant.

Hal shook his head.

I took a deep breath and got control.

We picked at our pasta.

"She needed lots of attention and Danny volunteered," said Hal. "She drained him. He might have needed to get away. You know, Chloe, sometimes you have to get away. I see it time and time again with the relatives and the lovers of people I work with. You have to and it's like behind you, you can hear the buildings crumble, the sky cave in, but you do it anyway."

It scared me to hear him talk that way. He was right across the table from me but there was no current between us, the way there always used to be. "You never left James."

"No. I never left James." He straightened up in his chair.

* * *

When we left the hotel it was chilly. I put on my black sweater. We stood together on the street. Behind us rose the hotel, pale stucco and red tile, balconied. Faintly you could hear music coming from the bar, tinkly piano-bar ragtime.

"How are you now, Chloe?" asked Hal. "I'll walk you home, then I have to get back to Tucson. I've already been gone too long. I want you to promise me something, okay?"

The lights from the hotel cast shadows on his face, emphasizing the deepening lines around his mouth, a bruised look about the eyes.

"Yes," I said. "Sure."

"Keep the doors locked at night, windows too. Don't answer the door unless you know who it is. I mean, I think this is all about Kristi, but stay safe, all right?"

I smiled. "I'll do my best."

Behind us the piano tinkled on, silly with its own virtuosity.

"Chloe," said Hal suddenly, "I never considered leaving James. I cared for him very much. Please don't ever forget that." He looked defeated.

"You don't have to tell me that, Hal."

I swallowed. What was happening to my family? First James and now Danny. My parents, so innocent in Italy; in Rome, to be exact, maybe at this very minute sitting at a trattoria in Trastevere. There was one there, Mario's, they especially liked that they talked about a lot. I could see my father calling Mario over, inquiring in his rough Italian about the tiny golden potatoes in the salad, had he grown them himself in his garden outside the city? How proud they were that they avoided the tourist places, got to know the people. They didn't deserve this and I wouldn't tell them, not yet. If Danny showed up, safe and sound, he wouldn't want me to have told.

Down the street where the streetlights lit the road it turned so you couldn't see far ahead anywhere. Dudley was so unlike the big city I'd left, where people lived their lives privately in the middle of crowds. Here I felt everyone watching. The whole town circled and curved like one of those mazes where at any corner you might turn and come across a hidden treasure or a minotaur.

chapter twelve

HAL WALKED ME HOME, OPENED THE DOOR to the carport with his key, made sure I had a key of my own, and then checked every room in the house. Then I walked out with him to the camper, gave him a hug goodbye, and watched as he backed out, watched his red taillights going down the hill, then I closed the door behind me, locked it, and started down the hill on foot.

I loved Hal, but his realm was interior, where one was brave and fought off demons and bad guys just like the cops, but I was thinking not of Hal but of Logan. Logan, who had taught me to shoot. So much of Logan's frustration when he had to go on disability came from having to make that switch from exterior to interior. He couldn't cope with being unable to confront problems straight on and shoot them dead. I could see how he felt as I headed down to Brody's shop.

The light was on. I knocked once, twice, and then finally he came and let me in.

"Hello," he said, his face turning somber when he saw me. "I heard about Kristi."

Seeing him brought me down to earth. He was wearing a

T-shirt silkscreened with the words DUDLEY, ARIZONA—RUBBLE WITHOUT A CAUSE. His Levi's were old and faded and his face was as plain as his jeans, plain ordinary but somehow charming and as American as if he were standing on a pitcher's mound, chewing gum, about to throw a curveball.

"Coffee?" he offered. "It'll have to be black, I don't have the fixings."

I sat on the old car seat. "Sure," I said.

"What I heard," Brody said as he poured coffee, "she was shot."

"Once in the head," I said abruptly. I didn't see why we had to talk about it.

Brody came over and handed me a mug of coffee and sat down across from me on a metal stool. "Nobody heard?"

The coffee was thick and bitter. I tried not to make a face. "Someone called the police but it was anonymous."

"Most people probably didn't notice 'cause lots of people around here like to fire a gun, no reason at all."

"Charming," I said.

"You shoot someone in the head, you want to kill them," Brody said. "So I guess they hung around to make sure they didn't have to do a second shot."

"I want to buy a gun," I said. "You seem like someone who might be able to help me do that. A .38, if possible. A snub-nosed .38."

Brody looked at me for a minute. "Good choice." He nodded his head up and down a couple of times. "Nice size for a lady who wants a higher caliber." He brooded a little. "You know how to use a .38?"

"Yes, I do."

Brody took off his cap, put it back on again. "Thing is, I could maybe get you a gun, but then you're on my conscience if you shoot yourself in the foot, say, or blow out the neighbor's windows, or, God forbid, if you should just happen to blow someone away."

You can only let them get away with so much. I could have fluttered my eyelashes delicately and begged. It would even have been kind of fun, since Brody had a muscle structure made to fill out a T-shirt. He would be easy to flirt with, tease, but I was too vulnerable, worrying about Danny, for that kind of detachment.

"Just for the sake of argument," I said, "let's pretend that I'm a responsible adult. Maybe I should mention I work for a private investigator. I own a gun and have a license for it but it's in New York."

"Okay, okay, I'll see what I can do."

There was a silence.

"I promise," he added.

"Right away," I said. "I need it as soon as possible."

"It's late. I'm not a magician." He paused. "Check back with me tomorrow morning, say around ten."

I looked away, then back at him. "They were asking me about Danny," I said, "like they think he might have come back that night and shot her. As if he's a suspect."

Brody looked disgusted. "Total bullshit. That's not our Danny boy."

"But Kristi had another boyfriend too, didn't she, Brody?"

"Who told you that?"

"Never mind. It's true, isn't it? Who? Give me a name."

"I have to think about that," he said. "Kristi have folks somewhere?"

"L.A. A mother and a stepfather. Plus a father, somewhere out there. Hal knows the stepfather."

"Hal? That faggot guy?"

I stood up. "You shithead! Hal's a wonderful person."

"I can't help it," Brody protested. "It's the way I was raised."

"My brother was gay. James." I felt myself choke on the name but went on. "He's dead. He died of AIDS, okay? It's a sensitive subject."

"I'm sorry," Brody said. "Okay?"

"No." I began to walk restlessly around Brody's shop, passing the Mercury, rounding it. It looked like a spotty dinosaur. I came upon myself in the side mirror, wan, eyeliner smudged. When we deal with pain and grief, part of us is in sorrow, the other part rebelling against shouldering its burden.

I'd actually gone into the bathroom before Hal and I went to dinner and applied blusher, a little lip gloss, eyeliner.

"I said I was sorry," Brody called to me.

"You're not really sorry." I was somewhat mollified but needed to punish him a little more. Vain, heartless, I fluffed my hair in the side mirror. "Not that you used that word. You're sorry I heard you say it. You'll use it again."

"I said I was sorry," Brody said.

"You're just a redneck." I licked my finger and used it to unsmudge my eyeliner. "A redneck bigot."

"A poor boy. Never went to college, never learned to think big good thoughts. Drunken father, hardworking mother." He raised his voice. "Used to watch my mama cry every Saturday night when my daddy didn't come home. Used to hold her hand tight. Bring her a can of Dr Pepper to cheer her up."

"Okay, okay." I came around the Mercury.

It felt like I could trust him, I wasn't sure why. It's funny how women, when they get close to a man, will tell him everything, and he remembers maybe a quarter and complains he doesn't understand her, where a man will tell almost nothing to a woman and from that she constructs a whole elaborate personality.

"The boyfriend," I said. "Tell me."

"This town's a rumor mill," Brody said. "Get seen with somebody once and you might as well be pricing the rings. So maybe all it is, is a rumor." He shrugged. "Not to speak ill of the dead, but Kristi was probably the last thing Danny needed in his life. She led him around by the balls and let him think he was taking care of her."

I said in desperation, "My brother's missing. His girlfriend's dead. Can't you see how important this is? I need to know everything I can about both of them. No one's really looking for him except me. Maybe they'll start, now that he's a suspect. But in that case I don't want them to be the ones to find him."

Brody got up, went over to the Mercury, and ran his hand along the fender. He put his hands in his pockets, then he turned back to me. "Duane," he said. "His name's Duane Taylor. Okay? Happy now?"

"One more thing," I said.

Brody led me up the steps with iron railings. Below was the town, closed down for the night, with only the lights of the televisions flickering like little home fires.

We had reached the top of the steps. The moon was waning but still bright. All the houses lay below except for the shack high on the hill above us. We climbed another set of cement steps, crumbling and uneven. A yellow ribbon saying POLICE LINE DO NOT CROSS stretched across the front porch. In the yard the grass grew in tall clumps, wild grasses sprouted during summer rains and now dried out. Seeds grabbed on to my pants legs, prickly, irritating.

We went up the rickety steps and crossed POLICE LINE DO NOT CROSS onto the porch. Brody took a mechanic's rag from his pocket, wrapped it in his hand, and tried the door. It was locked, but the window beside it opened easily. We stepped over the low sill, not needing lights, the moon shone in the windows so brightly. Inside, the house had been gutted.

But in the moonlight I saw not so much a room but a Buddhist shrine: the little table with Buddha's statue on it, the incense, the embroidered cloth. Other than that and a mattress on the floor, the room was empty. James had been a Buddhist once, spent time at Karmê Chöling in Vermont. The room made me sad, reminded me of the house Hal had fixed up for James when James was dying up in Topanga Canyon, that house so full of peace and sunshine it was as though Hal had the power to evoke them at will.

But not here. The moonlight blackened a stain on the floor near the low table. Kristi's blood? Had I listened to her stories with the right attention? *Kristi,* I thought, *I'm so sorry.* The shack was cursed now, I thought, always would be.

"Hal," I said. "Oh, Hal." I reached my hand toward the Buddha.

"Don't touch anything," Brody said.

"They found drugs here too," I said. "Cocaine and some kind of street drug." My voice rose. "Tell me who's dealing in this town, Brody. Everyone who has a coke habit or who's into drugs in a weird way."

"You think I'm nuts? You think I'd give out information like that?"

"Listen," I said to him, "I'm not here to bust people, just to find things out. For Danny. For Kristi too, she was so sweet, she didn't deserve to be murdered. Please help me."

Brody had his back to me, looking out the back window. I'd trusted him because he seemed to have none of the moodiness I'd fought so hard against in Logan: dark heavy moods that poisoned everything. How did I know that—just because he'd offered me a little piece of his past back at the shop? Or was it the near beer, a man who was trying?

"I wish I could," he said, "but I got no idea. If I were you, I'd be careful about asking questions, in case someone thinks you know something you shouldn't. Maybe be careful about answering them too."

When I got back, a car was parked down below in front of the house. It was close to two A.M. I hadn't seen it before, so I gave it a wide berth. Then car door opened and a man got out, came toward me under the streetlight. It was Jack Nance.

"Thanks for scaring me." I began to walk up to the carport.

"What else could I do?" asked Nance reasonably, coming along beside me. "Honk my horn at you?"

"This is a funny time of night to be here."

"It wasn't so funny when I got here. I've been waiting awhile."

"I guess you know about Kristi."

"Course I do."

"They found drugs in the house too," I said. "Is that why you're here?"

"Kind of."

"You might as well come in." I flicked on the light. "Cocaine and some kind of street drug."

He followed me in. "They haven't done the lab work yet, but I checked it out and I got a pretty good idea about the street drug."

"What was it?" I asked.

"Dream Queen."

"Dream Queen?"

"A designer drug," said Nance. "Some chemist messing around with the molecules. It's got something called fentanyl in it that ups the potency twenty-seven times. They had some near-fatalities in Tucson. Sure to be fatal if you don't get a doctor quick. It's been around Tucson for a while, but it's only shown up here recently."

"So," I said, "maybe whoever she got it from is who shot her. It wasn't Danny. Danny didn't kill her."

"I never said he did."

"So who? Who got her the drugs and then killed her?"

"Don't know. As for the drugs how does anyone get them?"

"I thought you were with the famous BAG, don't you know who's dealing around here?" My voice was snide. Probably Nance didn't deserve it, but I didn't care.

"Who knows where anyone gets drugs? Out of the blue. Out of the goddamn sky." He sat down on one of the stools at the counter. Every hair on his head was neatly in place, streaked with the marks of a comb. What tidy people cops were. I'd come upon Logan one morning ironing his jeans. The thought made me want to cry. Had Nance sat in his car, running a comb through his hair to keep busy, as nervous in his own secret way as a boy on a first date?

"So where you been?" he asked.

"Am I on parole here?" I asked sarcastically. "Supposed to report back to you?"

"Naw. Just a friendly question. You went out to dinner with that Hal guy. Then you went somewhere else. Who'd you see?"

"A friend of Danny's."

"Howard Brodman?"

I wrinkled my nose. "Is that his name?"

"That's it." Nance reached over and toyed with a penny lying on the counter. He set it on its side and twirled it like a top. For a few seconds it spun and we watched as if we were there for an exhibition of penny-twirling. Abruptly Nance reached over and put his thumb on it. "You should be careful who you hang out with."

I wanted to laugh, thinking of Brody with his red hair sticking out from his cap. "Why?" I asked. "Because he's got some kind of conviction from sometime long ago in Montana? So he's a bad guy the rest of his life? I think it was just a misdemeanor too. He's just trying to make a living now."

"Yeah, just remember I told you. You been finding any clues?"

"What do you mean?"

He shrugged again. There was just one light on in the kitchen, directly over the counter. Everywhere else was dark and we were suspended together in the circle of light. From outside you might look in and see the loneliness that surrounded us, but I was inside, part of the picture.

Lourdes Grijalva had said Nance's wife had left him for a Border Patrol man. He radiated a chemistry, the kind abandoned men send off no matter how they may deny it. I didn't want to think about it. No matter what you do to be free of your sex, nature is always there planning surprises.

"Why are you questioning me?" I asked. "Someone already questioned me this afternoon. Officer Bill Soto."

"He's the investigating officer for this case. I'm after the broader picture. You question people at the moment of bereavement, you don't always learn everything. Sometimes you learn more too, but you never know. I can't overlook the drug connection. Chip O'Leary. I'm here hoping you might remember something you didn't care to share with me before. Plus to warn you off again—this is not a game."

"I really don't have a thing to offer."

"This was a regular old town," said Nance disgustedly, "working-class people going to work, coming home too tired to get into mischief except on Friday nights, when a few heads got bashed down at the bars." He put his hand on his chest below his heart and grimaced. "I went away from here once when I was young, but I came back after a few years in time for the prettiest girl I ever saw to be grown-up. I got married. I liked it here best. I belonged here. Then the looney tunes started showing up and now nothing makes sense."

I suspected he considered me one of the looney tunes.

There was a silence.

"Got a bunch of fancy weapons recently," he went on, "and then when they break down there's no money to fix them so they're worthless. Got a big four-wheel drive Blazer they call Fred, with a camera on the top, thirty-foot mast. Guys driving keep running into power lines. It's supposed to be a prototype, but all it is, is just an expensive idea that doesn't work. It's the bad guys got all the money. I'd like my boys to go to college, get the right advantages, but I can hardly keep them in sneakers these days."

I felt sorry for him. "So what are you doing? Investigating beyond the call of duty? Making up for the odds?"

He put his hands in his pockets, his energy gone for the night. We were two neutral beings. "Who knows?" he said bleakly.

He blinked his eyes like someone just out of the shower. "You got one missing brother. One dead girlfriend. If you were smart you'd stay out of this. We can handle it." His voice was measured, like someone reading from a script. “We don’t need another corpse.”

“Danny isn’t dead,” I said. “You don’t know that he is.”

Nance reached in his pocket and took out a pack of Rolaids. He ate four. “No,” he agreed as he chewed, “we don’t know that he is. But Chip O’Leary is, and they were friends.”

chapter thirteen

I DIDN'T SLEEP WELL, BUT THE NEXT MORNING I woke up wired, overcharged, excessive energy eating away at my body. I had things to do, people to see: Kristi's counselor Mary Ann Cunningham; Duane Taylor, Kristi's second boyfriend; there was Darla, Chip's girlfriend—but the mere thought of talking to more people, people with no answers, made me want to cry.

I got up and went into Danny and Kristi's room. The walls were clean and perfect, painted a pale gray with white trim. Wally must have finished in this room before I arrived. Danny and Kristi had made it look like a crash pad, mattress flush on the floor, bed unmade.

Methodically, I started at the closet, small and crammed full of mostly Kristi's clothes, tight leggings, slinky long tops, several pairs of black jeans which were both Kristi's and Danny's, a short black dress and a short red one. I could see Kristi in the red dress: too clearly for comfort, stopping traffic. High heels stood forlornly on the closet floor, toes pointed in, looking vulnerable and uncomfortable to wear. Then there were several men's shirts, all white, as if Danny had found his style and was sticking with it.

The dresser drawers contained underwear and T-shirts. On

top of the dresser long earrings and necklaces lay in a tangle, beside a copy of Stephen King's *Pet Sematary* and a painted wooden dragon with wooden fire coming out of its mouth.

By the mattress was a pair of running shoes, women's, and under the bed along with the dust balls another pair, men's. There was an empty ashtray on the wicker end table. What did they need an ashtray for? Neither of them smoked cigarettes. The answer was obvious. Damn Danny for his carelessness. Careless, impulsive—but these were not things anyone deserved to die for. He lived his life on the edge and didn't even notice, never considered there were other options.

Addicted to a dizzying pattern of highs and lows. I could see so easily what had brought him and Kristi together.

I went out to search the van—Danny's wallet hadn't told me much, maybe the van would. In the glove compartment were the registration, insurance card, the usual warranties for brakes and tires whose fine print you should have read before you went to collect on the warranty, maps of California, Arizona, and Tucson, and an unopened letter from a congressman addressed to Resident.

Under the seat were two pennies, an old McDonald's fries bag, and a lot of the sand and grime that accumulates under the seats of infrequently tidied vehicles. Finally under the sun visor I found something of interest: a piece of paper torn from a notebook with an address, 21 Mescalito Drive, and a sketchy map of how to get there from the interstate. It didn't look like it had been there long, the paper still fresh and white.

So there was a chance that was where Danny had gone while Kristi was at the mall buying a dress to meet her father in—the father she had never seen.

Or maybe not.

I would go to 21 Mescalito Drive, maybe even today, but first I wanted to go back to Hal's other house, see it in broad daylight.

Yellow leaves from the cancer trees along the street floated down around my head forming drifts on the street beyond. At the first flight of steps I began to climb. Asters bloomed everywhere, the whole town awash in pink and gold. The iron railing was brown with age and rust, the cracked cement steps stamped with WPA. At the top, the shack on the hill looked shabby, lonely up there, away from all the rest and more a part of the mountain than the town.

Panting from the altitude, I crossed the potholed, dusty road and went up a shorter flight of steps to the house. The POLICE LINE DO NOT CROSS tape was still there, but it looked limp. I went up on the porch and peered in the window. Dust motes swirled in the sun and the room looked tranquil, resting in another age, still a good place to meditate if you could forget what had happened here.

But how could you?

Coming down from the porch, I walked around outside the house. Once it must have been painted white but was faded now to pale gray, with darker gray boards showing through. It really was just a shack. Pyracantha bushes covered with clusters of red berries grew at the side, the branches untrimmed and snagging at my clothes.

In back was an actual outhouse, the door hanging open and a musty fecund smell coming from inside. A roll of toilet paper down to the last few sheets hung on a nail and a bevy of spiders had cast webs back and forth from the nail to the ceiling. Beneath the back of the shack itself was a considerable crawl space with a door to get under. There was a rusty hasp on the door, the closure hanging free. I got down on my knees and swung the door open, leery of spiderwebs, but here there were none. The dirt was flattened down and smooth. Maybe Hal had recently stored things there.

The back of the shack shielded me from the rest of the town; behind, the red dirt mountain rose: rocky, the peak not far above. A lizard with a blue throat scurried in front of me, stopped, and began to do push-ups on a rock near my hand.

"Hey," said a voice, "you seen any javelinas?"

I jumped. I was down on my knees, a vulnerable position. But it was only a small boy, maybe eight or nine, regarding me through large round glasses that looked as though they were made for an adult. His face was dirty, his nose runny, and he wore a black T-shirt, adult-sized too, with the words MUD BOG RACES on it in red.

"Hi yourself." I sat back and brushed the dust from the knees of my black jeans. "What's a javelina?"

The boy sat down cross-legged. His hair was cut short but not well, with a little tail of hair in back, and he wore dirty khaki shorts and running shoes that were oddly new compared to the rest of him.

"Pigs," he said in a grown-up voice. "Basically. Wild pigs. Boars. They're really cool. I saw a mama javelina once with all her little babies. Hunters come up here and shoot them, if they can. I'm rooting for the javelinas." He wiped his nose on his T-shirt.

"You are, huh? What do they do after they shoot them? Make bacon?"

"Boy, that would be weird, they're covered with prickles. Yuck." He made a face. "My name's Aaron. What's your name?"

"I'm Chloe. Nice to meet you, Aaron."

"Are you a policewoman?"

"No," I said. "Why?"

He shrugged and pushed his glasses up on his nose. "Bunch of police were up here. Some of them are nice, some of them are mean. They all know me," he added with pride. "They bring my mom home sometimes. She hangs out in the bars and sometimes she gets so plastered she can't walk straight. A bunch of them was here 'cause someone was killed in this house. Her name was Kristi." He looked forlorn. "She was my friend."

His face got rigid and he blinked his eyes, picked up a stone, and threw it. It hit partway up the hill, then rolled down. We watched it. He looked down at his feet and tightened his shoe-laces.

"Those are snazzy running shoes, Aaron."

"Yeah, they're pretty cool. My mom's boyfriend bought 'em for me."

"You live around here?"

"Down there in that green house, but you can't see it from back here. It's the closest one to the top." He looked at me eagerly. "You want to come visit? You can meet my mom and have coffee. It's good for my mom to meet people and I make pretty good coffee."

"I don't know," I said. "Tell me about you and Kristi."

Aaron looked down at the ground and wiped a smudge from his running shoe. "She was really cool. Nice. She used to come here and do this thing called meditating. She'd sit real still for a long time, getting rid of strange thoughts. It was like she wasn't there. It's a cool thing to know how to do, 'cause if you're hiding from someone, they can't feel you there."

"You hide from your mom sometimes?"

"Well . . . mostly I hide from her boyfriends. She's got a lot of boyfriends. They're nice to me when they're sober, but then they get mean when they start drinking. Kristi was going to teach me to meditate. She said I'd feel better about things if I did. Is she really dead?"

"I'm afraid she is." I couldn't think of anything to say that would be reassuring. He wasn't likely to swallow *She's home with the angels* or anything like that.

"She'd come up here at night," he said. "She'd have a candle, then she'd blow it out and meditate in the dark." He paused. "Can you die from meditating?"

"No, never." I paused for a moment. "So did you never hear a shot, the night Kristi . . . ?"

"Nope." He opened his eyes wide and shook his head back and forth, staring at me. "No, I didn't. I *promise* I didn't." He looked at me suspiciously. "I thought you said you weren't a cop."

"I'm not. I'm the sister of Kristi's boyfriend. I'm worried about what happened, and I want to know more about it. Do you know Danny?"

He hesitated. "Who?"

"Never mind."

"My mom says not to tell cops anything. You never know why they ask you stuff and sometimes if you answer you get into trouble. My mom should know."

I stood up. "That cup of coffee sounds pretty good. Maybe I'll take you up on it, if your mom won't mind."

Aaron ducked his head. "Naw, she won't mind."

I followed him down the hillside stairs to the small green house Aaron had pointed out earlier. Brass wind chimes hung from the eaves of the porch; some of the chimes were broken and some of them dangled loosely, ready to fall off at the next chime. One of the steps was missing from the porch, but Aaron jumped up two steps lightly. There was an old couch on the porch with the stuffing coming out from under one arm. Aaron flung the front door open and said, "Hey, Mom, we got a visitor."

Inside, Mom was lying on the couch in the living room wrapped in an Indian blanket. Plates were piled on the floor beside the couch as if she had had several meals as she lay there. The TV was on, it looked like a soap, but the sound was off. Clothes lay in little clumps everywhere, and beer cans, and coffee cups half full of coffee. Ashtrays brimmed with cigarette butts.

The whole place smelled of stale beer, stale cigarettes, and unwashed clothes. Mom sat up straight on the couch when she saw me and put her hand to her hair: streaky ash-colored hair, frizzed in a perm. Like Aaron, she wore large glasses. She had green eyes and a cute little nose, and the whole effect was of an aging high school cheerleader gone bad.

"Excuse me," she said. "Aaron, what the hell?"

"She's a friend of Kristi's. You know. Kristi, the lady that got killed. The lady who was so nice to me."

Mom regarded me with something less than sheer delight. "Everyone's nice to you, Aaron, you're a charm-school boy. He is," she said to me. "A regular lover boy."

"I invited her to have a cup of coffee, Mom. You want a cup too?" He was already in the kitchen, bustling around efficiently.

"Aaron, this house is a mess," said Mom.

"Well, you did it."

"Don't talk back, Aaron," she said vaguely, looking at me and venturing a smile. "Excuse me, I had a late night last night. It's awful about that girl. Aaron didn't see or hear anything, that's what I told the cops too."

I hadn't even asked. "I'm sorry to barge in like this. Aaron invited me, and I didn't realize—"

She gestured with one hand. "Forget it. I'm Michelle, and I'm an alcoholic," she said in a mimicking singsong voice. "I used to be a recovering alcoholic, but right now I'm just a plain alcoholic again. I guess I'll go back to being a recovering one, one of these days. I got the record for sober for twenty-four-hours chips."

Aaron came from the kitchen balancing a cup of coffee in each hand. "Cream and sugar?"

"This is fine, Aaron," I said. "Thank you very much."

"Mom's doing better than you'd think," he said. "She admits it anyway. Miss Rubio's the social worker and she told me once someone admits it they're getting better."

"That cow." Michelle fell back on the arm of the couch. She looked over at me. "It sounded like some kind of drug thing to me. That's the most likely reason for someone to get shot around here."

"Maybe."

Michelle put her hand to her head. "Ooh. I feel like shit."

"So I guess you didn't see or hear anything either? The night Kristi died?" I asked her, though without much hope of a straight answer.

"I wasn't home," she said, sitting up again and sipping her coffee. "Circumstances happened and I didn't get home until the morning. Aaron's okay, he cooks for himself and the neighbor lady looks out for him, Mrs. Parker. Aaron goes to bed early, so that's how I know he didn't see anything."

She took a few more sips and then lay back on the couch again. "Another day in paradise." She groaned and closed her eyes. "Aaron, go outside for a minute, okay?"

After he left, she sat up straight. "Are you a friend of Danny's too?"

"You *know* Danny?"

"I know both of them. I didn't want to say this in front of

Aaron 'cause he loves—loved Kristi, but Danny was like her slave, you know?"

"Danny's my brother," I said.

"No shit." She looked at me with interest. "I heard a rumor he split, took off. Before she died even."

"More like disappeared."

"Same difference," said Michelle. "And I don't blame him—he took the rap for everything that Kristi did. How long can you do that for?"

"Like what? What did he take the rap for?"

She rolled her eyes. "It's all rumors. Take it for what it's worth. I'm only saying what I said 'cause you're Danny's sister, but I value my ability to know nothing about anything ever."

"Did you know Chip O'Leary?"

"No one knew Chip nowadays."

"Didn't Darla?" I ventured.

Michelle sat up suddenly. "I really like Danny—we always kind of had a thing, you know? Like we knew each other in some other century." She paused. "You know what, since you're his sister, I'll tell you this—there's Chip's brother. Talk to him. He's older, got big bucks, lives in Tucson. Roger, his name is, Roger O'Leary. I met him once and he's an asshole."

"Roger O'Leary," I said.

Just as suddenly, she shut down again. "Look, I don't feel that great, maybe some other time?" She lay back on the couch and closed her eyes.

Outside, Aaron was sitting on the steps.

"Come on," I said, "walk with me a little."

He leapt up.

"If you saw anything," I said, "it's okay to tell me."

"Aaron!"

Behind us, Michelle had come out on the porch and was looking down the steps at us. From a distance the sun gleamed on her hair and she looked young and pretty and innocent. "Where are you going?"

"I better go back." Aaron looked worried. "She sounds pissed."

We hesitated on the stairs. He looked at me intently. "Kristi wasn't crazy. Kristi said we could run away together sometime, run away forever from everybody. Except I wouldn't leave my mom."

"Aaron!" called Michelle.

"You called the police about Kristi, didn't you, Aaron?"

His face screwed up. "I went up in the morning, early, and looked in the window." He blinked rapidly. "I was scared Mom would get mad at me for calling the cops, so I used a pay phone."

"If you see anything going on at that house, anything at all, call me, okay?" I took out my notebook and scribbled Hal's number. "Or just come to the house. I live where Kristi lived."

"What if you're not there?"

"Well, then," I said, and paused. "Call Brody. Tell him to find me. Do you know Brody?"

"With the cars?"

"That's right," I said.

"Aaron! Goddamn it," shouted Michelle.

Brody was sitting on the car seat, holding a gun, pointing it at me. "What not to do with a gun. Here you go."

"Thanks." I took it. It felt warm from Brody's hand, the way a snake is when you touch it. Blued steel. There were guys who could get you a gun just like that, knew that world, and others who couldn't. I sat down on the seat next to him. "Guess you won't take a Visa card. I don't have much cash right now."

"We'll make it a loaner. You said you had a gun back in New York. You can give it back after you've shot everyone. It's loaded and ready to go. It's legal to carry a gun in Arizona so long as it's not concealed."

"Great. I'll take it out whenever I see a cop."

"Good thinking."

We stared at each other for a moment. "Danny left an address in the van," I said. "Twenty-one Mescalito Drive in Tucson? Ring any bells?"

"Nope."

"What about Roger O'Leary?"

"Yep. Chip's brother."

"You know him?"

"I met him once. Wouldn't care to repeat the experience. Even if he is a doctor."

"A doctor?" I was surprised.

"Dermatalogist. Got an office over in a medical complex on the northwest side of Tucson. Chip mentioned it once—kidding around."

Which meant he would even be in the phone book. Regardless of what seemed to be people's low opinion of him, a doctor sounded promising, someone who might tell me Chip's story without the accompanying paranoia.

"Brody," I said, "you are worth your weight in gold."

"Acapulco, I hope," he said.

chapter fourteen

JUST OUTSIDE THE CITY, I EXITED I-10 AT the Triple T Truck Stop and got a coffee to go. I sipped it in the van as I consulted the map of Tucson where I'd traced a line from the freeway to Mescalito Drive and to Suahuaro Medical Complex. I'd called the number for Roger O'Leary's office, saying I wanted to talk to him about his brother as bait and mentioning some possible mementos I might have. They gave me an appointment at one o'clock.

I wasn't familiar with Tucson—for all I knew, the Mescalito address could be a shelter for the homeless, a crack house.

Oh, Danny. How did you get so far away and where are you now?

The first time Danny got into trouble he was sixteen. The cops called my father from the police station and he drove over. Danny had been arrested with two friends for breaking into a house. The owners were rich and away for the winter. Danny and his friend hadn't stolen anything, just hung around in the fancy recreation room and played pool. Danny was good at pool. My parents didn't try to protect him, they made him go through all the procedures, in the hopes of making him take responsibility.

Danny was always a little bitter about that. Somehow he and his friends felt justified because the people were rich, the same way friends of mine in college felt justified in stealing from large department stores. Corporations and rich people didn't count. They saw it as a political stance. But Danny and James and I had been privileged too. James and I had never understood.

The freeway took me clear to the other side of Tucson and I exited on Orange Grove, passed businesses, fast-food franchises, a Mexican restaurant. I was in luck because the address of the medical complex was roughly in the same general area as the Mescalito address.

I had half an hour before the appointment, so I headed for 21 Mescalito just to check it out. I made a couple of turns onto streets that got progressively more residential.

Mescalito Drive was a street of neither crack houses nor shelters for the homeless but a very nice residential area: large stucco houses, low-lying, with red-tiled roofs, lay discreetly behind wrought iron fences and desert vegetation. Number 21 had a curving drive, but I parked on the street and walked up to the house. It was well landscaped with prickly desert vegetation, more sculptural than inviting.

The front door was a massive carved affair with an enormous knocker in the shape of what was possibly a gargoyle. It made such a gentle thud when I used it that I realized it was just for show. To my right I found a doorbell and pressed.

I heard it ring from somewhere inside, but no one came. I pressed again, listened, but heard only cicadas. They sang to a crescendo, stopped, and started again. Finally I turned away, trudged back down the curving driveway to the van, on to my next stop, keeping busy, busy, busy, so I wouldn't think too much about my brother most likely being dead.

* * *

Roger O'Leary watched me across the expanse of his oak desk. Photos faced him: wife, kids? I imagined he examined and treated people's skin in other rooms—those rooms with linoleum floors and chrome fixtures where they put you to stare at drawings of various brightly colored skin diseases while you waited.

The walls in here had framed photographs of scenic desert vistas, as yet untouched by development. On the floor was a Navajo rug. I sat in a reasonably comfortable fake leather patient chair that was probably almost but not quite as comfortable as the doctor's.

"I'm sorry about your brother," he said. "I believe Chip may have mentioned Danny, but I never had the pleasure of meeting him."

I stared back at Roger, trying for a neutral look. "Oh, dear," I said. "I was so hoping that you had."

The air conditioner was on full blast—I had little goose bumps on my arms, but it was only partly the air-conditioning. Roger hadn't inquired about the promised mementos, for which I was grateful, but other things were going on here for which I was not.

"No reason why I would, really." Roger had a round boyish face with cheeks like little apples, weathered by the sun, and wore a white doctor jacket, dark blue shirt underneath just visible. "Chip and I didn't, um, cross-socialize." He smiled.

I nodded.

"So what's the connection exactly between your brother and Chip?" He was still smiling, but behind the smile his eyes watched me carefully.

"It seemed to be at least in some part photography."

Roger looked blank, then he looked away. "They never charged anyone in that whole Chip mess. I didn't really think they would. Chip left his happy home and went someplace where not even our good old family name could follow him." He stopped. "I'm sorry, Miss Newcombe, I just don't seem to get the point of your interest in this."

I put my hands in front of me, palms together in an attitude of supplication. I wanted Roger to see me as a distraught sister, which I certainly was. "I don't know anything about my brother's life, you see. I'm trying every angle, hoping to find some connection that might help me find him."

He coughed. "No one was ever even named as a suspect in Chip's murder. There was a witness, supposedly. Some old guy who owns a junkyard out there, Carson's Junkyard, I believe it's called. Out in the Valley. Nothing much out there but chili farms and pecan orchards. Lots of illegal aliens cross through there from the border at night. Apparently this guy patrols the yard at night, carries a gun. I guess to shoot the illegal aliens. Or maybe the coyotes."

He winced a little when he said that, as if it had slipped out before he thought. I remembered what I'd heard about what the coyotes had done to Chip's body.

"Gus," he went on, "I think Carson's first name was, yeah, Gus. He called the police, all riled up, and said he'd seen a vehicle with two people in it down by his place, the night of the murder. But when they went to question him he clammed up, said he'd made a mistake—it was the night before."

Roger shrugged. "I see his point, I guess. Why should he endanger himself? Chip was already dead."

He fell silent, turning his head to look out the window. Bird-of-paradise bushes grew outside, blooming brilliant red. Behind them you could see the mountains. I didn't say anything to break the silence.

After a minute, he said musingly, "Chip was a lot younger than me, and spoiled. He was what they call a menopausal baby. Embarrassed the hell out of me, you know, having a pregnant mom when you're a teenager. Then, after he was born, he got away with mur—with things. Mother was too tired to be strict by then. He charmed his way out of every situation and she always fell for it. Charm, that's how Chip learned to get along in life."

I nodded.

"But they don't always care about charm out in the big world." Roger went on with some satisfaction. "Not if you're premed at the U of A. Believe me, I worked my butt off. Guess Chip thought he could charm his way through that too, but it didn't work, so he started to dabble."

"Photography?" I asked.

He nodded. "Chip bought enough equipment to choke a horse, but he didn't have any talent. I tried to get him a summer job doing promo work for some of my projects, but the pictures he came up with weren't slick enough. Look . . ." He paused. "I was wild and crazy in my youth. I traveled 'round the country, did all kinds of things, but then I came home and grew up. Chip never did."

I nodded again.

"Of course, our mother thought he had talent. She'd have bought him a gallery to show his work if he'd asked. She was devastated by his death. Now he's enshrined forever." His voice was bitter.

His mother's response seemed entirely natural to me. What mother wouldn't be devastated? But more devastated, maybe, than had it been the properly disciplined Roger. How charm lingers in the mind, the delight it gives smoothing the rough edges. Unfair, unfair.

"She even joined one of those support groups, Parents of Murdered Children. But she likes the position she has, those groups want everyone to get down on the floor together and mingle, so to speak. She didn't want to mingle. Now she sends them a healthy check and stays away."

"Weren't you . . ."—I struggled for a word—"curious about who killed Chip?"

Roger shrugged, his face distant. "Like I said, my brother was dead. I wish I could tell you more to help, but I didn't know about Chip's life. Once he switched from photography to drugs, I didn't care to talk to him. I'd had enough of druggies back when I was in my twenties. They're all alike. He threw his life away—his choice."

Roger looked blank suddenly. He'd said his piece about his brother, released a little chunk of destructive emotion, set it free. He looked at his watch and then stood up to indicate the interview was at an end.

"I'd love to talk more," he said, "but I have appointments. Sorry I couldn't be of more help."

I stood up too. "Thank you for seeing me anyway," I said politely. There was more I wanted to say, to ask, but I didn't.

Instead I turned and walked out the door, passing his receptionist and a smattering of women pretending to read magazines as they agonized over possible skin cancers. I went on through the outer door to the courtyard outside, which was full of exotic desert plants whose names I did not know. There I took a deep breath.

Roger was the man I'd seen arguing with Danny at the

airport. So he'd lied about knowing Danny, lied big. Now, why was that?

I stopped back at 21 Mescalito Drive before I left town, but there was still no one answering the door. On my way back to Dudley, I stopped in at the Benson Police Station. The alert-looking redhead I remembered from the first night looked out at me from the round hole in the plate-glass window.

"Rick Seed?" I said. "Is he in?"

"And you are . . . ?"

"Chloe Newcombe, my brother's missing?"

She nodded. "Sure. I remember now. You have a seat, I'll call him."

I sat on a chrome and vinyl chair, staring down at the beige flecked linoleum. After a while a door to the side opened and Rick Seed came out. Same graying hair, pouchy eyes. He sat down next me, hands clasped on his lap. "Nothing new to report." His blue eyes looked regretful.

"Well, I do." I told him the whole story, about seeing Roger and Danny arguing at the airport and Roger denying that he knew him.

Rick Seed was quiet for a few minutes when I finished. "Well," he said, "there's no law against arguing with someone at the airport or saying you don't know someone when you do. For all you know, your brother could have bumped into him or vice versa by accident and someone got riled up about it."

"For heaven's sake," I said. "He's Chip O'Leary's brother. Isn't that an awfully big coincidence?"

"I didn't say it wouldn't be." Rick unclasped his hands, rubbed his chin. "I know, I know, you're thinking, here's this hick cop, not like New York City, don't know his ass from a hole in the ground."

I felt my face getting red. "I never—" I began.

Rick Seed raised his hand to stop me. "You mention to this Roger O'Leary that you saw him with Danny, ask him what was what? Confront him?"

"No."

"Don't you do it, okay? If this guy does have something to do with your brother disappearing, he's not someone you want to mess with. I'll check him out, okay?"

chapter fifteen

I GOT BACK TO DUDLEY AROUND THREE-thirty. Wally was just coming out the side door hauling a bucket of Sheetrock mud.

"Someone's been calling you," he said. "Calling and calling. Every time I answered the phone they asked for you and said they'd call back, no message." He gave me a look. "It was a man's voice but not Danny's, if that's what you're thinking, 'cause he asked about Danny."

"Really? He asked about Danny? You don't have any idea who it was?"

"Not a voice I recognized."

Who knew? Not me. Wally must have been working in the living room; the pale gray Sheetrock was dabbed with mud and the couch was covered with plastic. I removed it and lay down on Hal's couch with the faded tropical flower-print cushions that once had borne the imprint of James's body, of Hal's, though there were no longer any imprints there, just the flatness of neglect.

Danny, where are you? If he were dead, wouldn't I know it somehow? I had a headache from all the driving. Worse, I was feeling utterly incompetent. Roger O'Leary had lied about knowing Danny, but what could I do with that information? Plus something about his round apple cheeks and his smile that didn't reach his eyes gave me the creeps. I closed my eyes and ignored the nagging worry that Roger had seen me at the airport, seen me with Danny, knew that I knew he was lying and the whole interview had been one big charade. Well, hadn't it been? I got up off the couch. I had to keep moving.

Catholic Community Services where Kristi's counselor worked was in an old red-brick building a block off the main street. A walk led up to it, hedged with privet, the dark glossy leaves shining in the sun. I went up the walk and poked my head in the door. A receptionist was sitting at a battered desk eating a slice of pizza. She was maybe in her late forties, with salt-and-pepper hair, big hoop earrings, and lots of makeup. Her smile was indefatigably cheery.

"Mary Ann Cunningham?" I asked her. "Is she around?"

She dabbed at her mouth with a napkin, leaving red lipstick smears. "Excuse me. There's never any time to eat lunch properly around here, we're so busy. Then they want to cut back our funding. Mary Ann's on her way back from Willcox. She should be here any minute."

An exhausted-looking woman and a pale and droopy middle-aged man sat on chairs, lifelessly leafing through old magazines with the infinite patience required of all those using grant funded services.

"She's already late," said the receptionist. "And these people are waiting, but if it's important you better catch her now, because she's leaving town right after work. Her mom's real sick."

"Maybe I'll wait outside, then, catch her on the way in," I said, not wanting to join the ranks in the office. "What does she look like?"

"Um. Dark hair, kind of heavyset."

I went out and sat on a wooden bench in front of the hedge. An orange cat came out of nowhere, jumped on my lap, and began kneading at me. Birds twittered in the trees. After a while a car pulled up, a white something or other, and parked near the walk. A woman stepped out, heavyset, all right, wearing sunglasses and one of those tunic tops so beloved of large women everywhere.

"Mary Ann," I called out to her. The cat jumped from my lap and scooted through the hedge.

She stopped in front of me, balancing a briefcase under her arm, glancing at her watch.

"I'm here about Kristi. Kristi Marsh. She was your client?"

"God," said Mary Ann, light glinting off the sunglasses. "This is not the time. Oh, dear, I'm so sorry. Are you a relative?"

"Danny's sister—Danny, her boyfriend?"

"I know, I know." She looked harassed, poised as if to run, her training holding her back. "Well, let me tell you, I only saw her twice. She came for an initial evaluation, then not for a long time. They wait, you know, until a crisis."

"A crisis? What was the crisis?"

"Look." She pushed her sunglasses up on her forehead. "Haven't you ever heard of client confidentiality? I don't . . ."

A helicopter flew low overhead, drowning her out, looking for what, illegal aliens? Marijuana in backyards?

"I'm concerned about what happened," I said loudly, as the helicopter droned off, wanting her to really stop and to focus on me. "Danny's missing, Kristi's dead. She can't be hurt by anything you could tell me. I know you're leaving town. This is my only chance to talk to you. Please won't you help? Danny's my brother, I need to find him."

"I'm just a counselor," she said. "How would I know where your brother is? I'm sorry."

"Roger O'Leary? Did she ever mention that name?"

"No. No, she didn't. She was weak in a lot of ways." Mary Ann looked sad. "Under that rebellious surface, overly influenced by people in authority, she was fighting that, I guess, and maybe Danny was too. . . ."

The helicopter had circled back, its noise filling the air with urgency, drowning her out once again.

". . . wasn't honest with Danny."

"What?" I said.

"Nor me either." She hurried to the door, attaché case tucked neatly under her arm, ample hips swaying. Then she turned. "You have to hope they're honest with you," she said. "You can never be sure, but in the end it's their choice."

I was desperate. I went home and called Brody, asked him for a date.

From one of the bars down on the Gulch, Garth Brooks sang about friends in low places. The Gulch was seedier than the rest of town. The buildings seemed faintly charred, the gutter held smashed beer cans. In a burned-out vacant lot to my right, a couple groped each other, unsteady on their feet. A parking lot to my left held a posse of pickup trucks. LEGISLATE CRIMINALS, NOT GUNS, said a bumper sticker. Once I'd liked shabby bars on shabby streets. This was real life, I'd told myself, but I'd tired of being groped by drunks, of dragging an incoherent and amorous Logan away in the early hours of the morning.

Now Brody and I walked together heading for the music, the fun times, at a bar called the St. Elmo, like a couple out on a date. He was wearing a clean T-shirt.

"You don't have to stick around," I told him, "once you point him out to me."

The St. Elmo was packed, full of men in cowboy hats, men in work boots and feed caps, women mostly of the bleached-blond, frizzy-permed variety, shouting over the noise of the jukebox. We wedged ourselves into two seats at the bar.

"Brody!" said the bartender.

Brody grinned. "Hey, hey, Jake. I'll have a Coke and . . ." He looked over at me.

"Soda water," I said, "with a slice of lime."

Jake brought our pseudo-drinks, then leaned his elbows on the bar. He looked at me out of the corner of his eye and said to Brody, "Haven't seen you here since the time we eighty-sixed Killer and he came back with the .357 Magnum."

Charming, I thought, staring at the back of the bar at a display of guns and old watches, arrowheads, sheriff's badges, and china figurines of happy drunks. Behind me a woman was saying, "Son of a bitch, son of a bitch," over and over.

"Maybe that was the reason why," said Brody.

"Naw." Jake scratched his head. "You joined up with A.A. or some fool thing."

"I just quit," said Brody.

"He just quit." Jake smiled at me. He had a big mustache and friendly eyes. "A quiet hero."

"This is Chloe," said Brody. "Duane Taylor here?"

"He will be. Count on it. Drowning his sorrows." He winked at Brody.

"He's here every single night?" I asked.

"Couldn't tell you that," said Jake. "I didn't work last night, but two or maybe three nights ago, I saw him. Romancing a lady."

"Who was that?" asked Brody.

Jake grinned. "Little old Susie Q herself."

A conspiratorial look passed between them, as if you could go to the men's room and find her name and number scribbled all over the wall.

The man on the other side of me began to sing over the jukebox. "Salvation Army, Salvation Army, put a nickel in the drum, save another drunken bum." He held out a feed store cap to me; there were already three pennies in it.

"You still want me to leave when he shows?" Brody asked me.

"Maybe not right away," I said. "Who's Susie Q?"

"Reba Jenkins," Brody said. "You might say she's the local crazy lady."

People began to dance, a solitary kind of dancing, each rapt in his or her own rhythms. The bar smelled of sweat and alcohol and cheap aftershave. It was too noisy to talk. How had Kristi met this guy Duane Taylor anyway? I couldn't imagine her coming here alone. Then, oddly, for a few minutes, despite or maybe because of the raunchiness of the bar, the smell of the drunks, the crush of pure undifferentiated humanity, I felt at peace.

Jake came back down the bar and jerked his head at Brody. Brody nudged me. "He's here."

He got up and I followed. Duane Taylor was just inside the door. He was good-looking, oh, was he good-looking. Curly brown hair and amber, confiding eyes; eyes that invited you to see the joke and share it. Then when you got close maybe not so good-looking after all. Funny lines around his eyes and mouth, and on his bare left arm a dragon swirled around and around.

"Hey, Duane," Brody said.

Duane looked at him. "Yeah, hey, man," he responded automatically, without recognition. "How ya doin'?"

"I'd like you to meet someone," said Brody. "This is Chloe. She'd like to talk to you."

More people were coming in the door. Duane backed up, keeping his eyes on me. "Hi, there," he said. "What about?"

I came close, trying to look a little dumb, a little helpless even. I didn't know how else to do it. "About Kristi."

Duane ducked his head. He reached in his shirt pocket and drew out a pack of cigarettes. He took one out and held it up. "Kristin," he said.

"Kristi," I said.

He put the cigarette in his mouth wrong end and lit the filter. He looked down. "Ah, shit," he said to me, "see what you made me do?"

"Could we go outside? Maybe just for a minute—talk a little bit." I made my voice soothing, as if I were speaking to a wild dog that had shown up at my door.

We went outside. Brody stayed behind.

Out on the street, it was still noisy. Duane and I walked down a ways to an alley with a wooden bench and a streetlamp overhead, and after I sat down, he did too. Out in the parking lot, a man was being violently sick next to a pickup. A woman stood by, holding his jacket like a second as he fought his manly duel with alcohol.

"You a friend of Kristi's?" Duane asked me. "Or what?"

"A friend."

"Me too," he said. Out here, he looked good again. The kind of good looks that drew your heart to him, while your brain went in the opposite direction, screaming back warnings. I was reminded of Danny, Duane's tattoo an obvious prison relic.

"A real friend," he went on. "That's what I wanted to be." He looked at me though his lashes, as if checking to see if I believed him.

I was silent.

"I mean, nothing else was happening. You know what she wanted to do? She wanted to get in my car and drive. She wanted me to drive her all over the county." He put his palms together, flexing his muscles, remembering. I could feel a tension in him like a coiled-up snake.

"We drove clear to Willcox once, got out, looked at a damn field, and then drove back. She'd be talking, talking, talking, like she was speeding except she never wanted to do any drugs. It was hard to listen, so I just looked at her. I never had an old lady looked as good as that."

"Ever do any Dream Queen?" I asked him.

"What the fuck kind of question is that?" His eyes darted away furtively. "Never heard of the stuff until the cops brought it up." He stared at the brick wall across the alleyway and massaged the dragon on his arm. He didn't seem able to keep still.

"I wisht I never met her," he said vehemently. "She was bad news. Lucky for me I spent the night she was killed with a lady friend, Lucky Lady, I guess I'll call her. Otherwise, with my record, I'd be up shit creek without a paddle, you know what I mean?"

I wondered what that record was exactly and about the lady friend, Reba Jenkins, just how good a friend she was. "Did you see Kristi a lot?"

"She had this old man, he used to go up to Tucson, maybe once, twice a week. She wanted to go too, she was pretty bored down here, but he wouldn't take her. I figured he had some lady up there he was balling."

I couldn't imagine that Danny was seeing another woman. He'd left Kristi alone sometimes in L.A. too. Across in the parking lot, the man had stopped being sick. The woman was holding him up now as he swayed back and forth.

Duane pulled out his cigarettes and lit up.

A truck drove by, honking, people standing up in the flatbed.

"It didn't have nothing to do with me, what happened to her," said Duane suddenly, violently. He took the cigarette out of his mouth and spat, "Maybe her old man knows. But he flew the coop, I heard."

"That's right."

"I figure he found out about us, 'cause after a while he started taking her to Tucson with him. Every damn time he went he took her. He'd drop her at a mall and go somewhere, Kristi told me, the last time I saw her. What'd she want to dump me for, so cold? I was nice to her, didn't play no games or nothing. Bitch. Who the fuck'd she think she was? Who told you about us?" he asked me suddenly. "You good old friends?"

"Not exactly," I said.

"You said friends." He looked at me as if seeing me for the first time. The look was menacing.

Involuntarily I backed away.

"Son of a bitch," he said. "I know who you are."

"Who?"

"You stupid cunt!" He jumped up.

The interview was at an end.

I peered into the St. Elmo—it was packed, I couldn't see if Brody was still there or not. It wasn't really that late, just a little after nine, but I was tired, too tired to look for him. I headed back to Hal's, wearily climbing the last stretch of hill. Somewhere in the dark a phone was ringing.

Hal's. It was ringing at Hal's. I half ran the rest of the way, through the carport, fumbled for the key, opened the door, went inside.

"Hello?"

"I'd like to speak to Chloe Newcombe." A man's voice.

"Speaking."

"At last. Hello, Chloe, this is Otto Marsh, Kristi's stepfather. I heard about Danny. No word?"

"No word."

"For heaven's sake." His voice sounded confident and controlled, not the sort of voice to pour its heart out over the phone or ever, even with a young daughter murdered.

I sat down at the kitchen counter. "Mr. Marsh, I'm really sorry about Kristi. I feel just awful."

"I appreciate your condolences. I know it's hard on you too, and then to have Danny gone as well. He told me about you. I understand you work for a private investigator in New York." His voice had a timbre to it that vibrated in my ear. I held the receiver away slightly.

"Yes," I said, "but I mostly just do—"

He cut me off. "I'd like to hire you," he said, the deep voice running on inexorably. "I'd like you to fly out to L.A. first thing in the morning if possible and talk to me and Abbie here in Venice. It's only a forty-five-minute flight. You could be here and back before dinner, so to speak. I will pay all expenses, of course. I don't know how much Danny told you, but there are things you should know."

chapter sixteen

MY FLIGHT TO L.A. WAS AT NOON, SO I LEFT before eight. Early morning sun streaked the little frame houses with light as I drove down the canyon. At various corners children were waiting for the school bus, little girls clustered in chatty groups and little boys chasing each other around, wielding lunch boxes like weapons. All the trees were golden. I felt full of a false nostalgia for my own school days, those fall days before winter sets in. In reality I'd always hated school, hated the cold mornings when I had to get up in the dark, knowing I would have to do it again day after day after day.

I'd given myself enough time to go back to the house at 21 Mescalito Drive. I didn't expect much, but it was worth a try. I drove the freeway again, past the exit for the airport to Orange Grove Road, exited, and drove to the residential area.

The cicadas hummed again and crescendoed as I pushed the doorbell and waited. But this time the door opened.

A woman stood there, a bit older than me but not much—maybe middle thirties, her long dark hair braided back in a French braid. She had the classic features that one sees on statues of ancient Greeks, anachronistic with the bright pink sweats she wore, which were stained here and there with different-colored spots. From behind her came the shouts of children.

I introduced myself. It was hardly a threatening environment, there was no reason to lie, so I simply told her that my brother was missing and that I'd found this address in his van.

She looked at me, wide-eyed. "For heaven's sake! It sounds just awful, I can't imagine. You must be worried sick." Her classical features took on expression and suddenly she looked quite contemporary. She brushed at the spots on her sweatshirt. "Be quiet for a minute." This last she said over her shoulder.

"I think he may have visited here on the day he disappeared," I told her. "So I thought I might learn something from you."

"I'm Jenny," she said belatedly, "Jenny Cohen. Come on in."

She turned and I followed. The braid extended down to her waist. I'd never seen anyone with such long hair. Unbraided, it would probably conceal all but her legs, Lady Godiva–style. From somewhere in the house I heard shouting, screams.

"Shut up!" she shouted.

She led me into a large and potentially elegant room, but for the tricycles, skateboards, Monopoly set, and various trucks and cars littering the Oriental rug. On the large dark leather couch a pack of cards was scattered and plastic robots were stationed on the two leather chairs. A small boy lay on the floor in a sleeping bag and on top of him a slightly larger boy, who appeared to be strangling him.

"Aaargh," yelled the smaller one.

Jenny put her hands on her hips. "Ethan, Ansel—both of you. You heard me. I said shut up."

The smaller boy lay still, looking plaintive, the perfect victim. "Ansel's killing me, Mom."

“Get off of him, Ansel,” said Jenny. “The minute I turn my back, you take advantage.”

Ansel rolled off his brother. “Ethan took all the cards and threw them ’cause he was losing.”

“He called me a midget,” protested Ethan. “And I wasn’t losing. He was cheating.”

“I don’t care what happened.” Jenny tossed her head. “We’re not talking justice here, we’re talking I’m the boss and we have a visitor. They’re sick,” she said to me. “Last day on the mend. School tomorrow.”

“Yesterday we were both throwing up,” Ansel told me proudly. “We puked our guts out.”

“Sit down,” said Jenny to me politely.

I hoped it wasn’t catching. I removed the cards from the couch and sat down.

She turned to the boys. “To your rooms. Now.”

The two boys got up and reluctantly left the room. “Mom’s a shithead,” one of them called back over his shoulder.

“Excuse me.” Jenny headed off in pursuit.

I felt I’d just been handed a clue to the basic nature of man right here in this living room. Alone, I looked around. Photographs, hung salon-style, covered the walls: good photographs, as far as I could tell. The photographer seemed to be in love with landscapes, even when he was not strictly photographing them. There were several photographs of parts of bodies laid out landscape-fashion, so it was difficult to tell which parts were involved: a face, with a nose rising serenely out of the bush of a mustache, a hip swelling into a dune. Jenny came back.

“In case you can’t tell,” she said with a grin, “my husband’s a photographer. He teaches at the U of A.” She looked at the walls a little sadly. "Sometimes I'd like a little color up there, you know. Maybe one nice painting."

"Interesting work," I murmured.

"Yes, it is, isn't it? I've been married to Josh seven years. Ansel was on the way when we did it. I was an assistant in the photography department and doing freelance work on the side. I was starting to make it, but my biological clock was running too, so we went ahead with our family. Once Ethan's adjusted to school, I plan to go back to work. I'm out of touch, with everything."

She sat down. "Josh's on sabbatical and he left yesterday for the White Mountains. He's camping out, can't be reached. So many students stop by here. He's very popular. When did you say your brother was here?"

"I'm not even sure, but it might have been four days ago."

"Four days ago." She rolled her eyes. "It was the day the boys started coming down with this stomach flu. I was pretty preoccupied. Someone showed up. I assumed he was a former student. They went into Josh's den. Josh has many former students, you understand. He teaches a special introductory course that lots of people take, without a commitment in the field."

I described Danny to her.

"I didn't actually see him," she said apologetically.

The U of A? Premed at the U of A, Roger had said, talking about his brother. And I already knew about Chip's interest in photography.

"Does the name Chip O'Leary ring a bell?" I asked her.

She smiled. "No, I'm sorry, it doesn't. I'm Josh's third wife. Josh is fifty-five. So much of his life has happened without me." She sighed. "I actually saw more of Josh before we got married than I have since. He's always running off somewhere. He was only back a couple of weeks this time." She looked disappointed and trying to be brave about it. “Josh was rather meditative after this guy left, but he didn’t tell me what happened. Usually I’d ask, but the boys were so sick. Then he went off later, to a workshop or something.”

“When will he be back?”

“Try calling in a couple of days.”

A loud crash came from down the hall.

“God, I’m tired,” said Jenny.

chapter seventeen

ON THE PLANE I THOUGHT IT ALL OVER. When you're working on something, you can run around for days without thinking and then sometimes find that whatever you were looking for has already been found. But you are still running, like those Road Runner cartoons where Wile E. Coyote runs off the cliff and doesn't notice until he's several feet out, legs still moving frenetically. I was feeling frenetic myself, and on top of that, discouraged.

How hard had the police looked for Chip's killer? Or was it just another drug killing? Had they even superficially checked out his brother Roger, who hated him? Checked out Roger's debits and assets—right up my alley—in case something was wrong there, something Chip might have alluded to, giving guarded hints to Roger, in public. Something that Danny might know about?

In the aisle across from me a young couple twittered together. She looked ordinary enough, brown hair, brown eyes, but he was obviously smitten, touching her arm, her hair, as we careened along high above the continent. Why weren't they in school or working at jobs, instead of sitting in a plane on a weekday reminding me of my contrasting solitary state?

At the airport I rented a car and got on Lincoln Boulevard. It was one of those rare smogless days in Los Angeles, so you could see the mountains. I'd come here to visit James when he'd only recently been diagnosed and had just met Hal, his rescuer, his savior. They were already living in Topanga Canyon, which had the same seedy picturesqueness that Dudley has, same frame houses.

James was not all that sick yet. Maybe he would never be, we told ourselves, maybe he'd been misdiagnosed. We drove around L.A. looking at the sights and had even gone to Venice where I was going now, to walk along the beach. James was still full of hope and quiet jokes, with all the news of the latest developments. Maybe he could beat it. All those maybes, not one of them panned out.

Marina del Rey glittered to my left, the good life, still looking like one of the reasons people moved to California and ended up living in Downey, Glendale, Reseda. Venice was once vacation homes for the rich, with the little twist of being built on canals, hence the name Venice, but Otto's address was on the blocks that fronted the beach itself, close to the line between Venice and Marina del Rey.

I parked behind in an alley and walked around to the sidewalk where the houses faced each other. At the end of the street was the beach, not crowded on a weekday. Sailboats flittered on the blue-green water and the air had a rich balmy scent, partly pollution and partly ozone.

The house was close to the beach, near Subway Street, a largish house, all odd angles and fancy windows, a rich lady going slumming. Bougainvilla spilled out onto the sidewalk. Whoever Kristi's father had been, her mother's second marriage partner wasn't exactly on skid row. I went up a little path and knocked.

A woman answered.

"Abbie?" I said.

She nodded. "Chloe?" Kristi's mother was probably in her early forties, younger than I'd expected, but then Kristi hadn't been very old, just out of childhood, with pieces of her still back in the fifth grade. "Please come in."

She had blond hair like Kristi's and the same blue-gray eyes, but she didn't have Kristi's nose, or her cheekbones. It was tantalizing, as if I could almost get a picture of Kristi's father by looking at the features her mother didn't have. She was very pretty, her skin just beginning to take on the appearance of crumpled rose petals.

"You wouldn't want to stay for the funeral?" she asked breathlessly, as we lingered in the hall. "I've lost track of so many of Kristi's friends or I never even knew them. It's at the Zen center and it will really just be meditation. Meditation's always been helpful to me, and to Kristi too. Everyone will be doing it together, sharing the experience."

I murmured that I had to get back, I needed to be around for Danny, in case, no, *when* he returned, sorry, etc., but I said that it sounded like a perfect funeral.

"We're worried about Danny too," she said. "Otto and I." Her eyes were dreamy, not stoned on drugs but rather on some mind-set. They were pink at the edges from what had undoubtedly been many tears, so the mind-set had not entirely taken over. "He'll be here shortly. He went for a swim."

From the forceful way Otto had spoken to me on the phone, I could see him swimming year-round, pounding on his chest as he emerged from the waters. *There are things you should know,* he'd said.

What?

"I don't know if Otto explained on the phone—he's Kristi's stepfather. He adopted her legally right after we were married. Kristi was three. Kristi's father Louis . . ." She paused. "It didn't work out."

She wore a long pale blue caftan of some filmy material; she turned suddenly and it swirled as she led me down a tiled hall. Her hair was long and loose down her back and she was barefoot, her gait soft and languorous. She might turn again, time would drop away, and there, standing before me, would be a flower child, circa 1967, eyes stoned and glowing.

We reached a large room that looked out at the ocean and Ocean Front Walk. The furniture was modular, covered in a wild black and white batik. There were thick Chinese rugs on the floor, a marble coffee table anchoring it all.

"Louis was wonderful in his way," she said. "Chloe, if you could have seen him the way I did. White, he wore white all the time, those Indian cotton clothes men used to wear. Why, he looked . . . he looked just like Jesus!" She seemed overwrought, maybe a little crazy. "Otto doesn't like to hear me talk this way. He's a therapist. I spent years of my life going to them, so I finally decided just to marry one. Did you know Kristi well?" Her voice was a little forlorn. Her clavicles at the neck of the caftan were delicately formed, fragile-looking. *Jesus,* I thought.

"No, I'd just met her," I said.

She sat down abruptly on one of the modular units. I sat too. choosing one with an arm.

"Maybe you'd like some rice cakes?" she asked, suddenly getting up again. "I know they don't feed you well on those short flights. And I have some seltzer water." Maybe rice cakes and seltzer water were de rigueur now in Southern California, but they had an odd ring, like prison food for yuppies.

But I was hungry. "That sounds wonderful," I said.

The seltzer water turned out to be flavored with raspberry and the rice cakes with garlic and tamari. They were delicious, but though I had several they had no effect whatsoever on my hunger.

Abbie politely pushed the plate of rice cakes closer to me. "Why?" she said. "A young beautiful girl. Why?" She put her hand to her throat.

Her fingers were covered with silver rings. It must have been a bore to take them all off to do the dishes. Or maybe Otto was the house-husband type. But I didn't think so. There was something puppetlike in some of her movements, as if someone else, maybe Otto, were pulling the strings. She asked, "You know about Kristi's illness?"

I nodded.

"It's from me. I have the same mood disorder. I taught her about meditating when she was just a little girl. Meditating has helped me so much." She shuddered. "I just don't know what to think." Her voice switched to automatic pilot. "It's only what we think that determines how we feel. Unpleasant thoughts can be filtered out. We can free ourselves of negative emotions."

Along with our sense of reality, I thought. I liked the real physical world out there; if you filter out too much of the bad, the good goes with it. But I had my own bad; other people's might be worse.

I heard the front door open and then reality strode in: a man, short, muscular, white-haired, wearing only bathing trunks with a towel around his shoulders. He grabbed both ends of the towel and rubbed his back with it vigorously.

"Chloe!" He gave me a practiced welcoming smile and presented his hand. Otto had a grip that would shame a used car salesman or a politician. We shook hands thoroughly. White hairs curled coyly over his chest, a young man's chest, well exercised.

He looked me squarely in the eye with none of Abbie's dreaminess and went straight to business. "Any ideas, clues, anything?"

"Not much. Apparently Kristi was seeing someone else besides Danny, a man called Duane Taylor. I talked to him. She didn't see him long and she'd dropped him before her death, at least according to him."

"Immaturity," said Otto. "Lack of self-esteem too. Such a beautiful girl, and she wasn't really aware of it. He a drug user?"

"Probably," I said. "When he realized I was Danny's sister, he stopped talking. He had an alibi, which I'll check out." I glanced at him nervously. "The police are considering Danny as a suspect."

Abbie wrapped her arms around her body and shivered.

"No way," said Otto firmly.

I nodded. "You said there were things I should know?"

Abbie's eyelids fluttered. She said in a wispy uncertain voice, "Yes. About Louis, Kristi's fa-father."

Otto put his hand on her shoulder and squeezed it. He said, "Kristi had the idea of her biological father stuck in her mind and absolutely nothing could dislodge it. What kind of man goes off anyway, without a word?"

"Oh!" said Abbie.

Otto raised his voice. "That's why Kristi got the job in the Play Room. Thought she wasn't good enough to try for something challenging. Thought if her father didn't think enough of her, no one else would either."

"The swims really get Otto going," Abbie said to me apologetically. "Otto loved Kristi so much."

"Of course I loved her." Otto's voice was angry. "I tried hard to make up for all these things, but she was already deeply scarred. Lou," he said, biting off the end of the name as if he had to diminish the man. "Lou Barnett."

"Louis." Abbie sighed. "We lived together in Seattle. It was an exciting place for young people then. I still love it, but I can never go back. It makes me too sad. I wasn't surprised when he left me. He always withheld important parts of himself."

"Like his heart and soul." Otto's voice was sarcastic. "Forget the guy. Enough is enough." He turned to me. "He walked out on her right when the baby was born, a woman and a newborn baby, alone and defenseless."

"I had friends." Abbie looked defensive. "Good friends, who helped me out. Listen to how judgmental you sound, Otto. You're supposed to be a therapist."

"I'm a human being first," said Otto.

I was beginning to like him in spite of my initial impression. Also to have the feeling I was being called on to act as an audience, a judge, for a protracted debate that had gone on for years.

Otto continued. "That was one of the major problems. Kristi always heard you defending him, glamorizing him."

Abbie suddenly looked stronger, less fragile and dreamy. If Otto won most of the skirmishes, it looked like she was still winning the war. But at what cost to Kristi?

"Back then it was considered moral to follow your feelings," she said defiantly. "You went where your feelings led you. The climate was different back then, especially the way Louis and I lived, we thought we were the new breed." She looked at Otto slyly. "But I mean, what do people follow now? The almighty buck."

"That's fine, Abbie," said Otto. "Fight back. It's good for you, but I have to tell Chloe, the almighty buck has been following me. I've done well for myself in this rotten world where everyone needs some kind of therapy. I've got lots of money. I'd like you to take this on. Name your price. I won't quibble."

We settled on a price, a little steeper than I made in New

York, but Otto was so easy I almost wished I were selling insurance.

"Kristi mentioned her father to me," I said. "She had this fantasy about meeting him."

"Which one did she tell you?" Otto said. "The one where she finds herself sitting next to him on a plane, or maybe the one where she goes to Paris with him, or maybe—"

"Las Vegas," I said.

"Ah," said Otto. "The Mirage fantasy."

"Yes."

The room was silent then. As if on cue, all three of us looked out the window, where we could see roller skaters out on Ocean Front Walk, sailing carelessly along, holding Walkmans to their ears.

Abbie gave a long trembling sigh.

Finally Otto said, "Louis Barnett was murdered fifteen years ago in San Francisco. Kristi knew that very well."

"Oh," I said. What was it Mary Ann Cunningham, her counselor had said? *You have to hope they're honest with you. You can never be sure, but in the end it's their choice.*

"Oh," I said again. I felt a sense of loss; lights going out, fountains running dry.

And now Louis's daughter maybe murdered too, as if she'd inherited some genetic tendency. "How was he murdered?"

"Arson. They had a suspect, but to my knowledge he was never charged."

"Arson," I said.

"Abbie never made any attempt to find Louis when he left. She thought she had no rights, that Louis was entitled to follow his whims. But shortly after we married, I hired a private detective, who found out that Louis had settled in San Francisco, where he lived with a woman, Cynthia Fuller. They died together in a fire when the house they were renting burned down. Apparently there was some bad blood with a neighbor and the police concluded it was arson."

"A neighbor? That's the suspect? Why wasn't he ever charged?"

Otto shrugged. "Once I learned Louis was dead, I didn't pursue the matter."

A light dawned. I took a deep breath. I knew my brother, the pursuer of lost and illegal causes. "But Danny *did,* didn't he? He pursued the matter."

"That's right. He was all fired up and I fed that fire, unfortunately. I thought Danny was a good, basically retrievable human being, and I thought it would be good for him to find a cause." He paused, blinked, and rubbed his eyes. For the first time he'd lost some of his confidence. He peered over at me like a man in a fog.

"He didn't tell Kristi he was looking for her father's killer. I don't know what he planned to do when he found him. Bring him to justice, I suppose. An act of retribution or something, so Kristi could move on."

Danny the crusader. I felt at a loss. I fumbled and asked, "What did Danny have to go on? Could you tell him anything?"

"Not much. I didn't know much about Louis."

"Do you have a name? A name for the arsonist?"

"That's the first thing Danny wanted to know," said Otto, "but that wasn't my interest."

Abbie rose and went to the window. She swayed, looking out at the ocean as though the conversation had no meaning to her. At least I thought she was looking at the ocean, but when I glanced at her, her eyes were closed so tightly her face was distorted.

"I gave Danny the name of the officer in charge of the investigation," Otto told me.

"I'd like the name of the investigating officer myself," I said.

"I wrote it down for you. I feel responsible if Danny's disappearance has something to do with this, Chloe. I want you to be very, very careful."

He walked to a desk, came back, handed me a piece of paper. "Phil Bates. A homicide detective with the San Francisco PD."

Abbie turned from the window and walked across the room. She walked so softly she looked as though she were floating. I thought the thing for me to do was get the name and leave at once. I didn't think my visit had been emotionally nourishing.

She left the room and then I heard the front door opening and closing.

"She's going for a walk on the beach." Otto's eyes were stricken. "I've been with her for years. Doing all the healing things I know, but she still loves Louis, in love with a dead man."

I folded the piece of paper he'd given me and put it in my purse.

Otto was looking away from me now. "Louis," he said. Suddenly with great force he raised his hand and brought it down on the marble end table. "That son of a bitch. That lousy son of a bitch."

chapter eighteen

I GOT BACK TO DUDLEY JUST AFTER MIDnight. My body was past the point of exhaustion, releasing the equivalent of speed into my bloodstream just to keep me upright. I couldn't stop thinking about Louis Barnett; a dead man, still powerful. Kristi dead as well. Their deaths seemed linked as my mind veered toward the occult—Louis reaching after her from the grave. . . . Hal's house felt eerie, full of hidden messages; as if Louis's ghost hovered in the shadows.

The red light glowed on the answering machine. I played it back, mostly little blips, then Hal's voice: "Hi, Chloe, I'm just calling to see if there's any word on Danny. Guess not, huh? I have to be in Phoenix for the next couple of days. I'll try to check in at the Windward House."

Guess not. Danny had been missing for days now. My mind tried to skirt around this fact. Maybe he was hiding out, afraid of the police, afraid to get in touch, but then again, maybe he was dead, like Louis, like Kristi. Lying out in the desert somewhere, food for coyotes, like Chip O'Leary. Until I found Reba Jenkins and talked to her, I didn't know how Duane's alibi for the night Kristi died would hold up. And Roger O'Leary, something strange was going on there, poisonous. Would Rick Seed even bother really checking or had he just been humoring me?

My mind ran on overtime speculating. What about Josh Cohen, popular professor at the U of A? A photographer—photography was springing up everywhere, but what was the relevance? Maybe there wasn't any, maybe Louis and Josh had known each other years ago in San Francisco. Could *Josh* be the killer? I wished Otto had known that neighbor's name. But would it have mattered? Surely he'd have changed it if he was wanted by the police.

Would Danny have just located a murderer at 21 Mescalito Drive, then picked me up and calmly driven to Benson? But he hadn't been calm, he'd been weird. Was Kristi's murder connected to all this? Connected to Danny's disappearance? After my talk with Abbie and Otto, I realized I probably couldn't rely on anything Kristi had told me—she'd talked as if her father were still alive, who knew what else she'd said had been mere fantasy?

Lou Barnett, I thought, Louis. A man who deserted the mother of his baby and evoked enough hatred in someone else to get himself murdered.

In my notebook I made a list of people to talk to next—there was the junkyard, Carson's Junkyard, with a possible eyewitness to Chip's murder. There was Darla, Chip's girlfriend, a potter here in Dudley; Phil Bates, the name Otto had given me, homicide detective in charge of the investigation in San Francisco. And Reba Jenkins.

I was overcharged, excessive energy eating away at my exhausted body. The mere thought of tracking down and talking to all those people made me want to cry, but I couldn't stop yet.

Had I searched the whole entire house? No.

In the living room I lifted up the pillows on the couch, found a dime, three pennies, and a scrap of paper. On it was written in Danny's handwriting, *Josephine Meadows. Golden Acres?* Golden Acres had a dreamy ring to it. Was that located near the Mirage? But it was something. Encouraged, I threw all the pillows onto the floor, but found nothing more. *This is all meaningless,* I thought, *meaningless and hopeless.*

I peered under the couch and found only a matchbook from the Copper Queen Hotel. Where Hal and I had had dinner only recently. What had happened to those conversations I'd imagined having with Hal on my way to Dudley? What was Hal doing right now, stretched to the limit already? I went into the bedroom where I was sleeping. The closet was full of Hal's old clothes. Hawaiian shirts from his California days, a dinner jacket, a suit, the black elegant suit he'd worn to James's funeral.

I could see him now in that suit, in my parents' living room before we drove to the church. We'd all gotten ready way too early, my mother tense and chattering, Daddy staring abstractedly out the window, Danny sulking in the kitchen. Sitting on one of the many battered recliners, Hal looked at the books all along the walls and piled on the chairs and tables and mentioned how a room without books was like a room without a soul. He admired the rubbings my parents had done in England and took my mother in hand, toured the house with her, and exclaimed at James's high school artwork, carefully matted and framed and hanging crookedly.

His presence, his voice brave and unafraid of memory, took charge, filling the nervous time while we waited, telling us how good and kind James had been as if they were useful qualities in a man nowadays, fighting in that jungle the world could be, to a man who was gay.

I could have sat there in Hal's house in Dudley for hours, loving Hal, as if to regain part of myself that I'd lost in the rush of finding things out. But Danny was still missing. I got up and rummaged through cardboard boxes just outside the bedroom door, full of books and household utensils apparently not needed here. Under a Crock-Pot and a couple of pot holders I found a school exercise book, a spiral notebook in fuchsia pink. I opened it to the front page. *Kristi Marsh* was written in the upper right corner, and below in the center was the word *Journal.*

My heart beat a little faster. It must have been very personal, for her to have hidden it even from Danny. I was full of jumpy guilt, as if she might appear suddenly and see me invading her privacy. The book was nearly empty, only the first couple of pages full of writing. The date on the first page was two months ago, as if it were a project she'd tired of almost immediately, the writing girlish, with circles where the *i*'s would be dotted. It was an exercise such as counselors sometimes assign clients to do, an exercise from Mary Ann, perhaps. Kristi had written:

GOOD	BAD
pretty, sometimes (do exercises more)	ugly, sometimes
smart, 25%	dumb, 75%
loving (when I'm not sad)	mean (when sad)
DANNY	dishonest

DREAM: Danny and I in car going to Mexico. In a cantina Mexicans ask me to dance, so I do. I dance all around the room and jump on the bar. All the Mexicans like me and they clap. But I see Danny is mad. I know if I don't stop dancing he'll leave but I can't stop because it makes me happy, I'll do anything to be happy. Danny leaves: I float out of the cantina and try to find him. I'm floating in the air, but I keep running into cactus. Big saguaro cactus, the kind with arms covered with thorns. Then I realize Danny is a cactus, and I say Danny stop, you're hurting me, but he just grabs me and hangs on. The only way I can get away is to hurt Danny but I don't want to.

The rest of the notebook was blank.

Exhausted but too wired to sleep, I turned off all the lights but a small one in the kitchen and went out and sat in the dark on one of the wicker rockers on the porch, listening to the crickets chirp. Somewhere a cat yowled, another yowled back. I closed my eyes, felt the night air cool on my skin. A little picture popped into my mind then, a memory from the office of Roger O'Leary—the office with the photographs of empty landscapes.

As if it were summoned up by this thought, I heard a knock on the door: a gentle *tap tap tap.* I glanced at my watch: one A.M. Late, too late for someone to be knocking. Had I locked the door? I stood up and walked barefoot through the living room to the kitchen and peered out. No one.

Tap tap tap.

No, someone: someone too short for me to see at eye level. Aaron. I opened the door.

Aaron scooted in and I closed the door, his hair scruffy, eyes big in the faint kitchen light. He was wearing the same black T-shirt with MUD BOG RACES emblazoned on the front. "I wanted to tell you something else," he whispered.

"Come on out on the porch."

He followed me out and we sat in the rockers.

"Where's your mom?" I asked him.

"Out in the Valley, visiting," he said in a normal tone of voice. "If I need anything I'm supposed to go to the neighbors'." He lowered his voice to a whisper again. "I wanted to tell you about the man. He comes over the hills, not up the stairs, down to the house where Kristi was. Not very often. Mom says I should never ever say anything to anyone, so I don't."

"What man is that?"

Aaron put his feet up on the porch railing and for a second seemed to contemplate his cool sneakers. "One time I left my Roboman up on the porch and I went to get it at night, and right when I was leaving I heard him, then I saw him back behind, but he didn't see me."

"Oh, yeah?" I said.

Aaron nodded. "After that I watched for him, he mostly comes when it's really, really dark."

"You mean when there's no moon?"

"Yeah. No moon. But I thought, well, maybe he might have been there when Kristi—"

I nodded. "Did you see what he was doing there?"

He shook his head. "I was too scared. I don't think he ever went into the house, just behind it."

Behind it, I thought, remembering the crawl space behind with the door closure hanging free and no cobwebs inside.

"Don't tell anyone I told you this, okay?" Aaron said anxiously. "My mom will get really mad at me."

"All right," I said.

"You promise?"

"I promise." I paused. "But Aaron, there might come a time when you want to tell more people."

He ducked his head. "Maybe."

"Okay," I said. "Maybe. It will be up to you."

He stood. "I better go. In case our neighbor checks in. I just wanted to tell you."

chapter nineteen

THE NEXT MORNING I WOKE UP GROGGY, still exhausted. The man Aaron had seen at Hal's shack, one more thing to check out. I should ask Hal, he might know. I gave him a call.

"I have no idea why anyone would go to that place, especially at night," he said. "That's interesting. Have you told the investigator?"

"I promised my source that I wouldn't."

"I'm pretty swamped up here," he said, "but keep me updated."

"I will," I lied.

The freezer was full of packets of coffee beans from San Francisco, a last remnant of Hal's former pleasant lifestyle, and I ground the beans in his Braun grinder and was brewing the coffee extra-strong as I heard Wally's truck pull up below. Not feeling sociable, I took my coffee and the phone into my room and shut the door. I dialed the number for the San Francisco police precinct Otto Marsh had given me and asked for Detective Phil Bates.

"I'm sorry," said a woman's voice, "there's no one here by that name."

"He was with the San Francisco police fifteen years ago," I told her. "A homicide detective with your precinct."

She laughed merrily.

"Well, could you switch me to someone who might know?" I said.

"I'll try," said the woman. "Can you hold, please?"

After a while someone came on the line. "Detective Howard here."

"I'm trying to get hold of Phil Bates. Could you help me?"

"Phil, sure. Lady, he retired four years ago."

"I gathered he was no longer with the force, but I wondered if you could tell me how to reach him."

"I don't think Phil would go for that. He values his privacy. Sorry I can't help you. If you know him, you could try calling his relatives."

"I don't know him. I was given his name. It's important."

"I'm sure it is, but lady, I don't know who you are or what your motives are in wanting to talk to him. You see my point?"

"Yes," I said wearily. "Thanks anyway." I hung up, feeling at an impasse. But then, I did know cops elsewhere, and a cop might tell a cop. Logan was two thousand miles away, it was okay, this really was a good reason. I sat nervously, cross-legged on the futon, marshaling my defenses.

All I had to do was keep reminding myself this was the guy who'd upended the kitchen table at his best friend Eddie's house, in front of Eddie's aged mother, when Eddie told him they'd run out of beer. Beer cans, plates smeared with take-out Greek salad from the Kolokithas Deli, glasses, knives, forks, all crashing to the floor. Logan looking wild and darkly beautiful as he did it. Everyone was afraid of him except Eddie's sister Wendy Sue, who ran in from the bedroom and whacked Logan with a broom.

It was turning into the kind of call cops hate most, but the cops were already there. Wendy Sue and I got Logan, mumbling heartfelt apologies, out to the car. I drove him home. It wasn't the only episode of this kind, only the one I chose to leave by.

I dialed Logan's number. "Hi," I said when he answered.

"Chloe, sweetheart. What's up?" As if I'd seen him yesterday instead of more than a month ago. It was his version of forgiving and forgetting. But his voice was nice, good to hear. He was often, I thought, a good person.

"Logan, I'm trying to locate someone. He's retired from the San Francisco police and they won't tell me where he is."

"I should hope not. I know you think we're just a bunch of fascist jerks, Chloe, but if we're lucky we get a few wild men off the street." He always spoke as if he were still on the force. "They don't know who you are, he has a right to his privacy. You working on a case?"

"Yes."

"You should come out to the island. The tomatoes are still hanging on, but I'm thinking about pulling up the plants and storing them. What's that recipe you told me about?"

"Green tomato pie." I closed my eyes. "I can't come out to see you. I'm in Arizona."

"Arizona? What the hell you doing there?"

He would be at the kitchen phone, probably, standing, looking out the back window, where fields that once grew potatoes stretched away to the horizon. Early in the summer we'd planted a garden together, first lettuce and radishes, then tomatoes, peppers, corn. Three hours later than here, it would be late morning, about the time we usually got up when I slept over, which had been nearly every weekend. We would read the newspaper, taking different sections and reading bits out loud to each other. I loved to take his face between my hands, kiss him hard on the mouth. Control this uncontrollable person, own him.

"I figured it was a safe distance," I said, feeling shaky.

"Safe from what?" His voice mocked me gently.

"Do you really want to go into it?"

"Sure. Why not? You're going to go on about my drinking. You don't understand it's just one of my habits. My friends drink too. Even my married friends drink. Their wives don't leave them. It's not like I ever hit you."

"Do you know what it's like being in bed with a drunk? It's like sleeping with a big wet dog."

"Ouch." I could hear the laughter in his voice. "That was cruel. Now, wasn't it?"

I rushed on, not wanting to let him pull me back. "The name of this guy is Phil Bates, a homicide detective. He retired from the San Francisco police four years ago. You could get his phone number for me. That's all I need. I need it pretty quickly."

"I'll see what I can do, okay? Give me your number and I'll call you back."

I gave him the number, possibly a big mistake. "I have to go out, but you can call me as late as you like tonight," I told him. "It's really important to me."

"Don't forget there's things in life beside work, Miss Financial Investigator. We had fun together, you forget that."

"You could have tried harder," I blurted out. "You only went to one A.A. meeting."

"And that was enough, bunch of losers. I couldn't relate."

"Bunch of ex-losers."

"Remember *Sea of Love*?"

"Logan. I have to go."

I hung up, keeping my hand on the receiver for a minute or

two, holding it down, in case Logan was still on the line. I wasn't going to let him get to me.

Then I hurried into the other room to talk to Wally.

The room where he was working was full of dust. Wally wore a white mask on his face, which he pulled down when he saw me. "Have you been outside yet?"

"No."

"The town looks like Christmas. They've got big red bows everywhere, on the streetlights, on all the fences, on the doors of the stores. It's Drug Awareness Week. The contemporary equivalent of a medieval holiday. It makes you think about our values, doesn't it? There's going to be a big rally this evening."

"A rally. Are you going?"

"I think I will."

"Do you know a Reba Jenkins?" I asked him.

He rolled his eyes.

I drove down Main Street humming the song "Sea of Love" to myself. Logan had gotten to me—just a little, I hoped. A big red and white banner saying DRUG AWARENESS WEEK was strung across Main Street. Another by the post office said JUST SAY NO.

Red ribbons were everywhere, with a large one on the old iron mining cart in front of the Mining Museum. People had on red ribbons too, mostly the people who looked employed. Did that mean everyone else was a drug addict? I don't know if I would have worn a red ribbon myself, although in front of the bank several sweet little old ladies were passing them out. It seemed too much like mind control.

I drove down Main Street, feeling sad, wanting to call Logan back, get him out here, to help. He'd be good at it. I could follow him around, be his admiring bimbo. The lure of bimbo land. I took a left onto the Gulch and drove down that for quite a ways, following Wally's directions.

"You bitch," Reba Jenkins yelled from her front porch. "You fucking bitch!" She wore black motorcycle boots, tight jeans, an olive tank top.

Her hair was dyed black, matte dark, so where the sun hit it nothing reflected back. Her eyes were heavily lined like a raccoon's eyes, peering at me timidly from inside two circles. They didn't belong with her words, her painted face.

From inside the house music blared out, screamed. Guns N' Roses singing "Sweet Child O' Mine"—oddly, for heavy metal, about childhood memories and bright blue sky. Reba closed her eyes. She swayed her body in time to the music. She smiled to herself.

I came up the path, past a cypress tree, its fallen needles under my feet. Under the cypress tree everything darkened. The music shattered the morning with screeches of pain, anger, despair, and underneath a hidden tenderness. I came just to the porch and noticed a spider tattooed on Reba's bony shoulder.

"I love that song," I said to her. "I've always really loved it."

Reba blinked her eyes. "Bullshit."

But it was true. I sang along, the lines about a warm safe place.

"I know why you're here, but Duane's a good boy," shrilled Reba over the music. "No one's ever been fair to him. Not ever. Fucking police, harassing him. When I hear that song I change the words, make them be him instead of her. Why not? It's a free country."

"I just want know if he was with you," I shouted. "Five nights ago."

"Yes, he was!" she shouted back.

"You don't want my love," screamed Guns N' Roses.

"He was, he was, he was," she shouted. "He was forever and ever, till death do us part, he always was, *he was, he was, he was,*" her mouth a snarl but her eyes still scared and vulnerable.

Please, I prayed as I drove past the Lavender Pit to Lowell, to Darla's studio, *let her be normal.*

This time the sign on the door said OPEN. I parked the van right in front of the studio and was getting out when a woman appeared in the doorway. Her dark hair was very short, moussed into little spikes, and she wore a paint-spotted apron, green squaw skirt, white anklet socks, and trendy big black shoes.

"Darla?" I asked.

"Isn't that Danny Newcombe's van?" Despite her bizarre clothes, her gray eyes were clear, her gaze level.

"Yes," I said, "I'm Chloe, his sister."

She gestured with her arm, pointing her finger to the side where there was a vacant lot between two buildings, fronted by a fence and a large open gate of corrugated tin. "Why don't you park it there?"

I got back in and drove through the gate. She followed on foot, pulled the gate closed behind her, and waited as I turned off the ignition and got out of the van.

"Sturm and Drang." Long chili pepper earrings dangled from her ears. She ran her fingers through her hair. "No, that's not the right term. Cloak and dagger? I'd just as soon no one sees you here. Let's go inside."

Early autumn was hot here in Lowell, with the abandoned movie theater, so cut off from the rest of town. Barren of trees or anything green except Darla's squaw skirt, which was decorated with silver and gold rickrack. I followed her as she clomped in her big black shoes to the back of the building, which was separated by a high wire fence from a desolate area that must be mine dumps.

Water, colored a brilliant deadly blue with chemicals from some long-ago leaching process, lay in poisonous pools that glittered seductively in the heat.

We went in through a back door, blue paint chipping off it. Inside along the walls were wire shelves with rows of plates, cups, pitchers, some bare and ready to be decorated, some already painted, ready, I assumed, to be put in the kiln.

"Who told you about me?" Darla asked.

We passed a large ceramic man pointing a gun, a dollar bill sticking out of the barrel.

"Stan at the photography studio," I said

We reached a long table.

"Have a seat," Darla said. "You might brush the chair off first."

I brushed off white powder and sat. She picked up a paintbrush: a row of cups lined the table; cups painted with spiked cacti; cartoon slogans and bursts of bombs going off; fanged frogs and comic-strip lettering saying Attack of the Killer Frogs.

"So," she said as she began to paint on a blank cup. "Why me?"

"Why anyone?" I said. I told her some of what I knew, including my visit with Roger and his denial of knowing Danny.

"Roger," she said flatly.

"Have you met him?"

She nodded, staring uneasily over my shoulder to the front of the shop, out through the plate-glass windows, and said musingly, "There was no brotherly love at all between Chip and Roger. Even when Roger looked like he was helping Chip it was somehow engineered to show Chip how incompetent he was.

"Roger gave him a job once, doing brochures. Anyone could tell it was way over Chip's head. I don't know anything about Danny and Roger, whether they knew each other, but if they did I can't explain why he would deny knowing Danny to you." She paused. "It's funny—Chip said to me once that Roger made all his mistakes away from home where no one was watching."

"What did *that* mean?"

"I have no idea."

From outside I heard the snarling noise of an inefficient car engine approaching. Darla tensed, held up her hand, and half rose to look out the window. The car noise receded. She relaxed, dipped the brush in black paint, and began to add a series of little teeth to a frog she had painted on the cup. On her wrist she wore a watch with a spiderweb marking the numerals and a spider ticking around the hours.

"What are you afraid of?" I asked her.

She concentrated hard on filling in the outlines of the teeth, not looking at me. "Not afraid." Her voice was resolute. "Cautious. I'd broken it off with Chip before he got killed, but not that long before."

She looked up at me then. "Beaten, then shot." She gave a nervous little laugh. "I never had a passionate thing with him. You have to understand Chip. He was such a cute guy. Cute's the only word I can think of. But no depth. And problems." She considered this. "Who needs a guy with problems?"

"Who does?" I echoed self-consciously.

"I was with Chip when he met Danny." She began to letter the word *Attack*. Her hand was a little shaky. After a moment she set the brush down. “Chip was wearing his camera, as usual. I bet he had the same film in that Nikon for years. Danny started asking him about photography, not technical questions but about the photography scene itself in Tucson. Chip knew everybody who was anybody in that scene from when he'd decided to be a big-time photographer. Danny wrote everything down in a notebook.”

“Chip took a course in photography from a professor at the U of A, Josh Cohen. Do you know him?”

Darla wrinkled her nose. “Josh is a guru-type, with an emphasis on the ladies, at least until this third marriage. The art department's full of gurus: professors that want to be followed around and worshipped by their students. Chip fell for Josh's line, of course. You should hear how he talked about him, like he was the man who'd invented photography. I mean, that human landscape stuff is not exactly a new or major breakthrough.”

“So it was just photography Chip and Danny talked about?”

“No, they got to be friends kind of.” Darla rinsed out her paintbrush and stood it up on the side of the cup she'd been working on. She reached into her overalls pocket and took out a pack of cigarettes. “Why don't we go outside? I don't like to smoke where I work.”

Out back we leaned against the side of the building as Darla lit up. I looked out at the mine dumps and the Pit beyond: the valley of the poisoned moon.

Darla exhaled smoke. “Danny's girlfriend was wild when she was up. I saw her a lot at the bars. She made things happen around her, made you see things in another way. I admire that. I know it probably had something to do with her getting murdered, but I can't help but admire self-destructiveness. It sharpens the emotional sense.”

She paused. "Still, are you going to throw your life away for a few really good ideas?"

She took a drag on her cigarette and blew out the smoke, looking as though she were considering this and not really rejecting it. She sighed and contemplated the end of her cigarette for a moment. "I guess you know Chip was into selling cocaine."

"I don't think Danny was dealing. I asked a friend of Danny's, Brody, and he said Danny wasn't."

"Well, if anyone would know, it would be Brody, if he's telling you the truth. Brody and Danny were friends?"

I nodded.

"I don't want to disillusion you, but Brody's not brand-spanking drug-free himself. That's no secret. He's been busted, you know."

"He told me. A long time ago in Montana."

"Montana?" Darla raised her eyebrows. She flicked her cigarette onto the ground, where it smoldered in the dirt. "He got busted here, and not all that long ago. He owned a lot of land out in the Valley, nice land, with a house on it. He'd rigged up this underground greenhouse for growing marijuana. The police waited until almost harvest, then they busted him. It was funny he didn't do any time."

"I guess he won't be showing up at any drug rallies."

Darla smiled. "I don't know about that. It would be just like him to show up, shake a few hands, and take advantage of the refreshments. If there are any.

"But listen," she said. "Roger's successful, but he's not a good person, even beyond the way he treated Chip. I know his ex from—from when I used to live in Tucson. She hung around the art scene. Kelly, Kelly Pomeroy. I don't know her number offhand, but it's actually in the Tucson phone book under *K. Pomeroy.*"

Darla wrapped her arms around her body and shivered in the heat. "I think maybe you should go now," she said.

Back at Hal's, I called Tucson information and got the number of K. Pomeroy and punched it in.

"She's at work." A man's voice.

"And that would be . . . ?" I said.

"Who's calling anyway?" he asked.

"A friend of Darla's."

"Darla. Sure. Here's the number."

I punched it in.

A woman's voice sang out, "Food Conspiracy."

I asked for Kelly.

"That's me."

I introduced myself. "Darla mentioned you," I said. "That you were married to Roger O'Leary."

"Roger." Her voice sounded flat. "Well, isn't that special. You know what? The last time I saw my therapist, about a year ago, she congratulated me on finally being able to go for several days without thinking bad thoughts about Roger. I can go for weeks now, weeks and weeks, so thank you very much for reminding me."

"I'm sorry," I said. I explained about my brother.

"I wish I could help," she said, "but I can't. I know nothing. But I can tell you this: if you suspect Roger of anything"—she began to laugh—"anything at all"—she laughed some more—"he's probably guilty."

I waited for her to stop laughing and maybe explain, but she kept on, and then someone hung up the phone and I was left with the dial tone.

I sat at the kitchen counter, feeling the muscles in my neck and back and shoulder blades tense up, tighter and tighter, with the urgency that had carried me along from the time Danny had disappeared. Nothing, I'd done nothing that had gotten me any closer, just spun my wheels. Now I had all kinds of facts and maybe lies too, all jumbled together, and it was no use, no use at all.

My ears started to ring with anxiety and I got up from the counter and went out to the van. I had to do something, anything at all; I had to act. I had to act and act and act, and then I wouldn't have to think at all.

chapter twenty

THE GUN THAT BRODY HAD GOTTEN ME WAS tucked in my purse, the foam dice were bouncing, and Danny's van clattered and swayed clumsily down the narrow highway through the Valley. If you could ignore the excessive amount of roadkill by the side of the road, mostly bunny rabbits, then it was another beautiful day in paradise, as Aaron's mother might have said. The wind coming in the window was spiked with oils from the roadside vegetation, dry and golden in the sunshine. To my left and to my right were fields, some still with crops growing, some plowed under, and the whole scene rimmed with hazy mountains. The road was empty except for the occasional pickup truck from out in the fields approaching from a great distance.

What had Darla been so scared about? I wondered, but now that I was doing something, the wind and the sunshine made me feel dreamy. I wanted to drive and drive in the sunshine and the wind until I reached the mountains, but my destination was more plebeian. You couldn't miss it, they said at the gas station where I'd stopped for directions, and then there it was: rows and rows of rusted cars, household appliances, furniture no one would ever sit on again, or lay dishes on, or sleep on. Things once treasured, saved up for, and now the whole mess was kind of blending into the earth.

The drive and the weather had stripped away my caution and made me silly. Beyond all the junk was a house with a patch of dirt in front where a gray pickup was parked. I pulled in behind it. Maybe once long ago the guy had had a wife, but she was most likely gone now, leaving only her rosebushes, woody, untended. Here and there trash had blown in from the junkyard, bits of it caught on the thorny branches and waving like blossoms.

I got out of the van, crossed the dirt to the house: square cinder blocks with an aluminum screen door. I opened the screen and was about to knock on the bare wood door behind when a man came around from the side. He was a gray man, wearing clothes that looked as though he'd picked them up at a junkyard too. Gray dirt covered his face, rimmed his eyes like some kind of weird mascara, exaggerating the blue of his eyes, which looked like bits of sky stuck in the ground.

"What can I do for you?" His voice was gruff and plain.

"Are you the owner?"

He hitched up his gray baggy pants, which were belted with a piece of rope. "Sure am."

I gestured to the bumper of Danny's van, which, luckily for my purposes, was crumpled on one side as if Danny had hit something, which was entirely possible. "I thought maybe you might have a bumper like this in stock and I could buy it cheap."

Carson went close to the van and looked at the bumper, looked at the van, and scratched his head. "No, ma'am, I wouldn't think so. Most of my vehicles are real old, though I do get the accidents out on the road when the big guys don't want 'em. Don't recall this kind of vehicle."

"Well, shoot." I put my hands in my pockets in what I hoped was a folksy way. "This a pretty neat place you have here."

Carson spit on the dirt, then rubbed the mark with his foot. "Ah, you got your privacy."

You sure did. There were no other houses for miles and miles. A buzzard, sun glistening blue-green on its wings, sailed in for a landing, coming to rest on the side fence.

"It must give you the creeps sometimes," I said. "I guess there was some kind of murder here a while ago."

"Lady." He spit again. His face turned ugly and bitter. "Lady, you come here to ask me some damn questions, you can get your ass off my property."

"I was just mentioning it. I—"

Carson had turned his back and walked over to the pickup, reached in the front seat, and pulled out a shotgun. *"Now,"* he said.

"Now," I echoed soothingly as I backed all the way to the van. I reached behind me and opened the door. I got in backward. Carson didn't move.

I started up the van, hoping the guy wasn't trigger-happy. People didn't just shoot each other out here, did they? The answer to that, at least in Chip's case, was yes. My gun was in my purse, but a shoot-out wouldn't help matters. I drove back onto the road. In the rearview mirror I saw Carson, shotgun now under his arm, still watching me. Then he turned and went into the house.

I drove slowly. My foot kept trembling on the accelerator. Unaware of my predicament, the weather kept being sunny and nice. Several miles down the road I felt a little better. I pulled the gun out of my purse and put it on the seat beside me. I drove lazily, imagining what it would be like to be a farmer out here.

They grew chilies, Roger O'Leary, that dog capable of anything according to his ex, had said, and pecan trees, but I didn't see any orchards. To my left was a big building with a sign in front saying REYES CHILI FACTORY. Past the factory from a road to my left an old nondescript pickup was coming, driving fast, leaving a cloud of dust behind. A farmer driving his chilies to market while they were still hot.

The pickup reached the main road with plenty of time to turn before I got to it, but it didn't turn, it stopped dead in the middle of the road. I slowed. The pickup still didn't move. It had probably stalled. Inside was a man in the driver's seat wearing, oddly enough for the warm weather, a knit cap, pulled down low on his face. The pickup backed a little then and turned toward me. The road was narrow, edged with ditches on each side, and the truck was smack in the center, so I couldn't pass it on either side. I felt the kind of recognition you feel when you realize the man close behind you going down into the subway is too close and you might be in trouble.

My heart started to pound. I stopped the van.

I reached for the gun. Unfortunately, when he'd taught me to shoot Logan had offered no pointers for shooting from a car while you were sitting in it. I wished I'd taken a few practice rounds recently. The pickup drove toward me and banged my front bumper, jerking me in my seat so that I bit my lip, hard. I could taste blood. Remembering something from some old cop movie, I grabbed the gun, opened the door, and got out, hitting the ground and twisting my ankle.

Standing up so the door shielded my body, I raised the gun and fired a shot into the air. The sun was on the windshield of the truck and about all I could see was that it was a man and he looked surprised. The pickup backed away. He must not have had a gun or surely he would have returned fire. For a second I thought he was going to ram me again. I fired another shot.

The sound of it hurt my ears. "You don't notice the sound when you're shooting at someone," Logan had assured me, so long ago on the pistol range. "What you're doing is so much louder."

Bullshit to you, Logan. "Don't shoot when you're feeling emotional," he'd said also. *How about scared?* The pickup backed off some more, onto the road where it had come from, then it came out, turned, and drove at me, but it swerved, passing me on my vulnerable side, but not stopping. I watched it go off down the road in the opposite direction, in the opposite direction, in the opposite direction. My mouth was dry but I didn't feel anything at all.

I got back in the car and took a pen out of my purse to write down the license number, but the truck didn't have a license plate. I wished I'd learned more about cars, from my various boyfriends who had loved them. To me, it looked like a mud-colored pickup truck. I'd seen several similar ones just on my drive here today. *It wasn't really old, Officer, and it wasn't really new. Mud color.*

I wiggled my ankle. It didn't hurt much, but it might be worse later. My lip already felt swollen. I rested my head on the seat back and closed my eyes. I was light-headed from shock, hyperventilating, and I wondered if anything in the van had been damaged in any serious way and if I would be able to drive it. I turned the key and felt enormous relief when it started. I drove on down the road. Nothing vital fell off.

Suddenly I recovered. If the Valley had looked beautiful before, it was twice as beautiful now. It was sheer poetry the way crops grew in the fields, in such neat rows, the way everything was washed with gold. A smile flowed over my face involuntarily. I whooped, shouted out loud, "I did it, I did it, I did it." On impulse I stopped the van by the side of the road and got out.

There were four bullets left. A jackrabbit hopped away from me on enormous hind legs, but I didn't shoot at it. I shot at a mesquite bush, I shot at a fence post, I shot the fence post again and saw wood splinter. Bingo. I was exhilarated, standing by the side of the road. I could have gone on shooting for hours, but I saved the last bullet, just in case.

Just me here alone, empowered, someone new and different, someone I'd secretly dreamed of being. If Logan could see me now.

The thought that he would be calling me later about Phil Bates hit me. I'd stayed away from him entirely for a whole month in New York and now I'd made the connection again. Like the reformed smoker who looks down and suddenly sees a cigarette in his hand, I couldn't visualize exactly how that had happened. No, I consoled myself, I'd had a good reason. Belatedly it came to my mind now that I knew at least two cops well enough in New York City who probably would have helped me. How could I have "forgotten"? I asked myself hypocritically.

Suddenly I wished I'd had an audience, like an actor who practices his lines, not quite on because no one is watching. No one but the man in the pickup. Shoot, he probably wouldn't tell anyone.

chapter twenty-one

DAMN BRODY, I THOUGHT AS I NEARED town. I don't know why he came to mind, I guess because he'd given me the gun. And lied to me, if not about Danny, at least about the extent of his own involvement in drugs. Though I'd never actually asked him. Now I didn't have anyone in town to trust. I should probably go to the police about the incident out in the Valley and then Nance would give me a little lecture. Or was it in his jurisdiction? Nance didn't seem to care about jurisdiction, though; he came and went as he pleased.

There was no doubt in my mind that the guy with the pickup had to do with my visit to Carson's, but on the other hand, he hadn't seemed to have had a gun, so it was probably meant merely to discourage me from coming back. Which hadn't really been necessary. My lip felt like someone had pumped it full of cotton and my ankle was throbbing.

Probably Brody hadn't mentioned his recent bust, I rationalized, because he didn't want me to think he was a bad guy. And who else was I going to trust anyway? Hal was in Tucson helping too many people already. I drove to Brody's shop, past the

Drug Awareness red ribbons tied onto everything and flickering merrily in the breeze. I parked the van and got out.

I hobbled into the shop. Maybe he had an Ace bandage on hand. Inside, he was happily spraying black paint onto the Mercury, using a compressor. He didn't look up until the compressor shut down, and then he did and saw me.

"You New Yorkers," he said. "You all come down here looking like you live in caves, and I bet you do. Take some time off, Chloe. Get some color in your face."

I collapsed on his car seat. "You slimeball," I said, though I like to watch my language. I closed my eyes but then opened them.

Brody was looking out at the van parked in front. "You really put a dent in that thing somewhere. You must be a worse driver than Danny."

Maybe he was getting a crush on me. Love affects some men that way. They just pick you apart until there's nothing left to love.

He came closer. "What'd you do to your lip? You look like a Ubangi."

"Just stay away from me with your racist talk."

"That's racist? What the hell is a Ubangi anyway, come to think of it? Aren't they those people who put plates in their lips? What's racist about that? They *want* to look that way."

"The dent was put there maybe half an hour ago," I said between my teeth; tough. "By some guy in a pickup out in the Valley who might have been trying to kill me. My lip I got when he banged into my car. I sprained my ankle when I jumped out of the van and shot at him. I shot at him twice."

Brody looked at me noncommittally for a moment before he spoke. "I hope to hell you missed."

I nodded.

"You like Mexican food? Chili rellenos, albondigas, caldo de queso?"

"I don't know."

"I'm going to close up shop. Since it's Drug Awareness Week I like to be out of town. There's a rally every day, but we won't be attending any. We could go across the line and eat in a Mexican restaurant. If we're lucky it'll be mariachi night. We'll leave this piece-of-shit van here and take my old red truck, 1955 Ford, big comfortable seats."

Brody drove slowly through town, which was fixed up, decorated like Christmas, then turned onto the highway, past the Lavender Pit and Lowell, through an overpass, around a circle onto another highway. I took off the flip-flop Brody had loaned me and propped my foot, ankle wrapped in an Ace bandage, up on the dashboard. It helped, to elevate the foot.

We were out in the open, the land stretching away on either side, dotted here and there with clumps of houses inhabiting the land futilely, dwarfed by the desert. A ways out, we passed a large Safeway and a few stores, a Burger King, the first fast-food place I'd seen in Dudley. We were headed for Mexico, another alien country.

The land had such a feeling of openness, yet no one I had talked to told me much. I didn't know this terrain or the people who lived here. We passed a sign.

SE PROHIBE
TIRAR BASURA

Not even the road signs made any sense.

Brody steered the big unwieldy truck like a ride at an amusement park. His red hair was shaggy, streaked here and there with gray, from his desperado life as a drug dealer, no doubt. A former drug dealer?

"Were you just plain dumb, Brody," I asked, "when they busted you? With the greenhouse?"

"Oh, shit, who told you that?"

Darla had said it was no secret, but I only said flippantly, "Common knowledge."

"I'm out of it now," he said, maybe a little too casually. "But anyway, dealing drugs is nothing new in this town. The cops are usually only after the big guys, unless you draw attention to yourself or someone turns you in. It was one of them damn churchgoing farmers out there in the Valley, thought he'd do his duty. I think it was just some bushwhackers that got old Chip, playing at it, wanting to be tough and it got out of hand. The big stuff comes from down south, but it doesn't stay here long. We're just a conduit."

"How does all this connect with Danny?"

"Your guess is as good as mine. Worst-case scenario is Danny's dead, of course, but maybe it didn't have anything to do with drugs, could be some whacked-out nutcase grabbed him, killed him for fun, and dumped him in the desert."

I put my head back on the seat and stared up at the ceiling of Brody's truck, biting my lip, a habitual gesture, and realized it was tender and swollen. "Maybe Danny's hiding out from the police."

"Maybe," he said without conviction. "I can't lie to you: I hope he's okay too, you know."

"I visited Reba Jenkins today," I said.

"Don't tell me. She had an alibi for Duane."

"Well," I said, "I'm not sure. What's she so scared of?"

"Nothin', nothin' and everything. She and Duane always did have something going. Kristi must have been pretty powerful competition."

So powerful, it wasn't even a contest. Poor little Kristi, playing so carelessly with other people's lives, Danny's, Duane's, Reba's, not even aware of her power.

Or was she?

"Darla? Is *she* scared of nothing and everything?" I asked.

The truck jounced and jostled as we hit a patch of bumpy road. Brody concentrated extra hard on his steering. "She's a woman, and women tend to be scared, I guess."

He hadn't denied her fear.

"Are you scared? Being a man and all?"

But he wasn't listening, or was pretending not to, or just didn't want to comment. I thought that was it, but then he said, "I worked on Darla's truck a while ago. She drives this big old pickup, but she takes good care of it, not like most women. Brakes went out on her all of a sudden. They were pretty new, but someone had worked on them and screwed up."

"Who worked on her brakes?"

"Not a goddamn mechanic, that's for sure. . . . Look, you got to make a choice. Live your life in fear or just go on living and enjoying yourself."

"Roger," I said. "Chip's brother." I told Brody about my visit with him.

"I got nothing in particular to tell you about this Roger guy," he said, "but you know, you're not doing Danny any favors if you get yourself bumped off."

I liked the way he said that, as if there were no real doubt that Danny was alive.

We drove across the border. It was twilight. The guards looked at us lazily and waved us on. On the Mexican side the guard grinned at us. Brody said, *"Comidos,"* pointing his finger to his mouth.

The guard laughed and waved us on.

Across the border, everything changed all at once. The air seemed to warm and in the dusk were trees, young ones planted in neat rows down the street.

"Naco got a grant recently, industrial development," Brody told me. "So they planted a bunch of trees."

"That's nice," I said. "Everyone should develop industrially in that way."

"What they got is *maquilladoras*. Factories producing goods for American companies. Sort of a hands-across-the-border: manufacturers don't have to pay union wages and people here get jobs. Course, a lot of the folks in the States lost some jobs 'cause of it too."

There was a dance hall, painted blue, a curio store, and a pharmacy. It had a Spanish old-timey look to it, as if Clint Eastwood just might ride around the corner, the lonesome stranger.

"Ladies come here on a regular basis," Brody said. "Stock up on Retin-A."

"How would you know?"

"Guess I know some ladies." He smirked.

We turned the corner and passed a pretty white adobe church with a wrought-iron fence. Twilight softened the poverty of the houses made of mud: battered cars in front, junk piled in the backyards, poor people's treasures. We parked in front of a big white restaurant with a tin roof and a sign with the words MARISCOS MARLIN.

The restaurant was cavernous, almost deserted. A mariachi

band strolled around. The music was mournful and, like lots of Latin music, sounded like unrequited love felt, but then they switched to a faster number. The waitress came over. She was heavily made up, Cupid's-bow lips, Kewpie-doll eyes.

"Shrimp's the best," Brody told me. *"Camerones rancheros."*

"Fine," I said.

Brody held up two fingers to the waitress. *"Dos camerones rancheros."*

"I think," said Brody, leaning at me across the table, "that you're wasting your time, all this running around chasing shadows. Can't blame you, though. What else you gonna do, after all?"

I was piqued. "I have a client, Brody, if you want to know. I'm actually getting paid for all this shadow-chasing."

"Oh, yeah? Who?"

"Sorry," I said. "Client confidentiality."

The mariachis stopped at our table hopefully, a trio of dark mustachioed men in big black hats embroidered with silver. They smiled at me and played a little harder, grinning as they strummed strenuously.

"Great," Brody told them. *"Fantástico."* We listened until they finished, then he gave them a dollar.

The waitress came with our plates. *Camerones rancheros* turned out to be shrimp with tomato sauce, rice and beans on the side.

We dug in in silence. To my surprise, I found I was really hungry. Near-death experiences are supposed to do that. From across the room a couple rose. Anglo, the man big, the woman tiny; teetering on four-inch heels, she only came to his shoulder. They walked across the room toward the exit.

"There she goes," said Brody.

"Who?" I asked, watching them.

The woman reached up and flounced her hair. She smiled up at her escort, then looked back across the room at us. I had a glimpse of a wide mouth, eyes enormous in the shadows, then they were gone.

"That's Luann," said Brody. "Last name used to be Nance. Don't remember what it is now. Pretty lady."

"She broke his heart," I said. Seeing her was something of a disappointment. She looked too little and fluffy to wreak such havoc on Nance.

"Hey, you give your heart away, it's your own fault if someone tromps on it."

"So I guess you've always kept yours right in your chest where it belongs."

"Damn shootin'."

We stared at each other, one of those loaded moments.

The mariachis had made the circuit, which involved only two other diners, and returned.

"Come on. Lighten up." He pulled a plastic rose from the vase in the center of the table and held it out to me. The mariachis played faster, all smiles.

I took the rose. *Damn shootin',* I thought, *what a guy.* We seemed to be reaching that point in our relationship, going from air raids to hand-to-hand combat. It must be that mariachi magic. The rose was bright red, just starting to open. Plastic.

I put it behind my ear. I didn't know any Spanish, but I searched for some word. "Tequila," I said finally.

chapter twenty-two

I FOUGHT OFF ANY DESIRE TO HAVE BRODY hold me in his strong and possibly untrustworthy arms—I didn't need any new problems. Besides, did I want to get involved with Brody? Not only a former drug dealer, but, even worse, a man who was not politically correct. Besides, Logan should be calling. At this last fact I pretended to feel totally, overwhelmingly neutral.

I got back to Hal's in time for the ten o'clock news, sat down in front of the TV, and elevated my foot. It throbbed. Drug Awareness Week seemed to be not just a local but a statewide event, and a blond female reporter was interviewing a young Hispanic, who looked about sixteen. He'd just been through a drug prevention class.

"Could you just sum up for us, Hector, what you got out of the class?"

He blinked a little in the lights, his chance for immortality. He had a cute baby face and romantic brown eyes. "I learned a lot," he said earnestly. "It's really a good course."

"Want to sum it up for us, Hector," said the reporter, time running out and the thought straining her voice a little.

Hector grinned, gaining confidence. "Sure. I learned that drugs aren't the answer. Guys I know, they think dealing's the solution, but me, I learned if I want to buy a Ferrari, I'll go out and earn that money, save up for it. I won't try to get rich quick dealing drugs."

Sure, I thought, *and when you're two hundred and fifty-seven maybe you'll have enough.*

The phone rang. I turned the sound down on the TV. "Hello?"

"Eight Cypress Way," said Logan. He paused. "Pine Grove." He paused again. "California," he finished. His voice was succinct and overly careful.

It was a voice of his I knew well. Damn. After midnight, one o'clock New York time. I should have known. I wrote down the address. "Phone number," I said clearly, the way you might to a child. "Not address."

"No phone."

"Are you sure?"

"Guy's an ex-cop." He paused as though contemplating this phenomenon. "Ex. Cop. Think he wants a bunch of losers calling him up?" Logan's voice turned maudlin. "Chloe, you a sweet lady. You're so sweet I wish—"

"Never mind."

"You need to talk to him? Fast? Drive up there. Not so far from you, California." Logan gave an uproarious chuckle for no particular reason.

"Where in California?"

"Mountains. Near, uh, yeah, San Diego. You listen to me, Chloe. I know about cops. Dress nice. Cops always like to see a little lady dressed nice. No jeans. None of that all-black stuff either."

"I don't want to talk anymore. You're *drunk*."

"What the hell you talking about? I'm not drunk. Chloe, you're a, such a, sweet lady. You be careful. I'm telling you that as your friend. Your good, good buddy."

"Sure."

"Who taught you to shoot? Who? Remember, it's not the faces that count, it's the hands. Wash their hands. Wash their damn hands."

"Logan. I'm hanging up and don't call me back."

"That all the thanks I get? I'm just telling you, don't forget to wash their ha—"

I hung up, trying not to think. I needed a California map and remembered there were maps in the glove compartment of the van. I went outside to check, hit pay dirt.

The very same address was scrawled on the face of the map and a red line was drawn up to Palomar Mountain, outside of San Diego, with a big red *X*. It was like a message to me from Danny. I called Southwest Airlines and booked a flight for early the next morning. If Logan cared at all, if he had any true desire to get back together, he wouldn't have called me drunk. Of course, when he was drunk he didn't have the sense to realize that.

I went into the bedroom, put on my nightgown, he'd always liked that nightgown, and lay down. We'd been through this over and over—why did I think it would ever change? Logan would be drunk every night for the rest of his life. Some other woman would love him, in spite of this—a woman weaker or stronger than I, I didn't know which. There was absolutely nothing I could do about it. It was as though he were behind a plate-glass window and I could scream and yell, but he wouldn't be able to hear me. He would look at me, but he wouldn't really notice I was there.

The streetlight shone through the curtains into my room, making shadows of the bushes, the trees around the house. I was following a trail that had already been followed by my brother. Would it lead me to where it had led him? Would I simply vanish one day, be gone like him? Except I didn't feel as though Danny were dead. Couldn't feel that his spirit had left, but wasn't that what Otto Marsh would call denial?

I could feel death itself, though, unconnected to Danny, its inevitability. Could feel that Logan and I were actually really through. We wouldn't plant a garden together, or go to raunchy bars, or make love, ever again.

I thought of the names I'd seen on the scrap of paper written in Danny's handwriting I'd found under a pillow on the couch: Josephine Meadows, Golden Acres. They were taking on a life of their own, more geographical than human, a sunny flat place with yellow grasses waving and purple flowers blooming. I could feel myself walking through the meadows, disembodied, empty: alone.

Except Logan was knocking at my door and calling, conjured up by my last waking thoughts. My watch said two-thirty A.M. The hell with him. I had a plane to catch in the morning.

I turned over, put the pillow over my head, but he kept on knocking and calling. Even with the pillow I could hear the knocks becoming louder and more urgent. *Shit,* I thought, *Danny? Or Aaron?* I got out of bed, hobbled to the kitchen, turned on the light, and if I hadn't been still half asleep I wouldn't have done what I did next, at least not without checking first to see who it was. I flung open the door. It wasn't Logan, of course, and it wasn't Danny or Aaron.

Duane Taylor stood outside, swaying slightly, holding a beer can upside down. "Howdy." He smiled, trying for charm, but the smile didn't reach his amber eyes. He flung the beer can over his shoulder casually, gracefully. It clattered onto the carport floor and rolled down into the street.

"Sorry," I said. "Some other time." I started to close the door.

But he pushed it open and came inside, blinking in the light. His eyes were bloodshot, his curls needed a shampoo. "Thought you wanted to talk," he said belligerently.

"We already talked." I backed away, putting plenty of space between us. "Not that I got any straight answers."

"Yeah," he said. "Like them tests, multiple choice but only one answer's right. 'Cause you made up your mind right away not to believe me."

"Not right away."

I leaned back against a counter stool and stared at him. The dragon spiraled up his arm, breathing fire where it vanished into the sleeve of his black T-shirt. He wore a greasy-looking leather vest, a metal-studded leather bracelet on his wrist, and heavy work boots. He didn't seem to have any weapons on him, if you didn't count sheer muscle power. My gun was in the bedroom. If I'd been thinking instead of overestimating the power of my charms, I would have brought it out with me.

"Maybe I got some questions too," he said. "Or is this a one-way street here? Maybe you're like Princess Kristi, thinking everyone owes you something but you don't owe nothing back."

"Ask away," I said.

He began to walk around the kitchen. He went over to the coffee grinder and pressed the button. It whirred uselessly. "Look at this. Grind your own fag beans for your fag coffee."

"That has nothing to do with anything."

He flexed his shoulders, eyes darting around the kitchen. They reached me. He looked accusing. "It was you sent the police over."

"It wasn't me," I said. "But it wasn't any secret that you were seeing Kristi."

"Thought they had the perfect fall guy." He went over to the shelf where Hal's collection of Lu-Ray cups and bowls and pitchers were carefully lined up and picked up a pale yellow cup. "Somebody dies, they look around and say, *Shit, we got Duane here. If he didn't do it, he must of done something, so let's stick him with it.* He held the cup by its delicate handle, suspended from his little finger, and swung it back and forth.

I watched it swinging. I wished he would put it down. "The whole town knew you were seeing her."

"Reba didn't." Duane winced, swinging the cup back and forth faster, precariously. "Reba didn't know shit, until the cops came. Took a whole evening to get her calmed down, and then what happens? Next day you show up."

I backed around the stool to the end of the counter. It wasn't far to the bedroom where my gun was. "So?"

"So?" His voice got louder. "So? So what? you mean." He was shouting now. "So what, who cares what happens to her? Just some crazy lady doesn't know her ass from her elbow. Who the fuck cares!"

"Don't yell at me," I said primly.

"Why don't you call the fucking cops?" he yelled. "Get rid of me." He made a sudden move and got to the phone on the counter. With his free hand, he pulled the plug out and threw the phone across the counter, into the living room. It hit the couch and fell back, bounced on the floor.

"Look." I raised my voice too. "You're the one who was seeing Kristi. Don't you think you should take some responsibility here?"

"'Responsibility'?" he mimicked. "You sound like some goddamned fucking probation officer or a goddamn fucking *school* teacher."

"Oh, Duane," I said sarcastically. "Such insults. I bet you were a big hit in school."

"They was all like you there," he said, swinging the cup. He sneered. "Saw what they wanted to see. So I gave them what they saw, what they wanted. A good excuse to get rid of me." He threw the cup hard. It hit the floor. It bounced, but it didn't break.

"That happens to be valuable." My voice was self-righteous. "A collectible. Pick it up right now." I didn't see how he could stand much more of me.

Besides, my words were absurd under the circumstances, but just as absurdly, Duane looked worriedly down at the cup. He bent to pick it up. I took the opportunity to run into the bedroom and grab the gun. I came back out.

"Okay, Duane." I held it two-handed, pointed in his direction but at the floor. "Leave." I had only one bullet in the gun, thanks to my target shooting, but I was hoping I wouldn't need it.

He didn't even seem to see it. Or maybe dying was something he had no opinion about one way or the other. "You know what," he said. "Kristi was dealing drugs, and that's the truth."

"What?" I said. "I don't believe you."

He shrugged. "Then don't. She was a bigger drug dealer than any of us other small-time folk, but nobody said a word 'cause she was so pretty."

"She was not dealing."

"Fuck you, then," he said. "Fuck you anyway, you went and saw Reba."

For a moment I stared at him, taking in this new information about Kristi.

"You made her hurt double. You don't care what you do to

people. You go ahead and do whatever you want." He came closer, menacingly. "Like she doesn't have *feelings*."

"Duane," I yelled, waving the gun. "This is totally ridiculous. Get out of here!" You were supposed to hold a gun on somebody and he did what you wanted. What was I supposed to do next, shoot him?

Duane looked at the Lu-Ray cup. "What the fuck am I doing?" He dropped it. He went to the shelf and swept it with his arm. Hal's entire collection—cups, saucers, bowls, pitchers—crashed to the ground, pastel pieces flying. One of them hit me on the cheek.

Duane kicked at the pieces. "Poor old Reba," he said, as if she were lying on the floor with the broken pottery. His voice broke, got maudlin. "Poor, poor little Reba." Tears came to his eyes. He wiped at them with his sleeve. "You fuck with her again, you so much as show your face near her place, somebody's going to get it," but his voice was suddenly useless, out of power. He gave a last kick to the shards of china, then crunched across the floor to the door.

When he got there, he paused. "Somebody's gonna pay." He raised his fist as he went out, slamming the door behind him.

I could hear his footsteps clomping down the street. Then for a moment everything seemed incredibly quiet.

Shit, I thought. I rubbed my cheek. The skin hadn't broken, but a lump was forming. Kristi was dealing drugs? I didn't know what to do with this information.

I looked down at the debris, what was left of Hal's Lu-Ray collection, carefully, lovingly assembled over time: *Hal,* I thought, bending over and picking up a pale pink pitcher, Sharon pink, the handle broken off. Almost everything was broken except a couple of cups. *Hal, oh, Hal, I'm so sorry.* People dying in his houses, cops questioning him, and now his entire Lu-Ray china collection broken. I sat down on the floor, holding the pitcher like a little china baby, and let myself cry. I cried for a long time.

Finally I got up, found a broom, and swept everything into a pile. I put all the pieces in a big paper bag. As if with patience they could all be glued together, maybe a little chip gone here or there, but almost perfect again, like poor old Reba's heart.

chapter twenty-three

WHEN JAMES AND DANNY AND I WERE KIDS, there was a period one summer when we went map-crazy. We drew maps of everything, real or imaginary. After we got tired of just making the maps, we made maps to go places with. James was eleven, I was nine, and Danny was six.

Behind our house was a woods, a jumble of undergrowth with little creeks running through. I don't know why James condescended that summer to spend so much time with Danny and me. The maps James made were beautiful, intricate things, with made-up names for ordinary places. He would produce a map in the morning and we would spend the day following it.

That summer James and I were nice to Danny. We followed Danny's maps too, exclaiming whenever we reached the spots he'd marked with an *X* and named. He was dinosaur-crazy that summer, so he had names like the Cave of Tyrannosaurus Rex, Stegosaurus Tree, Brontosaurus Creek. Now I was in a rental car following Danny's map again, to Phil Bates's house, in search of something just as primitive. Bates lived up in the mountains, 8 Cypress Way in Pine Grove: an appropriate name, because the road was thick with pines on both sides.

I followed a paved road to where it turned onto one that was unpaved. As I entered, a big sign on the right said PRIVATE ROAD, TRESPASSERS WILL BE SHOT. I parked my car just outside the driveway of Bates's address, metal number 8 nailed to a large pine tree, and went on foot over a carpet of pine needles, blue jays screeching at me.

Remembering what Logan had said about appearances, I was wearing one of my few nonblack items of clothing, a white blouse, with my black leggings and one pink ballet flat. Pink ballet flats were a nice touch, except the left one hadn't fit over the Ace bandage, so I was still wearing Brody's flip-flop. Sunglasses hid my eyes, swollen from last night's crying, but not my swollen aching cheek, my lip.

You could not see, but sensed the ocean somewhere over the mountains. The house was built of dark logs, with a wide veranda all around. A woman was sitting there as I approached the steps, reading a magazine. She was probably sixty but wore a halter top and shorts, exposing skin tanned to leather. Her hair was an elaborate arrangement of rolled sausage curls, a bright even orange, perched over her weathered and lined face like a wild banner of youth.

"Hi, honey," she said. "You lost?"

"I hope not. I'm looking for Phil Bates."

She regarded me with suspicion. "What about?"

From behind the house came the sound of a gunshot. I jumped, but the woman paid no attention.

"I'm looking for my brother," I explained. "He might have visited Mr. Bates a while ago. He's disappeared and I have no idea where he is. This is all I have to go on."

"Your brother a cop?" asked the woman. I just caught her words, then there were two more shots in close succession. "Lots of cops come up here to see Phil. Marry a cop, you marry the whole damn force. They get together, cry in their beer, then they go out and shoot at squirrels. That's what Phil's doing now."

"He isn't a cop. His name's Danny. Danny Newcombe?"

"Sure, I remember him. You're right, he did come up here a while back." She twittered and patted her curls. Danny must have made an impression. "I guess Phil won't mind talking to you. He's always liked to talk to the ladies anyway." She said this without rancor. "You come in and I'll get him. Care for a glass of iced tea?"

"I'd love it."

"Oh, honey, I didn't see you hurt yourself. Sprain your ankle? And your face too, you must have taken a fall."

"Yes." I walked up the steps, bravely holding on to the railing.

Inside was a small living room, dominated by a TV. There was a couch covered with a hideous mauve and yellow plaid, along with two brown covered chairs filled with stuffed animals, teddy bears, elephants, and Raggedy Anns and Andys.

"Just shove those little guys aside," she said. "That's my hobby. I'm Mildred, by the way."

"I'm Chloe." I sat down next to a Sunbonnet Sue.

She went through a door where there was a small kitchen and a back door. "Hey, Phil," she bawled with surprisingly hearty lungs.

After a while Phil came into the living room. He was a tall thin man, with a rakish pompadour and long Elvis sideburns. He had a pallor that hinted he might be sick, maybe even dying, but his bearing denied it. Mildred followed closely, carrying two glasses of iced tea. "Chloe?" he said. "Pleased to meet you."

We shook hands, then he sat down on a vinyl-covered recliner, moving a Raggedy Andy aside. Mildred placed a little plastic disk on the table next to me and another on the table by Phil. She set the glasses on the disks, dead center.

"Look, Milly, why don't you go skin some squirrels?" Bates laughed a sharp little laugh, then his face reverted instantly to serious. He began to cough. Mildred vanished out the back door. "Emphysema," he got out between coughs. "Hold on."

I waited until the coughing subsided, then explained why I was there. "Mildred said my brother Danny came to see you."

"He sure did," said Bates. "We had a long talk. Very nice sincere kid, your brother. Nuts too."

There was a silence.

"Well, not totally," I said feebly.

"Sorry, no offense."

"He's vanished. He picked me at the airport in Tucson, we stopped in some little town on the way back to where he lives, and he just vanished."

"How long ago?"

"A week."

"You talk to law enforcement?"

"I filed a missing person report." I hesitated. "Actually, I found out later someone saw Danny getting into a vehicle."

"And?" said Bates expectantly. "Were they able to ID the driver?"

I shook my head.

Bates looked at me for a minute. Then he ran his fingers through his hair. He said, "Cops aren't always as good at following up some of this stuff as they might be. Too busy, and then, maybe someone like your brother, he might have vanished on purpose. Some guy gets into a car voluntary, then he's not really missing."

I didn't want to get into another discussion along those lines, so I moved on. "He wanted to talk about a case you had fifteen years ago?"

"Sure did. Murder of Louis Barnett and Cynthia Fuller. Looked like a simple house fire, turned into murder one."

"Murder one?"

"Arson. Arson's always murder one."

"There was no doubt that it was arson?"

"No doubt at all. Guy could have burned down a department store. Multiple starts, use of an accelerant."

"What does that mean?"

"Multiple starts means it was started more than one place, not like your cigarette burning a couch. And accelerant is something that burns real hot and fast. Gasoline, in this case. In other words, someone slopped a whole bunch of gasoline all over the damn place. Victims were upstairs asleep in bed when it happened. Fire burns up, you know, up and out but they put it out pretty fast. Smoke inhalation was what killed them, so you might hope they died peaceful."

"Do you think whoever did it planned to kill them?"

"Law doesn't give a damn in the case of arson. The house was insured, so we checked out the landlady. She arrived home with the fire engines. Lived in the basement apartment. Turned out the house was insured but underinsured. No way she was going to profit from the fire." Bates paused to cough. He sipped iced tea and got it under control again. "Mrs. Meadows was the landlady's name."

I nearly dropped the glass I was holding. "Josephine Meadows?"

"That's the one. She was real broken up about those two dying. She identified the bodies. They weren't burned. It was sad; they had their arms wrapped around each other."

I was busy transforming a grassy plain into a landlady. I wanted to hug Phil Bates, but instead I asked, "But you had a suspect?"

"We did. Guy name of Frank Auerbach."

Frank, not Josh or Roger or whoever. Frank. I reached into my purse, took out a notebook and a pen.

"A-u-e-r-b-a-c-h," he spelled out for me. "He might not have been a suspect particularly, only he flew the coop right after it happened. We went to his house, just some routine questioning because the landlady said he was close to the couple. He left everything behind, 'cept for his credit cards. Food in the refrigerator, dishes in the sink. Like he just stepped out to buy a lottery ticket and never came back. Friends said he hadn't planned on going anywhere. Friends said he was always with Barnett and Fuller. They all had a little studio together where they showed their photographs, called We Three."

He ran his fingers through his hair. "Aw, who knows? Sometimes people real close get to hate each other."

"He was a photographer?"

"They all were: nuts about photography, the landlady said. Guess they were pretty good. Real nice people, all of them, from what everyone said. No motive we could find whatsoever. But what's motive anymore anyway?"

"Isn't it possible something happened to Frank too? I mean, it sounds like he was a suspect just because he disappeared."

"That could be, it could very well be," said Bates. "But we never found a body. And someone was out there. Charged a bunch of stuff up in Portland using Frank's credit card about a week later, photography equipment, clothes. Then he left Portland and a little while later he turned up in Tucson, we know that from stuff that was bought there. Also he made a phone call."

"A phone call?"

"Yep. Called San Francisco PD. Said he was Frank Auerbach, wanted for questioning, and he wanted to turn himself in and where should he go? Well, there's police stations all over Tucson. But he never turned up at any police station anywhere. Left a wide-open trail for a while, then he was gone, just gone from the face of the earth."

"That was so long ago," I said. "And there's so little to go on. You traced the phone call?"

"Pay phone. At one of them Circle K's." Phil smiled at me. "You want to know what I think? I think there's not a chance in hell Danny was going to find that guy. I mean, the police with all their resources couldn't. I even mentioned him getting *America's Most Wanted* interested, 'cause they do find people sometimes, but he didn't want his girlfriend to know. That's what I meant when I said your brother was crazy—crazy in love with that girlfriend of his, or he wouldn't have gone off on such a damn fool hopeless chase."

"The landlady. Josephine Meadows. What happened to her?"

"Moved to Phoenix to be near her son." Phil was beginning to look tired. He coughed feebly now. "I'm retired," he said. "I don't think about stuff anymore. I worry about what's on the tube at night, who's going to win the World Series. Don't have any address for Mrs. Meadows. Get on the phone, call all the Meadowses in the town of Phoenix, and pray her son wasn't from a first marriage."

"I think I have it. Golden Acres."

"Well, there you go."

Mildred came into the room. She had pine needles in her hair. "You didn't hit any squirrels for me to skin," she said.

"Do I ever?" Bates turned to me. "Mildred won't let me hit them cute little fuzzy things."

Mildred giggled, looking down at him. "You wore this old guy out. I hope you found out whatever it was, but you gotta leave now, 'cause he's tired." She gave him a look, so old-fashioned you could almost hear the strains of Tammy Wynette singing "Stand By Your Man" in the background.

"Oh, yeah," said Phil Bates, "if it makes any difference, Frank called the cops from Tucson sometime in the month of April." He grinned at me. "April, fifteen years ago. Well, you never do know."

"April," I repeated. "Thanks, thanks a lot."

I left and got in my rented car and drove off back down the dirt road, windows open. If I hadn't had Danny on my mind, I might have looked for the ocean not so far away, around a bend, and enjoyed the shouting of the blue jays and the seagulls.

It was late when I got back to Hal's, maybe eleven-thirty. On the counter was a note from Wally in big capital letters saying, *CALL JACK NANCE*, and a number. Under that was another note, saying, *CALL JACK NANCE IMMEDIATELY.* I turned on the answering machine and played the message back.

"Chloe," said Nance's voice, "Nance here, but where the hell are you? Hope it's not really San Diego. Call me at once, *555-2900*, that's a Tucson number, Chloe. This concerns your brother."

I punched in the number, my mouth so dry I wasn't sure I'd be able to speak. An operator came on and intoned, "I'm sorry, this number is not in service at this time. If you need assistance, please dial the operator."

"Shit." I banged down the phone, then called the operator.

"Where are you calling?" she asked.

"Tucson." I gave her the number.

"That's a long-distance call, ma'am, you need to dial a one and then 602."

I sat down on a stool and punched in all the numbers, trying not to think about anything.

"University Medical Center," said a woman's voice.

I explained who I was and that I had a message from Jack Nance. "Chloe," said Nance, almost immediately.

"Tell me."

"I been calling you since this morning," he said, rubbing it in. "Why the hell can't you stay by your phone? Your brother's a patient. I want you to get your ass up here."

"He's okay?"

"He's alive."

chapter twenty-four

IN A DARKENED ROOM, MY LITTLE BROTHER lay on his side in a hospital bed, knees drawn up, fetal position. He was hooked up to lines stuck in his veins. In the glow from the night-light, I could just see his face, his eyes closed. The only time I'd seen Danny in the hospital was when he had his appendix out when he was twelve. There was no comparison. But I had seen James not that long ago, an unrecognizable James down to matchstick thinness. Along Danny's jawbone was a purple bruise, and his hair was no longer slicked back, but dry and hanging over his forehead.

I pulled up a chair by the side of the bed and sat and held his hand. "I'm here," I whispered. "I'll take care of you, don't worry."

I squeezed his hand. He twitched irritably. Maybe I should call Mom and Dad. The parentials. But I waved that thought away, it was too traumatic. I thought back to Danny's maps and his perfect attendance button, about how James and I had teased him. Maybe we hadn't let his personality develop properly; we were always sitting on him. I wished I'd been the best sister in the world to him, wished I'd always looked out for him, listened to everything he'd said and believed it implicitly even when I knew he was lying.

"Oh, Danny," I said, my voice breaking.

A nurse came in and smiled at me. She was little, with a round pink face and pink-tinted glasses, what people call perky. On her name tag it said she was Melissa.

"Is he in a coma or what?" I asked.

"Not really, just in recovery. Your friend Hal was here, he stayed for a while. Wore him out, probably. He goes in and out of consciousness. One of his lucid moments he mentioned his friend Hal. I'm glad Hal came and now you're here," she said. "At first we thought he was homeless. Oscar's glad too, Oscar's been hanging 'round here the whole time."

Oscar had been with Nance when I arrived at the hospital. Oscar wore a brown hat with fur earflaps, two sweaters, a vest from a pin-striped suit, ragged jeans, and a pair of brown men's shoes with perforations that must have wowed the ladies when they were new sometime back in the 1940s. Oscar had looked glad to see me, like we were old friends meeting again after a long absence. I hadn't paid much attention, on the run to see Danny.

"Who is this Oscar?" I looked at the nurse. "I don't understand. . . ."

She raised her eyebrows. "Oscar got him here, he found him, out in the desert. Your brother wouldn't have made it without Oscar. He was admitted as a John Doe a week ago. You be good to that man, I know he's not pretty, but he saved your brother's life."

"It doesn't make sense," I said. "Danny wasn't homeless." In a way he was, though, by his own choice. "Is he going to make it?"

"He has so far. He's got a concussion. He's not totally unconscious, but he doesn't want anyone near him. He'll talk a little bit like he did with your friend Hal, but it wears him out. There's the concussion, some bruising, a broken rib."

"What are you doing for him?"

"He has to rest. His vital signs are stable," said Melissa. "And that's a good sign. If it's okay, there's an officer outside who'd like to talk to you."

"I want to spend the night here," I said. "Can I?"

"Sure. I'll rig up a cot. You go talk to that gentleman waiting just outside the door."

The gentleman was a cop, but not Nance as I'd expected.

"Officer Del Binkey, ma'am," he said. He was in uniform, young, thin-lipped, and sandy-haired. "I'd like to ask you some questions, if that's all right."

I followed him down the hall and into the elevator. We went back down to the first floor to the lobby, and sat down on a blue-cushioned couch in front of a glass-brick wall.

"You've seen your brother," he said. "All squared away now?"

"Hal was here," I said. "Did he tell Danny about Kristi?"

"The girlfriend," said the officer. "No. We discussed it. You ready for those questions?"

I nodded and turned sideways on the seat, so I could elevate my foot. I felt foolish carrying my foot around with me like a heavy package.

He looked at me. "Got a couple of injuries there."

I nodded again. I wasn't feeling articulate. Then my battered family struck me as funny. I started to laugh but suppressed it at once. If I didn't, it might go on forever echoing down the hospital halls, like a maniac's.

I took a deep breath. "Where's Nance?"

"Nance identified your brother. Guess they were looking for him in Cochise County. It was his interest in the case that got us looking to ID him there. Not even his case, but the guy wants to be a hot shot. Maybe they don't think about jurisdiction there. But we got some jurisdiction problems here.

"By all means," I said. "Of course. Jurisdiction."

"Your brother was found in Tucson. And from what we can ascertain, he sustained his injuries in Pima County. Any idea what could have happened?"

I told my story. The same one I'd told everyone else. "Doesn't help much, does it?" I said.

"Not much," he said.

I stared at the art on the opposite wall, art that was about nothing but pleasant shapes and pretty colors.

He scratched his nose.

"So tell me what you know," I said.

"We got this homeless guy," he said. "Lot of the homeless don't like cops. They think we harass them, and maybe we do, but a lot of good citizens feel harassed by them, so we got pressures put on us. Wasn't until Nance told him Danny was a possible homicide suspect in Cochise County that Oscar gave us some straight answers."

I nodded.

"Oscar and a buddy were driving here from Texas on the 110, see this guy staggering by the side of the freeway. They stop, pick him up, drive him over to Reid Park, where they figure on camping out. Guy, your brother, then passes out. They think he's drunk, see—he's been incoherent the whole time. Finally they figure he's not drunk, so they take him to a shelter. Shelter gets hold of the hospital and then us.

"So I guess the question is, what was he doing by the side of the road in the first place?" I said.

"Looks like his injuries were sustained from jumping out of a speeding vehicle or being pushed. Hit the side of the road, probably with his head, bounced, got a rock to his ribs; something like that. Probably okay until he landed. No sign of drugs or alcohol."

I shivered. "Officer, what if whoever was responsible decides to come back and finish him off?"

"We're not releasing any information about him," said Binkey. "Certainly not the name of the hospital. If you want to tell friends about this, as a precaution you can be discreet yourself." He stood up. "Thank you for your time. I guess Detective Nance would like to talk to you. Don't you let him harass you, now."

I looked up and saw Nance hovering. His blue eyes were rimmed with pink, like a rabbit's. Behind him stood a man, ageless the way street people can be, not young and not old because nobody looks that close. Oscar. I didn't really understand what was going on, but if the nurse said Oscar had saved Danny's life, I was willing to ignore the rank smell that rose gently from Oscar's garments.

"Thank you," I said to him, extending my hand. Then I gave him a hug. There was not much to him under his clothes. He grinned at me, half his front teeth gone.

"Don't you worry about your boy, now," he said. "Oscar took care of him."

I steered Oscar a little ways away. "What happened?" I asked him gently. "You found him?"

He bobbed his head up and down. "We was driving down the freeway, me and Will, and we see this guy, kind of staggering. 'It's one of the boys,' I said to Will, and Will stops his truck, backs up, and we stopped. He didn't make no sense, but we thought the cops would pick him up for sure, so we drove him into town. No one knew who he was. But no one knows who I am either, and I'm standing here talking to you."

"But Oscar—you didn't see any other vehicle on the road, maybe up ahead, slowing down?"

"It was real dark," said Oscar. "Saw a bunch of taillights and a bunch of headlights all going seventy-five, eighty miles an hour."

"And Danny didn't say anything?"

"He got a lady friend, name of Crystal? Christine?"

"Kristi."

"Yeah. He kept saying Kristi, something about all of Kristi something, something, something." He wrinkled his forehead. "When I think too much I get these headaches. But yep, that's all he said, I can remember. He was looking for his wallet too."

"It's been so long," I said, giving up.

Oscar grinned at me proudly. "I don't usually tell them damn cops nothing."

"Danny didn't have any ID on him." I turned. Nance was standing behind me. "Now, why was that?" he went on. "Someone stole his wallet?" He looked at Oscar for a moment reflectively.

"Not me." Oscar glanced at his arm, pantomiming looking at a watch, though he wasn't wearing one. "I got to go."

"I have Danny's wallet," I told Nance.

Oscar backed off, looking at Nance furtively.

"Oscar, thank you again," I called to him as he receded. I turned to Nance. "Danny left his wallet at the garage." I stood up. Dots flashed in front of me. I bent over. "I could use a cup of coffee."

"What the hell you been doing?" he asked me. "Playing in traffic?" He took my elbow and propelled me down the hall. I didn't want Nance leading me by the elbow, but I knew I needed the support. My legs weren't functioning well, with only one reliable foot. "Where are we going?"

"Boy, are you paranoid." He moved away from me, spoke from a distance. "I thought we could get some coffee in the cafeteria."

The cafeteria was brightly lit but deserted, closed down for the night.

Nance got two coffees from a machine and we sat in a corner. The coffee was awful, but I drank it fast.

"What about your folks?" he asked. "I mean, you got some, don't you?"

"Yes, I got some," I said sarcastically. "I'm going to wait on that. They're out of the country. They'd be upset and worried and have to fly back."

Nance nodded, both hands around his coffee cup as if to warm them. I wondered about his boys, where they were now, who took care of them while their father was out investigating.

"I lost my dad to a heart attack a while ago, my mom to cancer. I'm sorry now I didn't tell them more." He shrugged. "But what the hell, if they were alive I still wouldn't. You get to be a cop for too long, you don't know how to tell civilians anything, and that's the truth."

"What about other cops? Don't you talk to them?"

"Used to be closer to my fellow officers, I mean the ones in my own territory. Hell, we all got the same problems, but you look at Binkey there, for instance. All worried about procedure, jurisdiction. Get guys in the department squabbling about stuff like that and you forget why the hell you even got on the force. Then you wonder why you should trust them at all."

"Well, you have to a little bit, don't you?"

"Sure," he said. "You have to a lot. You can trust 'em with your life, but not your wife." He laughed. "Ah, that's not fair. Can't trust your wife, then you can't trust anyone else either. If you can trust her, then what's the worry?"

I said nothing.

"I was real close to the other guys once." He picked up his coffee cup. His hands were shaking slightly. I wondered why. Fatigue, maybe, nerves. "Like it was my religion—you know, your friends. Lost my faith. Lose your faith and what do you got?"

"I don't know, Nance. What do you got?"

He reached in his jacket pocket and took out a bottle of Maalox. Cherry cream. He took a swig.

"You switched brands."

"Ah, you develop a tolerance or something. Used to take Tagamet, but started to upset my stomach. Whose car was your brother in? Got any idea at all?"

"None." Now would be the time to tell Nance about Danny's search for Kristi's father's murderer. But what did I really know? Frank Auerbach could even be dealing drugs now, why not? It could all tie up in a neat little package. But I decided not to say anything, at least until I talked to Danny. "By the way, no one I've asked in Dudley thinks Danny was dealing drugs there."

Nance looked at me in mock surprise. "How about that? Nobody I talked to said he was either. Ain't that something?"

The coffee hadn't done much for my stomach. I was beginning to feel the effects of the last twenty-four hours. It seemed like years ago that I'd talked to Phil Bates. Another cop. The lights of the cafeteria seemed too bright and Nance very far away. He didn't move except to tilt a little more in his chair. Maybe he'd tilt right over, break the mood.

"I'd like to get back to Danny." I stood up.

"Wait a minute. You look like hell. You know that? You want to talk about it?"

"No."

"Heard you talked to Mrs. Booth."

“Who?” Then I remembered—the woman from the Laundromat. “Anything wrong with trying to find out what happened myself?” I began to limp away.

“Depends.”

“Don’t get up,” I said.

But he tilted his chair forward and stood in a hurry. “You haven’t been straight with me.”

I continued walking. “What now?” I said over my shoulder. “Should I get a lawyer?”

I reached a long hall with more vinyl and chrome seats on both sides.

“Not a lawyer,” called Nance, pursuing me, “but you need a cop. You could use a little protection yourself. I mean, look at you. That’s what comes of poking your nose into things you shouldn’t.”

I sat down abruptly on one of the seats.

He sat across from me and gave me a Cheshire cat smile, except he didn’t vanish. “Duane Taylor, Reba Jenkins, nice down-home folks. Then there’s Carson’s Junkyard.”

I closed my eyes.

“Like stirring up a hornet’s nest.” Nance’s voice droned on. “Got people out in the Valley are still back in the pioneer days. Hell, they even catch little wild animals, skin them, and sell the pelts. Don’t give a damn there’s a law against it. They have their own laws. How’s your friend Howard Brodman, by the way? Are you dating now? Those known felons are a kick, aren’t they?”

I opened my eyes. “I don’t know anyone in town. Brody’s a friend of Danny’s. Another known felon, remember? He’s not allowed to show me around? Of course we’re not *dating.* God, Nance, you’re so corny.”

“I’m just an old-fashioned boy at heart.” He gave a toothy grin.

I got up again, playing musical chairs. *"Hal,"* I said suddenly. "I need to call him first thing in the morning."

"Yeah, sure, that guy, I guess he was here earlier. But how about a little trust for your friendly local law enforcement? Hell, it might even save you some doctor's bills."

"Nance," I said suddenly, taking him up on it, "what about Kristi?"

His eyes were opaque. "Nothing up at Duane's place but dead cockroaches and one still living. We got no witnesses. Oh, yeah, the gun left there at the shack was the one killed her, it checked out. No big surprise. Typical drug-dealer gun, serial number filed off—no help at all."

I thought they should go ahead and arrest Duane Taylor. Not because there was a whole lot of evidence but just in case. It's amazing how your sense of justice breaks down at a time of crisis.

"Keep me posted, anything you find out," Nance said. "Always good to hear from a fellow professional."

If he hadn't kept throwing out snippy little remarks like that, I might have told him more from the start, like the fact that Kristi was doing some dealing herself, but I just plain didn't want to, plus he'd try to tie it into Danny somehow because of Danny's record.

I slept fitfully in the cot by Danny's bed. The strange hospital room was bare as a prisoner's cell, but it seemed full of people, questioning me: Kristi, Abbie and Otto, Phil Bates, Lourdes. Aaron. Nance. Duane and Reba. I had my brother back and yet I didn't have him. Like hearing Hal's voice on the answering machine, right there, his voice for sure, but no one really there at all.

Hal had been here at the hospital, but he hadn't stayed, wasn't there for me now, like I'd always imagined he would be in time of real need. You try to hold on to someone, hold tight, and feel them slip away like water.

"Hello?"

I looked over.

Danny's voice, through a kind of fog.

"Hello," he said again.

I woke up completely.

Danny was sitting bolt upright in the bed. "Chloe." His voice was clear and sounded nearly normal.

"Hi, Danny." I said it softly. I wanted to hug him, but I didn't know if he could sustain an embrace.

"Kristi," he said. "Where's Kristi?"

I came over and sat by the bed, took his hand, and told him.

chapter twenty-five

DANNY'S EYES WENT BLANK, THEN CLOUDY, then bright. "I knew it." He closed his eyes and lay back down on the pillows. "I could feel it almost. I was trying to save her and I couldn't. I knew it right away, but I didn't want to know. I didn't want you to tell me because then it would be true."

"I'm sorry," I said.

"I didn't catch it in time," he said. "I didn't bug her soon enough about taking her medication. She must have been on a downslide. I never thought I'd get to keep her," Danny went on. "Remember those animals we used to save when we were kids? Rocky Raccoon? Tweety Bird? How Dad made us let them go when they were better? Kristi was like that to me. I was going to make her better, then I'd let her go. She was too young to be stuck with me, some guy makes his living cleaning out swimming pools."

"You got good grades, Danny," I lied. "You could go back to school even now. Do you ever think about that?"

But he wasn't listening. He'd heard me before. I was just part of the scenery. He went on. "Hal stopped by. We talked for a little bit, but I was really tired." He paused. "That job he has, it's really hard and depressing, he doesn't need any more grief. Bet he wishes he never met this family. All we've ever done is cause him heartache."

I didn't know what to say.

"Anyway," Danny went on, "Hal knows Otto, Kristi's stepfather—he's a therapist too, so Hal had me and Kristi to dinner. You know, like two young people, why not? Jambalaya. I can still remember, but I could hardly eat—it was like sparks between me and Kristi, right away."

I nodded.

"We used to hang out on Venice Beach—she had a job for a while walking dogs, there was this one Doberman, bigger than she was almost. She was really thin, so you could see her little bones sticking out like a bird. She was staying with Otto and Abbie to get over some guy. Guys were always hitting on her and she didn't know how to resist, or at least hit back. Back then when we were getting to know each other I'd use the same tone of voice I used to use on Rocky Racoon. Even the Doberman liked me."

"Dogs always liked you, Danny," I said reassuringly. "You have a way with animals."

"Anyway, after a while we started living together. Damn." He clenched one fist, wadding up the bedclothes in it. "Shot dead. How the hell did she get hold of that Dream Queen stuff, anyway?"

"Danny," I said. "Who do you think got it for her? Any idea?"

"No."

I bit my lip, which was recovered now and ready to be bitten. "Duane Taylor?" I asked softly. "Could it have been him?"

"I shouldn't have left her alone so much. She got stir crazy. If he had anything to do with this, I'll kill him."

I was sorry I'd mentioned Duane at all, but Danny wasn't going anywhere. "Maybe Duane, maybe not. Someone used to go up to Hal's house at night. A man."

"A man." Danny looked blank. "Well, I couldn't tell you. I never went there. It was Kristi's private place. Who told you that?"

"A little boy called Aaron. He lives in the closest house."

"Michelle's kid? Michelle lives around there?"

"Right. You know her? She's not much of a mother."

"Aw," said Danny. "It's not her fault. I see her in the bars. She's hooked on alcohol. When she's sober and not hung over, she's real smart. Pretty too. She doesn't pick the right guys." His eyes got a little dreamy and he spoke in his crusader voice. "She needs to find a good man and Aaron needs a father." Danny let go of the bedclothes and seemed to shake himself.

"What I thought was," he went on, "if I could find the man who killed Kristi's father, it might make her better. Why did I think that anyway? I was just stupid as usual."

"No," I said. "You're not stupid, Danny. You were never stupid and you're not now."

"Do you even know what I'm talking about?"

"Yes. I know lots. I went and visited Abbie and Otto. Otto hired me to investigate. I'm on the case, Danny. Now that I have you, we can figure it out."

"Figure what out?" Danny sat upright again. "Figure what out, Chloe?"

"Where Frank Auerbach is. Who killed Kristi. Whose car did you get into, in Benson? We need to tell the police right away, so they can arrest him."

"I don't know whose car I got into. The last thing I remember is leaving the gas station and walking across the street."

"What about at the airport?" I said. "Remember that? You were arguing with someone—"

"Yeah? Who?"

"Chip O'Leary's brother Roger."

"Chloe, give it a break, okay?"

"You know what, Danny? Roger told me he'd never met you. Why would he say that?"

"How would I know?" Danny fell back on the pillow. He closed his eyes. "He's a pompous idiot. Anyway, Frank Auerbach and Kristi's father have nothing to do with whoever killed Kristi, Chloe."

"How do you know they don't?"

He threw up his hands. "Why would they?"

"And Josh Cohen, you went to see him, how does he fit in?"

"Look, Chloe, I want you to stop investigating this Kristi's father stuff, okay?"

"Why?"

"Because." Danny looked exhausted. "I don't even care about Frank Auerbach anymore. Kristi's dead. Let Otto hire someone else if he wants to know. I don't see why, though. He never cared before."

"It might be connected to Kristi getting murdered," I said softly. I felt a little guilty, grilling him like this, but not enough to stop. "Don't you see?"

"Sure I see, but if it is connected, you think I want my sister to be next? The only sibling I have left?"

"But—" I began.

"No," said Danny. "No buts or anything. Let it be. I want you to promise me, okay, Chloe?"

I crossed my fingers. In my family it was fair when you lied if you crossed your fingers. "Okay," I said.

chapter twenty-six

"PARTIAL AMNESIA," SAID THE DOCTOR. HE was dark and bearded and wore glasses with thin black frames, trendy glasses like those worn by Sylvester Stallone. "Not uncommon at all. Remember the Central Park jogger got attacked by some sort of roving gang? She forgot everything surrounding the traumatic event." He gave me a look. "That was up in your neck of the woods."

I felt in some subtle way he was blaming me for coming from New York, as if crime had followed me here.

"Lots of people carrying around missing blocks of time," said the doctor chattily. "It's the brain, that tangled knot. Maybe he'll recover some of the memory, maybe not. Why don't you count your blessings? The prognosis is pretty good—I'd say brain damage is minimal."

I thanked him and went to call Hal to tell him what the doctor had told me.

"That's a big relief," he said. "So they finally found you. That Detective Jack Nance could work a little on his PR skills."

"I told Danny about Kristi."

"Can I help? Do you want me to come over?"

"It's okay. I'm probably as much as he can handle. He should rest."

"This is hard on you too," said Hal. "Don't think I don't realize that. You're not far from me. I'm in Armory Park. Can you get away? Why don't you come over and have lunch?"

Armory Park was shabby, wide streets lined with orange trees and palm trees, run-down picturesque houses from the 1920s. Windward House was stucco, Southwestern English Tudor. Hal told me to try the office next door first, but no one answered.

I went over to the house and knocked on the big wood door. A young man answered. He had enormous brown eyes and he was thin, oh, so thin. I caught my breath.

"Chloe," he said. "Hal went to the corner grocery to get some sandwiches, he'll be right back."

We stood in a foyer, with a couch against the wall. Laughter came from what looked like the living room. Sunlight streamed in the windows. It might have been a fraternity house, but it wasn't, or maybe it was a house for a different kind of fraternity.

"I'm David," he said. "I feel as though I knew your brother. Hal talks about him." David had a bandage on his arm with a needle under it.

I sniffled. I couldn't help it. Memories flowed back, in the hospital, James making jokes, chiding me, saying, "You know, Chloe, men aren't like nice places to visit, quickie vacations."

"No," I'd bantered back, "they're learning experiences."

James, wanting to get me settled and happy for my old age, the lucky one who got to have one. While his dying hovered over us, making everything else devoid of meaning. Had I hugged him hard enough, that last time; hard enough for it to accompany him wherever he was going?

"Oh, I miss him," I said to David.

David opened his arms and I went over and hugged him for James. "There, there," he said. His bones were like a bird's, his thin, thin shoulder blades.

"I miss him so much."

"That's good," said David. "He needs to be missed."

We stepped apart, the front door opened, and Hal came in, carrying a brown paper bag. He was smiling, but he looked even more tired than he had when I'd seen him last. The lines on his face had deepened and he looked maybe five years older. Once again I was afraid for him, and I had an intuition that death had placed a little finger on him, just a touch, just a reminder.

Tears were streaming down my face. David vanished and came back in an instant with a Kleenex. I grabbed for it. "Oh, shit. I'm sorry."

Hal stood there. I could feel his tension. "Tears are permissible, Chloe, for God's sake. Come on. I can't leave, but we can sit out in the courtyard."

"Goodbye, David," I called back.

"You come back, now," he said. "You hear?"

Sniveling, I followed Hal down the hall and outside. In the center of the courtyard was a little Mexican tiled pool with purple verbena and alyssum growing around it. Three deck chairs and a wrought-iron table were arranged under a flowering tree.

"Pretty, isn't it?" Hal said. "It's *Chilopsis linearis*. Desert willow. This one flowers way into the fall. We take good care of it."

Flowers were falling from the tree. They looked like miniature orchids, rose-colored, marked with purple. "Sit down," Hal said.

He put the paper bag on the table. "I'll get us something to drink. Diet cola, right?"

"Right," I murmured.

The courtyard was like an oasis. I moved my deck chair out a little and held my face to the sun. Hal came back with a Coke and a diet Pepsi and set them on the wrought-iron table. He wore a blue striped shirt, khakis, and boating shoes. He looked pale, yes, but like an Italian painting of Christ on the cross, pale with suffering. He stood directly in front of the sun as he set down the food. A halo bloomed around his head. Maybe I was getting delirious, sitting in the autumn sun in Tucson, Arizona, swollen-eyed, spent.

Hal sat down and and crossed his legs, ankle to knee. "What was that all about, back there?"

"Nothing." I didn't want to put him through the paces of grief.

"Did any more of Danny's memory come back?"

I shook my head.

"Maybe we should all be so lucky. All our traumas obliterated from our memories, the whole world walking around like mindless children."

"It wouldn't be fair to the dead."

"Let the dead bury the dead," he said abruptly.

We sat in silence for a moment. Then he said, "I didn't mean that. What about Kristi? Is there an ongoing investigation or what?"

"I guess. They don't tell me anything." I put my hands to my face and rested on them. Between my fingers, I looked at Hal. "Your Lu-Ray china collection . . ."

"What about it?"

I explained about my own investigation into Kristi's death, Reba and Duane; Duane's visit.

Hal stared at his hands. He shrugged. "That's the least of my worries, my Lu-Ray china. If you can find out what happened to Kristi, feel free to throw in the rest of my belongings too."

"The shack, Hal. I went up there a couple of times. It's amazing, the way you fixed it up."

"I didn't have any real use for it. I guess you could call it an excessive need for roots. I didn't want to fix it up to make it rentable. The Buddha, the cloth, were James's. It's funny, James had so much of his past he carried with him. When I went through his belongings I recognized that it was my past too, though we hadn't lived it together. What had I done with mine? I moved around, threw things away. I missed my past, when I was youthful and foolish, and here was some of it in James's things. I wanted to make a place of peace."

"Do you use it much?"

"Basically never. Just a few times in the beginning. Then I got swamped here in Tucson. I had trouble even making it back to my regular house. When Kristi mentioned liking to meditate, I knew it was perfect."

He opened the bag and took out two club sandwiches. They sat on the table between us. Neither of us took a bite, as if they were props for a play we were rehearsing together. "I talked to a little boy from the neighborhood. Aaron," I said. "He told me a man was there sometimes, at night, I thought maybe it was you."

"I think I can safely say I haven't been up there for six or seven months, and never at night."

"You didn't store anything underneath the house?"

"Never," said Hal. "And after what's happened, I feel like selling it. It'll never be a good place for me now. I was relieved when Kristi started using it. I guess it was a way of doing something for her to excuse the fact that I never really did anything for her before. Just like with you, Chloe, I haven't done enough for you. I'm sorry to say that once again. Sometimes I feel I've chosen all the wrong things to do the right things with. Hurt the people I should have helped."

"You can't save the entire world, Hal." I took the turkey out of the club sandwich and ate that. I wasn't really hungry. "You're not personally responsible for every soul on this earth."

"One of these days, Chloe, you're going to look at me and realize I'm not the great person you think I am."

"I saw how you were with James," I said. "I would never change my mind about you."

"I don't know that I haven't thrown away my entire life." Hal looked out at the little pool. There were orange carp swimming in it and flowers floating on the surface. The carp came up, nipping at the flowers, retreating. "You look back and you find the turning points; I took the easy way every time."

"You took the hard way, Hal." I thought of my many relationships and how I'd run from them all instead of trying. Or tried when I should have run. "You've been too hard on yourself and now it's catching up with you."

"The hardest thing for me," he said, "was acknowledging I was gay. I still wonder if I shouldn't have married a woman, had kids, brought them up to be loving and accepting of everyone. Maybe I should have just grown like the flowers." He smiled, but without humor. "My father was a Baptist minister."

"I didn't know that." It wasn't surprising. He'd never spoken of his family before, but I knew he was from a small town, back East, down South. Georgia, was it? or North Carolina? "Where is he now?"

"My parents were old when they had me," said Hal. "They're both dead."

"I've never heard you talk about them."

"My father wasn't a warm man," he said. "He might have been once, but not when I knew him. I think I understand him better now. Like me, he was essentially in a helping profession."

I crumbled a piece of bread and threw it into the pond. It vanished in a swirl.

"In the so-called helping professions there's a known burnout rate," Hal went on. "I'd say half the counselors out there are burnt out and have been for years. But they chose a profession, got advanced degrees. They have families, bills to pay. What are they going to do? So they go on. They have all the manipulative skills down and they start to turn them on people, not to help anymore but to watch them react, to study them. They begin to get pleasure from pulling strings. They think they hide it, and sometimes the patients never seem to realize it, but I think deep down every patient does, some part of him is touched by that essential coldness. Not only patients, but the people in the other life of the trained helper."

He seemed so bitter.

"And you think that's happened to you?"

"I came to the profession late," said Hal, as though he hadn't heard me, "through a man who loved me. My mentor. He got me into graduate school, pulled strings. He knew a lot of people in the profession. I observed, took notes in my head. There's a poem, starts off, 'They that have power to hurt and will do none . . .' It has the famous line about lilies that fester . . . Do you know it? It's Shakespeare, but I got it from an Isherwood book."

I waited for him to quote it, but he didn't. Shakespeare. I would look it up. "Is it a sonnet?"

"Do me a favor, Chloe. Don't look it up. Don't take everything

I say as gospel. Don't you know how hard it is for me, being who you ask me to be?"

He was probably right, but I was stung. I tried not to show it, but it must have shown.

"Come on." Hal put his arm around my shoulders. The trained healer. "You didn't eat your sandwich and neither did I. Haven't you noticed we never eat when we're together? What good are we for each other?" He paused. "I certainly haven't helped much lately. This man you told me about? Who comes to the shack?"

I nodded. "Aaron said he does it on a regular basis—but only when it's really dark."

"A new moon, you mean," said Hal. "You told me that."

"Yes."

"You know what? That's coming up in a few days—it might be interesting to be there at the shack. No lights on, just waiting. That's something I just might do."

"Hal!" I said. "No."

"And why not? What have I done so far? Nothing."

chapter twenty-seven

SINCE I WAS IN TUCSON I BORROWED THE phone at the Windward House and called Jenny Cohen. "Is your husband back yet?" I asked her.

"No, did they find your brother?"

"Not yet," I lied, because the cops weren't releasing any information about Danny.

"I'm so sorry. I did speak to Josh."

"And?"

"And forgot your brother's name. The boys were acting up so much when you were here. Josh will be back late tonight. He'll be happy to talk to you."

"I was wondering," I said. "How long has he been teaching at the U of A?"

"I couldn't tell you exactly," said Jenny. "Maybe seventeen, eighteen years? Why?"

"Oh, nothing." I felt a little ashamed.

"Call me in the morning," she said. "If it's okay we can set up a meeting for you with Josh."

Then I called information in Phoenix for Golden Acres, got

the number, and called it. The woman who answered told me they did have a resident by the name of Josephine Meadows.

I looked at my watch. It had been an early lunch; Phoenix was two and a half hours away. Phoenix and Josephine Meadows and Golden Acres. I could go there and get back in time for dinner with Danny.

At Golden Acres assisted living, the old man in the wheelchair was nodding. His shiny head, decorated here and there with a strand of white hair, bobbed up and down, his gnarled hands were clutched in front of him. When he saw me, he raised his head and his eyes came alive. They twinkled. "Hi, honey. Come on over here."

"Good afternoon, Mr. Flanagan," said the nurse. "How are you today?" She was tall and well built, with a pleasant face, worry lines etched between her eyes.

"You come too," said Mr. Flanagan. "And bring your friend."

"You'd be too much for her," said the nurse. "She's here to see Josephine."

Mr. Flanagan rolled his wheelchair a few inches toward us, but it seemed to be too much of an effort. He stopped and his head resumed its bobbing.

"They get lonely here," said the nurse. "Even when there's relatives they don't visit as much as they could." She set her mouth in a disapproving little moue. "Josephine's down here in the recreation room. We're proud of our rec room."

The recreation room was large, with a stone fireplace at one end and long windows, floor to ceiling, that looked out on to a view of the distant mountains.

"That's Josephine," said the nurse. "The lady with curly white hair and the earrings."

Josephine, wheelchair-bound, was sitting at a table playing cards with a man and two other women.

She put a card down, splat!, on the table. "Trumped your ace," she was saying triumphantly as we approached.

A plump nurse stood behind her chair. "No, Mrs. Meadows, hearts is trump this time, remember? It was spades the last hand."

Josephine looked surprisingly rosy-cheeked, until you got close and realized it was due to two spots of rouge placed somewhat haphazardly, one on each cheek. She had thin white curly hair and long dangly earrings. She glared at the nurse. "Well, I got a heart too." She snatched up her card and lay down another one.

The other players sat benignly, holding their cards tightly in front of their chests.

"You have to follow suit, Josephine. Clubs was led and you still have clubs."

"Ah, the hell with it." Josephine wheeled herself back from the table.

"Visitor!" said my nurse cheerfully. "This is Chloe Newcombe. She'd like to talk to you."

Josephine looked at me merrily. "In the nick of time," she said to no one in particular.

The nurse pulled up a chair at the bridge table. "I'll sit in," she said.

I walked, Josephine rode energetically, over to a quiet corner. I could see how she might be a handful. I sat down in a big old plush armchair. We had a good view out one of the tall windows. Outside was a cactus, with many arms, and large evil-looking thorns all over them.

"I'd like to talk to you about some people you knew a long time ago," I said. "If it's all right with you. People you knew back in San Francisco. When you owned a house there?"

"Sure did," said Josephine. "It burnt down. Can you believe it? I didn't like insurance people, so I didn't get much insurance on that place. My fault, but I still hate insurance people. Hell, they don't care. What people?"

"Your renters," I said.

She looked at me shrewdly. "Who's asking?"

"I am."

"Some guy was here not long ago asking too. He was bossy, like it was my duty to tell him things. Who says, is what I say."

"I don't expect you to tell me anything," I said, "unless you feel like it."

"The cops asked me a lot of questions. Guess they thought maybe I burned the place down myself. I didn't trust them. The kids didn't trust them, so why should I?"

"The kids?"

"My kids," said Josephine. "My renters. Cynthia and Louis. Oh, that Louis."

"I'm not a cop," I said. "I'm a private investigator, and I'm representing the parents of Louis's daughter."

She looked interested. "Louis had a daughter? The devil." She smiled wickedly.

"They had a friend. His name was Frank. Frank Auerbach?"

"Frank didn't have a thing to do with it. I can tell you that, I knew him. I don't care how much evidence you got on that boy. He was the most gentle creature. And he loved Louis and Cynthia. If he ran, it was because he was hurt and scared. Wouldn't you be? Your two best friends murdered and maybe whoever did it's coming for you next."

She paused, looking out the window. She pointed at the cactus. "Look at that thing. Ugly as sin. You wouldn't see that in a San Francisco garden. I only live here because of my son. I don't know why. He's never here. When he comes I kid him, I say, 'Do I know you?' But he doesn't even have a sense of humor. Not like Louis and Cynthia and Frank."

She stopped again. She took a strand of hair and twirled it around her finger, like a young girl might. Her earrings glittered.

I asked, "Did they have a sense of humor, Louis and Cynthia and Frank?"

"You should have seen them. Alike as three peas in a pod. All had the same length hair. It used to make me laugh, except Cynthia's was dark, Louis's and Frank's were light."

I nodded.

"Saddest thing when I identified the bodies—" She gave me a quick glance. "They weren't even singed. It was the smoke that did it. Asphyxiated. It made me sick, identifying. I threw up afterwards. Louis and Cynthia, arms around each other."

A little tear came out of one eye and rolled down her cheek to her mouth. She licked it away. Her face softened. "A daughter. Oh, my. I never knew that. Is she pretty?"

I hesitated. "Very."

Abruptly she began to wheel away from me. "Come on. Let me show you what I got in my room."

I followed her as she went at a fast pace, down the hall and into a small room. There was just a bed, an end table, one armchair, and a chest of drawers with photographs on it.

"I've been trying to get a Victrola," she said. "So I can play records. I got me a Cat Stevens album."

"Cat Stevens?"

"He did the sound track." Josephine raised her arms, moved them back and forth like a hula girl. "'Do you dance?' she asks him. 'Do you sing and dance?'" She tossed her head.

She had lost me.

"Maude says that, to Harold. Of course he doesn't dance, but she teaches him. 'It's best not be be too moral,' she tells him, 'You cheat yourself out of too much of life.'"

"Harold and Maude."

Josephine laughed delightedly. "You've seen it?"

"Yes," I said. "Years ago."

I even remembered the line now, about being moral. It was when Harold and Maude were sitting smoking some kind of dope from a big hookah. A kid and an old lady. Everyone I knew loved it; we clapped, we cheered, and we came back to see it again. It told us we could do anything. We were happy to hear that.

And what was it we wanted to do? We hadn't a clue. Everything was different. How can you keep up when the world reverses itself with such ease? How can you tell who you are?

"I was lonely," said Josephine. "After Lee, my husband, died. I watched TV, I went shopping for food. Once a week, mah-Jongg. I pretended I didn't care, being all alone, then Cynthia and Louis moved in. One afternoon, Louis knocked on my door. 'We're going to the movies,' he said, 'just you and me, Jo-Jo.' That's what he called me, Jo-Jo. And that's what we saw, *Harold and Maude*. She began to hum tunelessly, then broke into song. "Cause there's a millions things to do, da da da da da."

"It was a great movie," I said.

"Louis didn't need to take me to the movies. He could have gone with anyone, but he chose me. I was proud, walking into the theater on the arm of such a good-looking man. Oh, my."

"And Frank?" I asked tentatively.

"Good-looking too. In fact . . ." She put her finger to the side of her nose. "I got a picture here of me and Frank. Those three took pictures all the time. We used to joke this was a wedding picture. Me and Frank were going to get married. 'Cept we grew up in different time zones, so to speak."

"I'd love to see the picture of Frank," I told her.

"I got it right here on the dresser. Lots of stuff burned in the fire, but this was saved."

The photograph had been tinted sepia to make it look old-timey, set in what looked like a funeral parlor, probably Josephine's living room. Backed by a large spray of gladioli was Josephine herself, hair not so stringy, her lips curving into a modern smile, wearing a long dress and a shawl. Beside her was a man in a top hat.

"That's Frank," said Josephine over my shoulder. She touched the glass.

He was good-looking, with a wide brow, narrow patrician nose, mustache. I was sorry to see the mustache, obscuring his mouth, making him harder to identify years later. His hand rested lightly on Josephine's shoulder, paternally in spite of his youth. What does a murderer look like? Anyone.

"But don't you have a photograph of Louis?" I was intensely curious to see what Kristi's father had looked like.

"Got one of Cynthia." She opened her drawer and reached under some lingerie. She looked up at me slyly. "Louis is in it too.

She handed me the photograph. This was more of a snapshot and burned all around the edges. Cynthia looked out at me, a dark-haired young woman with short spiky hair and big hoop earrings. She had a pixie face, smiling out at me from the lost days of never again. Someone had come up behind her, clowning, and made a pair of horns over her head.

"Louis's hand." Her eyes twinkled as if she'd just played a joke on me. "He was a kidder, but he was the serious one too. People listened to Louis when he spoke."

"And Frank? Did they listen to him?"

"Frank," said Josephine. "Him you just wanted to hug. He was a cutie-pie."

A cutie-pie? I wanted the photograph of him like crazy, but I knew she would never give it to me.

"Do you think I could copy this?" I asked her. "They must have a xerox here."

"You after Frank?" she asked suspiciously. "Can't you tell he wouldn't hurt anyone? Didn't you listen to me?"

"Josephine, I'm after the truth. Do you have any idea what that might be?"

"Somebody killed those children. All they wanted to do was go around taking pictures. And then somebody killed them. Jealousy, maybe, 'cause they were all so pretty. Killed the two and blamed it on the third. It wasn't Frank, and that's the truth. I've forgotten everything else. You find Frank and clear his name. Then tell him to come visit me. Before I die. Just one more time. He didn't have family, you know. Parents were killed in a car crash and he used to say I was his granny and mom rolled into one. My son here, he's okay, but compared to Frank, oh, compared to Louis, he's just another insurance salesman."

Another tear rolled down her face.

The nurse appeared at the door. "Now you've upset her." She looked at me sternly. "I think you'd better go. Josephine is a sunny person, usually. Aren't you, Josephine?"

"Says who?" said Josephine indignantly. She waved the photograph. "I need this thing xeroxed right away."

Danny had just finished dinner. He'd eaten everything but the fruit cocktail. He held the remote control for the TV in one hand. The TV was on, but the sound was off. He flicked the channels: actors moved their lips strenuously, cars careened around curves, a woman in a spangled dress sang her heart out silently.

I could see he was tired. I didn't have a change of clothes and I planned to drive back to Dudley that night, but I wanted to stop in and see him.

"Say hi to Wally," Danny said. "And anyone else that shows an interest."

"I won't be really broadcasting that you've been found," I said. "For your own protection. Maybe Brody, though—"

"Brody?" Danny started to laugh. "You've met Brody?"

"What's so funny?"

"Nothing," Danny said. He laughed some more.

"I mean, is he reliable, trustworthy?"

"Up to a point."

"So maybe I shouldn't tell him."

Danny leaned back and closed his eyes. "No, it's okay. Tell him I said hi."

"Go to sleep, Danny." I kissed him on the forehead and left the room.

Driving back to Dudley, even though I had a picture of Frank, I felt discouraged. Maybe Josephine was right, he'd been framed and someone else had murdered Cynthia and Louis. Could be anyone, in that case, and no clues, so long ago. What did it matter?

But someone had killed Kristi, and that was new and fresh and whoever did it was out there now.

chapter twenty-eight

I GOT BACK TO DUDLEY AROUND EIGHT AND took a shower immediately. Surprisingly, I wasn't tired. I looked through Hal's freezer and found nothing but coffee packets and Lean Cuisine, which was fine with me. It usually tasted better than anything I cooked myself. I heated up cheese cannelloni in the microwave, then I sat at the kitchen counter. Because I had nothing else to work with, I studied the xeroxed picture of Frank as I ate.

After all, Danny had moved here. He'd always been fond of Hal, of course, but was that enough to move to where he lived? What if he'd had other reasons? What if Frank were in Dudley all this time and that was why Danny had moved here, in pursuit of some obscure clue?

Maybe I'd seen him already, wandering down the street. I covered up his mustache with one finger and added on fifteen years. People age differently, of course. Would his hair be gray now? He looked like no one I'd run into lately. A cutie-pie?

When I finished eating, I called Otto Marsh. He still didn't know Danny was alive. I gave him a quick rehash of the Danny story.

"Well, thank God," said Otto. "But amnesia. Damn. It's a lot more unusual than people think. So near and yet so far, huh? If only he'd regain his memory of the event."

"I wish I didn't keep thinking that the only thing that's saving him now is that he hasn't," I said.

"So maybe he just doesn't want to." There was a pause then he asked, "They got a guard on him or anything?"

"No, but they're not releasing the name of the hospital. If anyone calls, they're not saying he's there. Anyway, if it was supposed to be murder it was pretty spontaneous, the way it looks. And not very effective. If you're really after someone, you don't push them from a vehicle and hope they get hurt bad enough to die so they won't tell anyone you did it."

"I see your point," he said. "But he could have jumped out to get away."

I couldn't think about it. "Anyway, before this whole Danny thing I talked to Phil Bates, the investigating officer in San Francisco?"

"And?"

"He connected me up with the landlady of the house in San Francisco. She gave me a picture of Frank."

"How's Danny taking the news about Kristi?"

"It's still sinking in," I said.

"Let him talk about it," said Otto, "as much as he wants and for as long as he wants."

"Understood."

"Course, you've got Hal there. A first-class therapist."

We hung up.

I wished I had Hal here now but all I had was Brody. Brody was okay in his way, but he wasn't Hal. And why was Nance always asking me about him and why had Danny laughed?

But I could trust him, Danny said so. Up to a point.

I applied full eyeliner and put Frank's picture in a manila envelope from Hal's desk. Was there a point to this? I wondered. Most of the evidence was circumstantial. Even the phone call to the San Francisco police might have been a cry for help—help that never came. I might be carrying around a photograph of yet another dead man. I took the photograph out again and held it under the light.

Frank's face looked back at me, his eyes calm above the mustache. Maybe it was the effect of the xerox, but his face seemed soft and vulnerable. A victim, not a killer? His hand so protective on Josephine's shoulder, but unable to protect himself? I thought of all the mad men in the world today: arsonists, serial killers, motiveless in any human way, unfathomable. I could go crazy, doubting everything.

I shoved the xerox back into the envelope and took a walk down the canyon. The lights were off in the garage and the sign said CLOSED, but there was a light near the back. I banged on the door. After a while another light came on and I could see Brody through the glass. I felt relief. He opened the door.

"Well, I declare, it's Miss Chloe Newcombe." He held a chicken leg in one hand. "What'd your folks give you that old-fashioned name for?"

"So I'd be an old-fashioned girl."

"Heard they found your little brother."

"What? It's supposed to be a secret. How'd you know?"

"Small town," said Brody.

A small town where information flowed freely to the cognoscenti, myself not included.

"He doesn't know what happened to him," I said. "A couple of guys picked him up by the side of the freeway, staggering like a drunk."

" 'Cept he wasn't," said Brody.

"Nope, he just had a concussion, a broken rib, and bruises."

"Had a broken rib myself once. It's okay, if you don't breathe much. Come on in. You like chicken? This is that Banquet stuff, I just nuked it." He was dressed informally, in jeans and a white T-shirt, spotted with little holes in the tummy area, probably from welding sparks.

"I've eaten, thank you." I followed him through the garage.

"You've never been to my bachelor quarters. Bet you thought I slept in a sleeping bag on the floor of the garage."

"Something like that."

We passed the Merc, walking to the back, where he opened a door. Light streamed out. "Guy I bought the garage from built this addition, then I kind of renovated," said Brody. "Didn't do much to the outside, why advertise? Come on in."

I stepped into a wood-paneled living room with a counter on one side, beyond that a kitchen, and another door half open leading to the bedroom, but I didn't look. There was a dark leather couch, a rocking chair, a CD player, large-screen TV, VCR. Everything looked new, no springs popping out of the furniture, wall-to-wall carpeting in your basic masculine beige. "Very nice," I said.

Brody waved the chicken leg modestly. He walked to the counter, hurled the leg at a trash basket, and picked up a wing from a plate on the counter. He crunched it. "Sure you don't want some of this? If I'd known you were coming, I could have made a salad. Maybe added some radicchio. You thought I wasn't hip to radicchio, I bet."

I wandered a little, stopping at a bulletin board between the kitchen and the living room. A couple of photographs were stuck up with push pins. One was what you would call a glamour photograph, where the photographer takes pains and an airbrush to make you look sexy, of a young woman with an elaborate hairstyle, and a face like Dolly Parton, had Dolly been not quite so sweet. The other was a young woman in a parka, boots, and sunglasses, standing somewhere in the snow. It was impossible to tell what she looked like.

"Who's this? I mean, them?"

"Wives," said Brody. "Those are my ex-wives."

"Two of them."

"That's not bad. I'm no spring chicken."

"Girlfriends?"

"Girlfriends I keep in the bedroom, in the drawer where I keep my shorts."

I went and sat on the couch. "A man of endless surprises. Things must be pretty good in the auto restoration business."

"Yep."

"If that's the business you're in."

"Hey," said Brody. "What else?"

"You got off pretty easy with that place you had out in the Valley."

He threw the chicken wing at the trash basket. "Good lawyer. Some of those public defenders know their stuff."

Maybe he was lying, but I couldn't think of a better explanation. I took the picture of Frank out of the manila envelope. "Come look at this, Brody, and tell me if you know this person."

He came over and squinted at it. He pulled some reading glasses out of his pocket and took it over to the kitchen light. "This from some archives or something. Somebody's great-granddaddy and their great-great-great-grandmammy?"

"Oh, forget that. It's supposed to look old-fashioned, but it was taken fifteen or so years ago. It's a guy called Frank Auerbach."

"Not good-looking like me." Brody handed back the photo "Don't know him. Should I?"

"Not necessarily."

"Not going to tell me more then?"

"You have enough secrets to keep just from me," I said. "Why tell you more?"

"Any secrets I got are things you shouldn't know for your own good."

Whatever that meant.

Brody looked at me for a moment. "You got to get your mind off all this shit sometimes. Recreate." He went and switched on his CD player. "Come on, darlin', let's dance."

He stood in dance position, one arm held up, like kids used to do in junior high. He probably pumped his arm up and down while he danced too. Snapped your bra strap.

The music came on. "Oh, no, Brody, *Neil Young.*"

"You don't like Neil Young?"

"Of course I do."

It was easy to relax into Brody. He wasn't much of a dancer, he just sort of swayed. Neil Young was singing "Cowgirl in the Sand." His plaintive voice went right through me, and I felt like I was a teenager, incredibly excited about everything, except school. Oh, parents everywhere, tell your children to study harder or they'll end up private eyes. For the second time in as many days I started to cry.

"Heartbreaker, isn't it?" said Brody, unperturbed.

"Things were better back then," I sobbed.

"Ah, who knows? We were younger. You're just crying for your youth."

I inhaled his scent which was half gasoline and half aftershave. I whispered in his ear, "Why does Nance keep asking me about you?"

Brody held me a little tighter. "Used to go to concerts," he said, ignoring my question, "Neil Young. He always looked like he was stoned out of his mind, especially at the end."

"You're a one-man drug propaganda force." I leaned into him, feeling the urge to go to sleep, resting on his shoulder, as though I'd come out of a storm into an emotional safe harbor.

"Naw, pretty much wasted the guy, I guess. But he cleaned up okay in the end. Some guy we don't even know coming into my living room and breaking our hearts. Makes you think."

"Did you deal coke, Brody? Or just marijuana?"

"I always did good in the car business. Never needed outside help. Just marijuana."

"So Nance keeps his eye on you."

"Whole thing's a game," said Brody. "Cat-and-mouse. Smarter one wins. But, hey, Nance isn't all that worried about me. Guy's just a worrier. I'm out now anyway; classic case of the small businessman getting squeezed by the big guys. I'm a traditional guy, grow a crop, sell it, mostly. Times I used to fly in stuff across the border every now and then, back a few years, but the plane crash-landed and wiped out not only me and my partner's investment but our capital as well."

He did a little turn, a dip.

"Why?" I asked him.

"It was an exciting life, and besides, I wanted my share of the American dream. When they sell that dream they're selling dope too, to all the unhappy people who can't have a slice of the pie. All I sold was a little quiet escape from tension and stress, occasional users, not near as much on my conscience as your standard liquor store owner."

Suddenly the music was gone. Brody and I stood in the middle of the floor, holding each other. It was hard to think clearly, but I did get a glimmer of our possible future together. Me and Brody in a little house, surrounded with a bare dirt yard piled high with junk cars, and Brody in a little shop out back, welding.

Someone was pounding on the door. I pulled away.

"Shit." Brody went to the door and looked out. "It's that damn Nance."

I followed Brody through the garage.

"You got a warrant?" asked Brody, when he opened the door. He didn't sound worried.

Why didn't he seem worried?

"A warrant?" said Nance, hands in his cop windbreaker pockets. "For a little talk among friends? Did I come at a bad time?" He looked around Brody at me.

"What the hell do you think?" Brody said.

"Me?" said Nance. "Not much. Anyway, Chloe here says you're not even dating."

"Chicken?" Brody said to Nance.

"What kind?" asked Nance.

"Banquet."

"Fried?"

"Fried and microwaved."

"Nah, can't take the fried stuff," said Nance. "You got some crackers or something?" He removed his windbreaker. Underneath he wore a green plaid flannel shirt, a white T-shirt peeking coyly from the neck of the shirt, new, stiff jeans.

I was sitting on the couch. The atmosphere had changed considerably. Brody and Nance sounded like old friends. Well, Brody had said Nance was a car nut like himself.

Brody put a big box of saltines on the counter. "Near beer?"

"If that's all you got." Nance picked up the crackers, took a near beer from Brody, and carried them over to the rocking chair. "You give up everything, Brody?"

"Not everything."

I crossed my legs primly.

"I'm thinking about starting to work on this car I got parked out in the Valley," Nance said to Brody. "Nice little Ranchero."

"Yeah?" Brody opened a near beer. "What year?"

" 'Fifty-seven."

"Good year." Brody sat on the couch by me. "First year they made 'em. Got those single headlights, looks better than the double ones they put on in '58. Course, '58s got the big block engine. Gas hog, but that engine is pretty potent."

"Hell, I don't care about that," said Nance. "Want to show it off to my brother-in-law, guy that married my little sister. They live over in El Paso. He's a damn dentist. He's got himself a Porsche."

Brody's lip curled in a sneer. "Porsches. Nothing but a glorified Volkswagen. You tell him that, see what he says. All those Porsche guys know is price tags."

I shifted restlessly on the couch, feeling like part of the furniture. I yawned. Still, I felt the need to contribute. "When my father was courting my mother," I said, "he had a little Studebaker."

They looked at me politely for a moment, eyes glazed over.

"Well, never mind," I said.

"No, they're pretty collectible now," said Brody, "the '51s."

I rested my head on the arm of the couch. Something was

nagging at me. Nance hadn't known I was going to be here. He'd shown up at the door like someone who did it all the time.

Nance was consuming cracker after cracker. Cracker crumbs were falling on his shirt and he looked almost sloppy, as though Brody were working a subtle influence on him.

"Do you have any Pepsi?" I asked Brody.

"In the fridge."

I got up, went out to the kitchen, and opened the door of the refrigerator. Inside was a jar of salsa, hot; a stack of tortillas, the edges curling up; a container of moldy potato salad from the Safeway deli. A near beer and three Pepsis. I tried to think what I'd told Brody that I hadn't told Nance. I'd been so close to trusting Brody.

I stood blankly looking into the refrigerator, forgetting why I was there. In the other room they'd moved on to dual carbs and pistons. I shoved my hands in my pockets and encountered something, a card. *Victim Witness Program,* it said, and underneath two names were scribbled, *Ruth* and *Annie.* The two women who'd been at the house when I'd found out about Kristi. I started to crumple it but didn't. Guilt, maybe, that I hadn't availed myself of their services, allowed them to be helpful and kind. I put it back in my pocket.

Then I grabbed a Pepsi and went back to the living room.

Nance was standing up. "Guess I should be going. Don't want to bore Chloe to death."

I blinked politely like I had no idea what he meant: I sat down on the couch while Brody showed him to the door.

When Brody came back, I was waiting for him.

"I didn't know you knew Nance so well," I said accusingly. "That you two were such good friends. Did you tell him everything we talked about? Is that how he knows so much?"

"You don't have to be friends with a guy to talk cars," protested Brody. "I haven't told him anything. And you never told me much."

"Thank God I didn't. You were setting me up, weren't you? Trying to get me to tell you things about Danny or what?"

Brody sat on the couch. He slumped back and stared at the ceiling. On his face was a look of utter despair. "What is it about you women?" he asked. "No matter what I do, it's not right or it's wrong or it's not enough. Everything was going fine. And then, darn, it's not."

"Don't talk to me like I was some sort of generic woman. Like I don't even have a point."

"Damned if I know what it is."

"Maybe I should talk to Nance."

Brody grabbed my wrist. He held it tight, not tight enough to hurt but tight enough to get my attention. "Don't talk to Nance. Leave Nance alone. You got it? Do what I say, all right?"

"Why should I? You and Nance are hiding something you don't want me to know? Don't I have any rights?"

"Trust me. Okay? Just trust me."

Trust me. Sure.

I walked down the canyon in the dark. Under the streetlights the gold trees whispered and shivered. Leaves fluttered softly down around my head like little doubts. I passed the Baptist church; the stores that sold postcards and turquoise and earrings, two pairs for five dollars; the Co-op, where they sold drug-free veggies.

I remembered the look on Brody's face. Maybe I was being a little paranoid. Maybe I was just a snob, who didn't want to get involved with a guy who worked on cars, just wanted him to answer my questions, provide temporary comfort, Pepsi-Cola, and free Mexican dinners.

But what about those pictures of his ex-girlfriends he kept in the drawer under his shorts, what about those ex-wives? I ranted on self-righteously. Kids, did he have kids? Was he providing them with *child support*?

But by the time I began to climb the hill to Hal's, I had shifted gears, gone into a deeper zone. It had been a while now since I'd done it, but I began a series of arguments with Logan in my head, about his drinking, about his going to A.A.—arguments that were cool and calm and articulate. They lacked the fervor they'd once had, residual emotion of a cause already lost. I walked up the last of the hill and into the carport. I could almost imagine, since our phone call, Logan figuring out where I was, catching a plane out here, waiting impatiently for me right now in Hal's house. I didn't really believe it, though. And when I opened the door and went inside, the house was empty; empty of Danny and Kristi, empty of Hal and Brody and Logan.

chapter twenty-nine

I CALLED JENNY COHEN THE NEXT MORNING as soon as I got up.

"Josh will be happy to talk to you," she said. "The boys were so excited to see him they were faking tummy aches to stay out of school, but I packed them off this morning."

"Could I come see him late this morning?"

"That's fine. He'll be home all day. I asked him to tell me what this was all about, but he said if he did, it wouldn't make any sense."

Nothing was making sense to me. Last night had robbed me of some essential will and I woke up more exhausted than when I'd gone to sleep, as if all this running around had finally caught up to me.

So what if Nance and Brody were friends? I packed an overnight bag as Wally lugged the ladder around from the other room. I wanted to forget everything, be a simple person again and live an ordinary life. I believe we all know more than we are consciously aware of. Maybe I knew what I was going to find out at Jenny Cohen's husband's house.

I had to do something to get back in the groove. I took out my photo of Frank Auerbach and carried it into the room where Wally was sanding.

"Do you recognize this guy?" I asked.

He took the xeroxed photo from me and looked at it carefully. He scratched his head. "It has a strange flavor to it, I can't say what. The man looks a little bit like Billy Daniels."

"Who?"

"Billy Daniels. You can see photographs of him at the library where they have the historical photographs on display. He was a handsome devil—a famous sheriff here back in the late eighteen hundreds."

"This was taken fifteen years ago, Wally. It's supposed to look old, but it's not."

"Then that explains the flavor. I haven't seen anyone that looks like him around here."

Once again I parked the van on the street in front of Jenny and Josh Cohen's house. Carrying the manila envelope with the photograph of Frank, just in case that rang any bells, I walked the long curving driveway past the desert vegetation, ignored the door knocker in the shape of a gargoyle, and rang the bell.

Jenny answered the door at once. Her hair was down, curled into a cloud, and she wore a long red skirt, purple T-shirt, and Indian jewelry. Dressed for her husband. I felt like a traitor coming to her door right in the middle of a happy homecoming.

"Now we'll get this settled," she said brightly. "Once and for all." She smiled at me over her shoulder as she led me into the living room. She seemed lighter, more girlish.

"Here's Chloe," she said.

"Hi, Chloe." Josh got up from the couch to greet me. The room was relatively clean except for camera equipment strewn around and a backpack in the corner. He was a good-looking man, with what they call a leonine head, massive like a lion's. His graying hair was wild and bushy and he wore tortoiseshell glasses, which I could imagine him taking off, discreetly, when wowing the ladies. But he was a settled man now, with a family.

"Danny Newcombe." He smiled wryly. "I remember your brother well. It was an unusual visit."

"What did he want?"

"He didn't know what he wanted," said Josh. "Not exactly. He had a rough time frame, is all. He thought April."

"Yes," I said, remembering what Phil Bates had told me about Frank's call. "That would be about right."

"I lead a pretty routine life, do the same things over and over. Aprils, one of the things I do is take a bunch of photographers out to the desert and we have a seminar. Anyone's invited, the general public, anyone interested in photography."

"So?" I asked.

"It's pretty well advertised. I usually get an interesting bunch. Most of them I don't remember unless they follow up, take a course from me, or are in the profession."

I pulled the photograph of Frank out of the manila envelope. "This is Frank Auerbach. I know Danny was looking for him. Is that the name he gave you?"

"That's the name, all right."

"It's just a xerox," I said. "It looks a little odd, because the original was tinted sepia."

He looked at the photograph. "Sepia tinting. That was quite a fad for a while, especially with the hippies, getting dressed up in their hippie clothes. They looked like people from another time period. You know, they'd make movies, westerns, and hippies would get jobs as extras and they wouldn't even have to change clothes."

"Do you recognize him?"

"Not that guy, no." Josh handed the xerox back to me. "Come on, let's go into the den."

I followed him into the den, where there was a big easy chair, an enormous desk, and masses and masses of photographs all over the walls.

"Sit down," he said. "Frank Auerbach, that's the guy Danny was asking about; not the guy in the photograph."

"But that's Frank. I know it is. It was given to me by a reliable source." I thought of Josephine: her love for Frank and Louis and Cynthia. Her stubbornness and her wicked smile. "I think it was a reliable source anyway."

Josh smiled at me as though I were a student who hadn't quite gotten the point. "Let me just tell you what transpired. That's all I know. It's what I told Danny. I remembered the name Frank Auerbach, because I wrote it down."

"You wrote it down? When?"

He raised his hand. "Let me go on. First of all, the guy was obviously a professional. He had good equipment, and he knew what he was doing. Also he repeated his name to me and to everyone there. 'Hi,' he'd say, 'I'm Frank, Frank Auerbach.' To tell you the truth, it was so long ago, I probably still wouldn't have remembered all this if it weren't for one thing."

"Which is?"

He put his finger to the side of his nose like a scholarly Santa Claus. I could tell he was enjoying talking, stringing things out, letting go in front of a captive audience hanging on his every word. "Well, we were taking pictures of the desert. It's an interesting challenge, the lights and shadows. But every now and then we'd get a figure in the photograph. Frank didn't want to be photographed. He said he was like those guys in Africa, think a photograph takes away your soul.

"We all kind of laughed at that. I mean, here we were, a bunch of photographers taking pictures of people every day. You realize that a photographer has eight zillion subjects. Everything's subject matter. It's the way you take it, the way you handle the negative, that makes the photograph. And like I tell my students, take a lot of photographs, don't be stingy with your film. That's my philosophy because there's another element that's equally important. You know what that is?"

Get on with it. "No," I said politely.

"Serendipity!" His voice was triumphant. "Some of the best photographs are accidents, luck. God-given moments. You ever read those Carlos Castanada books?"

"No," I said. "I mean, yes, of course. Don Juan?"

"Right." He looked approving. "The artist is the warrior, he keeps his tools sharp, in this case his camera and his expertise, so he's there and ready when the God-given moment is handed down. I hope I'm not digressing."

"Oh, no," I murmured, making myself smile. "Of course not. It's very interesting."

"Anyway, I guess the devil was in me that day. The guy was kind of an interesting subject. So I shot him, figuratively speaking. I don't think he even knew it."

"And it turned out?"

"Sure did," said Josh proudly. "Which is probably the main reason I remember the name. When I realized the negative was worth playing around with, I wrote down the name of the subject while it was fresh in my mind. I took the picture just to be obnoxious, but if it was going to be one I was going to display, I wouldn't have wanted to do it without consulting the subject. Never did see him again, though. No one knew him."

"Could I see it?"

He smiled. "You're standing not two feet away from it right now. It's over on the wall to your left."

I turned to my left, walked over to the wall, and looked. The young man in the photograph had turned an exquisite profile to the mountains, though his body faced forward. The sun had been behind the mountains, and they formed wings on each shoulder. Somehow, in the taking of the photograph or else in working with the negative, Josh had caught a transparent effect, so the young winged man looked ghostly, like an angel caught briefly in a short visit to earth.

"*Mountain spirit,* I call it," said Josh.

I laughed. "You're wrong. You've shown me the wrong photograph. You've taken this more recently."

He took it off the wall. Behind it was a cleaner spot, as if the photo had hung there for a long time. He turned it over. *"Frank Auerbach,"* he read, *"April 1975."*

"That's not Frank Auerbach. You've made a mistake."

"That's the first thing Danny said to me too," said Josh. "That's why I had to show you. I couldn't have said to you on the phone, *I got a picture here of Frank Auerbach, but it's not Frank Auerbach.* It's funny. You have a picture of Frank Auerbach too, but it's not Frank Auerbach either."

"I can't explain. Please, Josh, if you could lend me this for just a while, I'll bring it back. I'll take good care of it. I'll explain later."

* * *

In reality, I didn't know how to explain anything: *I need help,* I thought as I drove away from Jenny and Josh's; *I need help.* On Speedway there was an inordinate amount of traffic. They were widening the road on each side, which added to the congestion, and I hit every red light. At the University of Arizona droves of students were on the sidewalks, crossing against the light and swerving dangerously on bicycles, as though they owned the world. I too had owned the world when I was a student. *I want it back,* I thought, *oh, God, I want it back.*

I finally reached Campbell, where the University Medical Center was, and turned right. I pulled into the parking lot and drove around and around visitors' parking until finally someone pulled out. I parked and walked up the entrance, past the hedges of pyracantha, past the lineup of wheelchairs, folded up and waiting like little taxis in front. I went inside, past the glass brick wall and the people in the front waiting room, past the boring art and the display of photographs of the hospital staff, and got on the elevator and went up to Danny's room.

I looked in. He was asleep. His face was thinner now. He'd lost weight from his ordeal, but he was free of the contrivances they'd rigged up to him, free and getting better. He knew, I thought, he didn't have amnesia, he was faking it. *He knew.*

Let him sleep. A nurse was passing by, and I stopped her. She was plump, a little sour-looking, as if nursing wasn't agreeing with her.

"Could you tell my brother—he's in that room—that I stopped by to see him? His sister. Just hi to him from me."

The nurse looked impatient, as if she'd been shouldered with a herculean task.

"I just don't want to wake him." I tried to give her a smile.

"All right," she said, and hurried on.

I left the hospital. A clump of people were standing in front, cars were pulling in and out. Here I was in a big city—well, medium-sized anyway—no one to stop and buttonhole, no one to tell what I knew. I got back in the car and drove to Windward House.

In the office, a handsome young man was manning the desk.

"I'd like to see Hal," I said. "It's kind of an emergency." My fists were clenched and though it was very nearly hot, on this autumn day in Tucson, my hands were cold.

"He took the day off," said the young man. "Went to his place in Dudley. He's been pretty strung out lately."

"I know," I said. "I'll catch him there, then."

"I guess it's some kind of significant day," he said. "Or night."

"What do you mean?"

"New moon. He said he had to be in Dudley for the new moon."

When it was dark, the man came when it was dark, Aaron had told me and I'd told Hal. Damn it, what did he think he was doing?

I got on the I-10 and headed back to Dudley. The traffic was heavy until past the Triple T, then it slowed. I drove seventy-five miles an hour to Dudley, thinking of the day I'd arrived, driving this way with Kristi and Danny, watching the tail end of the monsoons thicken the clouds. Kristi had been so alive, and she might still be if I'd only been alert and thinking. It wasn't that many days later, but the monsoons seemed to be gone. It was close to five when I hit Benson, where Danny had vanished. I still had no explanation, but I was getting closer to one.

I got to Dudley around six, driving over the pass, down Main Street up to Hal's. His camper was parked in the carport. I parked down the street, got out of the van, and walked up the hill to the carport.

"Hal?" I called when I got inside, but no one answered.

I stood in the kitchen drinking glass after glass of water. The way I had when I'd found out about Kristi. There were no Victim Witness women to try and calm me down, to call all the right people if I wanted them to. Where was Hal? Not far, with his camper in the carport. It wasn't close to dark yet, I only had to wait and he would show up sooner or later. Waiting is hard.

"You ever notice it's women do the waiting?" the waitress had said back in Benson. Instead of waiting, I took a walk down the canyon to Brody's.

The big doors were open at the shop and he stood with another man in front of a pickup with the hood raised. They were conferring together. I couldn't hear what they said exactly, but they had the intent absorbed look of men talking about cars, inanimate objects.

More serious, more real than flesh and blood.

"Chloe," said Brody when he saw me. "You okay?"

But I was already turning around, going back. It was starting to get dark and I knew where Hal was, suddenly. Back at his house, I picked up the picture of Frank Auerbach and the picture of the young man who was not Frank Auerbach—which was which, I didn't know. I wasn't really thinking straight—It wasn't raining, but I found a raincoat in the closet and put it on. Then I got the gun I'd bought from Brody and stowed it in one of the pockets. It made the coat hang kind of funny. I wasn't entirely stupid at this point, though close to it. Then I went down the hill and around and climbed the long stairs to the shack on the hill.

chapter thirty

I OPENED THE GATE, WENT INTO THE YARD. The POLICE LINE DO NOT CROSS ribbon was gone. The little shack looked dark, deserted. I went up the steps and knocked on the door. I hadn't thought at all for hours, in limbo waiting for an explanation.

"Who is it?" said Hal's voice from inside.

"Me," I said, "Chloe."

"Come in."

The town lay below me, lights just beginning to come on. People finishing dinner, putting the kids to bed, watching television. I went in and closed the door behind me, closed the door on ordinary life. I felt like someone who'd gotten the verdict on an illness—and the verdict was terminal. Everything was charged with new meaning.

Hal sat cross-legged on a mattress. He wore a loose white Mexican shirt, a guayabera, and khaki pants. There was just enough light left to see a kerosene lamp, unlit, on the table made of boards and cement blocks, a poster I hadn't noticed before: the Maharishi looking down, smiling beatifically. *Welcome to 1967, where nothing has happened yet.*

"Hi," I said. "Am I bothering you?"

"No." He smiled at me, as though he were the host at a tea party and I an invited guest. "I'm just waiting. I thought I was going to meditate, but too many extraneous thoughts kept coming."

"Strange thoughts," I said.

"What?"

"Nothing. Just something a little boy said to me once. People meditate to get rid of strange thoughts." I had thoughts too strange to think, too scary.

We sat there for a while. In the near-dark, Hal's face seemed illuminated by some inner light, the kind of light you see in the face of an actor, ordinary, even plain, before he walks onstage and is transfigured once he gets there. He'd always been on a stage: playing to some higher power. *How am I doing, God? Not so good, Hal.*

"I like this room, Hal. I guess I told you that already." My voice was placating, as if to tell him he had nothing to fear from me. I had an inane smile on my face.

"It's myself," he said, "before I knew myself."

"Do you know yourself now, then?"

He looked down at his hands. He folded them, then began to move them in an old childhood game: here's the church, here's the steeple. He stopped at the steeple. He looked oddly childish.

"I told you my father was a Baptist minister," he said. "My parents were old when I was born. I was the only child. I guess they tried to love me, but they stifled me. They had no concept of beauty. I'll always remember sitting with them in the dining room where we ate dinner. They had a mahogany dining room suite. My mother was so proud of it. She was a house-proud woman and it was an expensive item inherited from some relative who was dead. It was dark, dark wood. It stood on a dark rug and not one picture hung on the walls, not one plant grew in that dark house, as we sat there and ate starchy horrible food, vegetables cooked in bacon grease. We sat in complete silence. They were old. They had nothing left to say to each other and they couldn't think of anything to say to me. The room bore down on us and I promised myself I'd never live in darkness again." He paused. "Yes," he said. "I know myself."

I took a chance, drew a breath, and asked, "Frank?"

He didn't seem surprised. "That's what Danny said to me when he got in the camper. I saw him over at the gas station. I thought he was alone, on his way back to Dudley. I knew he went to Tucson a lot. I waved at him and he came running over. He got in the camper."

He paused and said in an aside, "I'd light the lamp, but it might scare the man off."

"Do you think we'll catch him?" I said.

"We're going to try."

"I was coming back from the retreat," Hal went on. "It was in the White Mountains and I'd stopped in Benson to get gas on my way to Tucson. Danny got in the camper. 'You're just who I need to see,' he said. 'Let's go for a drive, Frank.'"

I held my breath for a moment, then exhaled. "And what did you say?"

Hal looked at me. "I said, 'Frank who?'"

I felt a wave of relief. For a second, I stared at him. "What do you mean?"

"He didn't know what he was talking about. I told him so. He got mad. Meanwhile, I just drove. I drove back onto the freeway. I wasn't thinking clearly."

I took a deep breath. "Things are getting pretty crazy, Hal. It's all mixed up and we have to figure out how it got so mixed up."

I opened the manila envelope and slid out the photograph of the man Josh Cohen said was Frank Auerbach, handed it to Hal. He held it in the light of the lantern.

"Well, I can't say it's not flattering," he said. "Where'd you get this?"

"It's you, Hal, isn't it? The man who took it says he took it in 1975, in April, at a photography seminar. Josh. Josh Cohen. He says you were there and he took a picture of you."

"In 1975? I don't recall someone taking a picture of me in 1975, in the desert."

"He said you didn't know he was doing it. He said you told everyone not to, that taking pictures steals your soul."

"And maybe it does," said Hal. "Maybe it does. Well, I wanted to be remembered. I guess I was, with a vengeance."

I pulled out the other picture and handed it to him. "This is a picture of Frank, supposedly. Obviously not you."

He took it and looked at it. He didn't look at it closely at first, as if he already knew it. He looked up at me, then back at the photograph, the xerox, as if drawn irresistibly. He looked at it for a long time. He traced the elements of it with his finger. Then he lay it on the table, facedown. "The landlady. We used to call her Jo-Jo."

"No," I said. "No, Hal. What are you talking about?"

He wasn't listening to me. "She loved us so much. She saved me. At least I thought she did."

"This isn't a photograph of Frank? She gave me the wrong photograph. To protect you." But it didn't make sense.

"You always did like all the details," he said. "But that's good. A probing mind. I can't say I ever expected you to be my nemesis."

"You'd better keep explaining. You know I don't want to be your nemesis."

"I know," said Hal. "All you want is what I can't give you. But Danny kept saying to me, 'I saw a picture of you at Josh Cohen's with your name written on the back.' I didn't really know who Josh was. Then he explained and I remembered. I hadn't known he'd taken a picture of me. Here I was in danger all these years, that photograph ticking away, set to go off years later."

I bit my lip, still waiting for the explanation, the redemption. "Then you are Frank? Does that mean you did it?"

"Did what?"

"Murdered Louis Barnett and Cynthia Miller. Set fire to their house, did you do it, Hal? Or do you know who did and you had to run away? Are you protecting someone or what?"

"Danny kept asking me that. 'Who are you trying to save?' he asked. Danny wanted me to explain it and make it go away. That's what you want me to do, isn't it? Make it go away."

"I don't want there to be anything that has to go away."

"He kept going on and on. Asking the same questions over and over. *James's brother,* I kept thinking, *this is James's brother.* Danny was obsessed with what he thought he knew. I don't think he ever thought about the effect it would be having on me if it were true. James's brother, the one good thing I ever did, the one thing I thought could save me. I kept driving. There were tears in my eyes. I could hardly see, I could hardly steer the damn camper. It was crazy.

"Then Danny said, 'I can't be in the same car with you. You killed Kristi's father,' and he opened the door and jumped out. Crazy. Like a little kid who was pissed off."

He rubbed his beard, looked around the room, slowly turning his head until his eyes met mine. I could make out only the whites, disembodied. "You want to jump out too?"

"But you let him? You just drove on?"

"No. I mean, not on purpose. I couldn't stop right away, there was a massive truck behind me and on those freeways you have to keep going. I checked the milepost where I was and drove to the next exit, got off, before I realized I couldn't get back on and drive back. I had to go to the other side, drive that way, to the next exit on the other side. When I finally got back to where Danny had jumped, he was gone. I got out of the camper and walked around, called his name. I have a flashlight, a really good one, that I use on retreats. Very high-powered. I shone it around. I kept thinking about what he'd said when he jumped: 'You killed Kristi's father.'"

"Oscar. Oscar probably had already picked him up."

"Anyway," said Hal, "I searched for a long time, I even walked down into the desert, god, maybe a mile or so, calling his name.

"After a while I had to give up. So I got back in the camper and drove into Tucson. The only thing I could see that could have happened was that he hadn't really been hurt, that he'd caught a ride from someone. I didn't know what he planned to do next. He's an unpredictable person, your brother."

"And now you know," I said. "Whatever's going on, Danny's protecting you. Whatever's going on, he forgives you, because he's lying about the amnesia."

"He never said that directly to me at the hospital," said Hal, "but I knew he was lying to everyone."

"Anyway," I said.

"Back when it happened, I couldn't figure his thought processes, what he planned to do with his knowledge. I put it in the hands of fate. I'd done that once before in my life and I guess I thought it would work out again. That I had some special purpose, and that made me protected. Whatever happened, happened. I spent the night at the Windward House. I was emotionally spent. I couldn't sleep. I was half waiting for Danny to show up, or even the police. I kept on thinking about what Danny had said, 'You killed Kristi's father.'"

"But you didn't, did you?"

"All those years, and everything wiped out." He put his hands over his eyes.

I began to weep.

Hal lay down on the mattress. "Cold," he said.

I took his hand. It was like ice. I took off my raincoat and covered him with it, forgetting about the gun in the pocket. It clunked and I took it out and set it on the floor. I wasn't afraid of Hal. How could I be afraid of Hal? I realized I'd been in love with him for years, always hoping he would reveal himself to me.

I lay down beside him as if to warm him. I still loved him; silly, I kept thinking about Jane Eyre and Mr. Rochester. She gets him in the end, when he's finally reduced to an invalid, when the spirit she secretly loved him for is gone. I'd stopped crying.

"Even when I came to Dudley the next day," Hal went on, "I thought I could get hold of Danny, talk to him, persuade him he'd made a mistake. I had to hope he wouldn't tell you about it first. But if he did, I thought I could convince you otherwise."

"I'm easy," I croaked. "Palm me off with a poem. Convince me now, Hal. Tell me. Tell me the story."

"Frank's dead; he's been dead for fifteen years. I set fire to the house. The fire that killed Frank and Cynthia. Cynthia was beautiful, everyone thought so. But not as beautiful to me as Frank. I'm not Frank, I'm Louis. Louis Barnett, Kristi's father."

"But how—I mean, Danny just happened to meet her," I said.

"Of course not. I set it all up. I tracked Abbie down. Poor little

Abbie. Of course she would marry a therapist. I arranged things so I would meet Otto at a conference. I wanted to make a connection with Kristi, but I couldn't tell the truth. So I had Danny and Kristi to dinner."

"She was just his type," I said sadly. I closed my eyes.

"It was the best I could do—if I told her who I was, then I was facing a murder charge."

"What now?" I said.

"It's the new moon and we're going to sit here and catch whoever it was who killed my daughter," said Hal.

chapter thirty-one

"LOUIS," I WHISPERED.

I thought of Abbie, still in love with him. Jo-Jo too. After a while Hal felt warmer.

"What time is it?" Hal said in the darkness. He whispered too.

"Still early," I said. It seemed natural to whisper now, here in the realm of secrets. A new moon and all the stars closer, here in the mountains. I thought, *You want to know everything about people; why?*

"My daughter," said Hal. "If I'd come sooner, if I had handled it differently, realized what was really going on . . . If Danny hadn't jumped out, we could have come back here, all of us, and she would have been saved."

"And you would have been caught." I was glad of the dark. It was easier to talk. My words lingered in the air, then sank under their own weight. I had to wait for Hal to be ready if he was going to explain.

"I came up here early to try to communicate with her somehow. Dumb, huh?" He paused. "If nothing happens tonight, I'm not going to give up."

"Me neither," I said.

"I always struggled against being gay. All the things men say to each other with contempt involve being gay. There's so much hatred and fear."

Now that it had been dark for a while, my eyes had adjusted and I could see better.

"I knew I was gay pretty early in my teens," Hal went on. "I seduced a friend, telling myself it was only an experiment. He wasn't unwilling, and anyway I was always able to seduce everyone around me. I had this power. In high school girls would call me up all the time. I went out a lot and I was proud that I never took advantage of them. That was what I called it, taking advantage, like my father would have."

The moon was new, but the stars shone on the mountain behind the house, where javelinas and other wild beasts roamed. Where men hunted and shot them. Out in the Valley they killed small wild animals and sold the pelts. They didn't care about the laws. Men hunted each other now in places like New York and L.A. and didn't care about the laws either. I wasn't thinking about where Hal's story was going to lead, but I was preparing myself for it.

"I went to college in Washington State. It was as far away as I could get from where I was born. After my experience with my friend, I was determined to be with women. In college I had several female lovers and it was enjoyable. I told myself it was the real thing. My friendships with men, I told myself, were good strong friendships. The hippie movement was in full swing and everyone loved everyone. People were demonstrative, caring. I loved it. I thought I'd come to heaven on earth, a heaven my father would have despised. When I met Abbie, she was determined I would love her. I'd never met anyone as determined, and her illness made me feel responsible for her. I wanted to save her.

Saving her was very seductive for me, as seductive as anything I'd felt up to that time."

He started to shiver again. I sat up on the mattress and tucked the raincoat around him. He went on. "Then when the child was born, I went to see her in the hospital and I knew I had to escape right then or I would be drawn in further and further and I would not only hurt Abbie but the baby too. She didn't even have a name, I left the next day."

I could imagine him as an L.A. hippie, they were the prettiest. I could see him with long, long hair, dressed in a white embroidered shirt, white pants, maybe carrying a flute. Like Jesus, Abbie had said. He would be tanned, his green eyes magical. In the sixties and seventies people were either spiritual or political, James had told me. You could take either route, but some took it too far, some were destroyed by it.

But Hal's story wasn't going to be political or spiritual.

He went on. "I ended up finally in San Francisco and met Cynthia. She was a free spirit, she didn't bind me the way Abbie had. She got me interested in photography. I was still just a hick from the South underneath and she represented art to me. That was how we met Frank, at an opening. I fell in love then for the first time. With Frank. The three of us did everything together. We'd lie on our bed and watch TV, listen to music together. We were physically very close, all of us. It was a natural way to be back then. You shed your character armor. I shouldn't have shed that armor. It was vital to me, a shield I needed."

I wanted to turn the photograph over and look at Frank again, to discern the secret of the power he'd had over Hal, but I was afraid to break the spell of Hal talking.

"I thought Frank loved me, the way I loved him. It was our unspoken secret. But Frank had a secret too. He was in love with

Cynthia. Pretty Cynthia, with her boots and embroidered dresses. Then I caught them one time, embracing, not like friends, like lovers. They didn't see me." He put his arm over his eyes.

It's all right, I wanted to be able to say to him, *I still love you,* but I couldn't.

"After that, everything was poisoned. I wasn't experienced in unrequited love. I couldn't handle it. I set a trap, said I had to go up to Seattle, see some old friends. But I stayed in San Francisco, waited. I didn't have to wait long. Frank was up at the house the very day I left. I used my key, snuck into the house. It was nighttime.

"I thought I just wanted to confront them, have it out, but when I walked into the house, clothes were scattered everywhere, in the kitchen and the living room. Frank's pants, his shoes, Cynthia's boots. Shed on the way to bed. I knew they had to be upstairs in the bedroom. I took Frank's wallet, his keys, out of his pants. My idea was to keep them, then show them to Frank at a psychological moment, tell him when and where I'd found them. But I couldn't wait. I was in a rage, Chloe. It was horrible, it took over my mind."

A crime of passion. He'd always led me to believe passion could be controlled, it was only an illusion, one he'd mastered, and if you followed him, you could master it too. He could show you a world of poetry and art instead. Little samples of other people's passions, safely under control.

"And so?" I asked. My voice came out in a croak.

Hal didn't seem to notice. "I got a can of gasoline from the back porch. I sprinkled it everywhere. It was an automatic reflex, one step after another. I went to the door outside and threw in a lighted match. It took a few matches before things started to go."

Use of an accelerant, Phil Bates had said. *Guy could have burned down a department store.*

What did it matter? I was sitting on the floor now, leaning against the wall. I could hardly hear Hal, but his words reached me clearly anyway. Maybe we were communicating without speaking aloud. A child's temper tantrum, gone adult, gone berserk.

"How did you get away with it? Josephine said it was you in the bed with Cynthia."

"She saw me as I was leaving. She was coming home. It was only for an instant and at the time I wasn't sure it even registered. We were close in a strange way. Josephine was sharp under her silliness. I think she understood everything. I think she wanted to save me."

"Maybe she did," I said.

"Anyway, it was in the papers, on the news, the landlady had identified the couple as Louis Barnett and Cynthia Miller. I was going to turn myself in. I thought my life was over. Funny how it was just beginning and I didn't even know it. Funny how small a thing my feelings for Frank really were."

That gave me the chills . . . I, I, I, I thought, my, my, my.

"I knew it was a sign. A sign that my life wasn't over, wasn't supposed to be."

According to who, Hal? Who did he think was protecting him?

"I stopped at Frank's," he went on. "I had his keys, just long enough to get a few things. I knew the cops would show up pretty fast. I had his wallet, his credit cards. I went up to Portland right away, in the bus, used the cards long enough to establish that Frank was still around then headed to Tucson. I went to that damn photography seminar to get people to remember my name. The phone call to the police was the last thing I did as Frank. After that I hitchhiked to L.A. I was Hal from then on."

I knew how hard it was for people to disappear. There was always a trail. "How did you do it? There's IDs, Social Security, everything."

"It was only the middle seventies. People disappeared for good reasons as well as bad. And I had my looks. I went to L.A. and right away I found someone to help me. He was an older man, an architect, respected in his field, just coming out of the closet. He was easy to seduce."

Easy, I thought, *everyone's been easy for him. Except Frank, so what did Hal do? He just killed him.*

"I told him I'd been on the run for years, a draft dodger. I told him I needed a new identity. He fixed me up, got me into graduate school. My parents thought I was dead. No one else cared about me. My relatives, I didn't care about them, backwards people, of no importance."

"But James?" It was all I had left now of Hal. "Did you love James?" He seemed far away from me across the tiny room. My words drifted over to him. They sounded plaintive, childish.

"Yes, Chloe," he said. "I loved James. I've tried to have nothing but love in my heart for everyone after James. I felt it was the closest I'd come to redemption, that period with him. When you met me, you met a new person, just born. Ever since then, I've tried to be totally unselfish. To leave as much good in the world as I could to make up for what I'd done. I don't think it's up to courts of law, do you? I think it's up to each individual to find his salvation."

I didn't know if I believed him, not really. It sounded like a plea for me not to tell. Like he could still manipulate me any way he wanted. The gun was still lying by the mattress. For the first time it occurred to me, if I didn't do what he wanted, he had it in him to eliminate me. I didn't say anything. I was colder than the cold air around me.

"Are you angry?" whispered Hal, like a lover after a minor quarrel. "Are you mad at me, Chloe?"

I thought about Abbie, and Kristi, and Danny. Frank and Cynthia. He'd hurt all of them. "I don't know."

"I don't care if I live or die," he said. "Maybe dying's preferable."

I didn't know if he meant it. I moved closer to the mattress, scuttling across the floor, reached the gun, and held it up.

"Go ahead," he said. "Shoot me. You think I want to go to prison? Someone like me? I wouldn't survive it." He smiled at me in the moonlight, in the old way, loving and caring. Manipulative.

You could hardly hear the mechanics of it grinding away. I'd never felt the mechanics of it anyway, my instincts had never warned me, and what could you trust in the end, if not your own instincts? Worse, even now I still trusted him.

"We need to be quiet now," he said. "It's time."

We sat in silence for a long time, me holding the gun at Hal and knowing I would never shoot him. I figured it was the last of my feelings for him. Sitting like that in the dark, we heard the noise outside, around the back.

Our eyes met.

chapter thirty-two

I STOOD UP SLOWLY, SO AS NOT TO MAKE any noise, and, placing each foot carefully in front of the other, crept over to the window that looked out onto the back, onto the mountains and onto the stars. I peered out the window.

Hal came up behind me and put his hand on my arm. You couldn't see anything with the angle of the window. We could hear someone out back, furtive sounds, as if they were walking carefully, so as not to be heard. I turned from the window.

Stay here, I mouthed to Hal, but he shook his head. The two of us went through the room and out onto the porch. I had the gun in my hand.

We went down the steps and to the side. Hal was right behind me. When we got to the corner, I started to look around, but Hal took my arm and tried to pull me back. I resisted.

Someone called from the back, "Who's there?"

We stood together holding our breaths. A man came around the side suddenly and said, "Police."

It was Nance.

"Shit." But I held my hands behind my back, concealing the

gun. I didn't want Nance asking questions about where I got it. "Damn you, Nance." I exhaled. "It's okay," I said to Hal. "He really is the police." Under the circumstances, that fact might not be reassuring to Hal. I took his arm. "Don't worry." I wasn't about to turn him in, not now, anyway.

"Chloe," Nance said. "What the hell are you doing here?"

And then it hit me: *What the hell was Nance doing here?*

"Officer," said Hal. He sounded calm and together. "I own this house. I don't have to explain my presence here and Chloe doesn't either."

"You could explain yours," I said to Nance.

"You know mine." Nance wiped his forehead with his arm. He was wearing the same plaid shirt he'd worn at Brody's.

Brody's. I had just been there. It was hard to fathom. Brody must have known or suspected something when he told me not to talk to Nance, but I hadn't trusted him. Or was Brody . . . ?

"I'm conducting an investigation," Nance went on. "Someone was murdered here, don't forget." He said it sarcastically, as if the survivors were careless and he the only one still on the job.

"Murder," I said. "Oh, I guess I did forget."

I was cold. I wished I had my raincoat. It was in the shack. I wrapped one arm around myself to keep warm, and with the other hand kept hold of the gun I held behind my back. I took a few steps, moving to keep warm. Hal stayed with me, moving too. Walking got us clear of the shack, so we could see around the back. For the first time, I noticed that Nance had a gun.

Watch their hands, Logan had said. Nance wasn't wearing his police windbreaker over his green plaid shirt. He wore a down vest. On the ground behind him was a backpack, a strange thing for a cop on an investigation to have. The door under the shack was open wide.

"Course," said Nance backtracking, "she might of done it to herself, after all is said and done—pulled the trigger."

"Sure," I said.

"I happen to be a thorough investigator." His voice was fanatical. "Not too many of them left, you know. Guys who want to see things through to the end."

"You lied to me." My voice was shrill, indignant, as if Nance owed me something. "You were up here from the beginning. When Kristi died."

"What's that supposed to mean?" said Nance. "The investigator was Soto. I was called in later."

"They never called you in, Nance," I said. "Are you kidding? You're all so busy squabbling over territory." My voice was triumphant. I couldn't see I was being a total ass. I wasn't scared of Nance. Silly me. I walked around him and over to the backpack and kicked at it. It fell open. Packages wrapped in brown paper.

How many times had I seen cameras on the news panning over the latest score by the drug police?

"What's this, Nance?" Still being silly me.

"Drugs are being concealed under this house." Nance's voice was taut, strained. "I've been watching here for a long time."

"And you brought your backpack," said Hal, stepping in for the first time. "Just in case you needed to confiscate some?"

"That's right." Nance stepped back. "I did." He had both me and Hal covered by his gun.

Hal moved slowly, keeping his eyes on Nance. He moved until he was standing in front of me.

"You brought it to drop stuff off," I said suddenly. "You've been hiding stuff under the shack, Nance. Stuff you skimmed off of seizures. Right? If you can't beat 'em, join 'em. Did Kristi—" I stopped, suddenly realizing the implication of what I'd been about to say. What was the expression? Your mind is on vacation while your mouth is working overtime?

"No." Hal took my arm and squeezed it hard. "You know that's not it, Chloe. This man's a police officer. He's obviously conducting an investigation here. We'll let him get on with his work."

"Interrupted work," said Nance. "Maybe you left the stuff here and came back suddenly. You drew a gun on me. You think I don't know you've got a gun, Chloe? Twenty years on the force and I just didn't notice? I didn't have any choice but to shoot. That's just hypothetical, of course."

"Maybe you had a good reputation once, Nance," I said, "but not anymore. You make everyone nervous." I pointed my gun at him. "Chip. That's what makes you so jumpy, Nance. You're scared if they know about the drug stash, they'll connect you with Chip. All that investigating was to keep everyone else away."

"O'Leary," said Nance. "No one cared about that blabbermouth kid. His own fucking brother probably would have handed me a medal."

I held the gun out, steady. "It's okay. We're not concerned about Chip either."

"You shoot me and your friend dies too," Nance said.

"I don't care about that," said Hal, "and Chloe knows I don't. I'd just as soon die now."

Nance sneered. "Sure."

"I'm not about to shoot anyone." I was coming to my senses. Because I knew Nance and had talked to him, seen his vulnerability. I'd been careless. "This is crazy. What are you doing? What about your boys?"

"This is for them." Nance laughed wildly, with no mirth. "What am I doing? What every son of a bitch now is doing. Making money where there's money to be made. I got a wife left me for some Border Patrol guy, two boys, can't even afford to send them to college. Why should the dope dealers get all the breaks?"

"That's right." Hal's voice was soothing, hypnotic. "Why should the drug dealers get the breaks? I can understand your situation, Officer. I can understand your anger. Who's to blame you? You must be outraged. And then Kristi—why?—"

"She found out—hell, I don't know how."

But I did. Aaron. Aaron must have told her about the man coming over the hill at the new moon.

"Nothing ever stays here longer than an hour or two," Nance said. "And no one ever comes up here. It's safer than any place in town and not connected to me at all. How was I supposed to know someone's in there sitting in the dark, doing nothing? I look up and there she is, right in front of me, staring at me." He spoke in a rush, relief in his voice, as if he'd been waiting to tell someone, anyone. "She said, 'Don't worry, I won't tell.'"

"But you didn't believe her."

"I did believe her, she said she only wanted drugs, so I'd leave her a little from time to time. This was a while ago, but I'd see her around town, see how flaky she was. So I got in touch, asked her to meet me here, I had some super stuff. I told her that back when they brought it in, I took a little of that Dream Queen from the evidence room, kept it on me. Had a rig I'd confiscated too."

He laughed again. "When she came up the hill I was waiting." He shrugged. "I shot her, then waited till I was sure she was dead." His hair fell over his forehead. He pushed it back with his free hand. "I left drugs there so they would think it was a dealer who did it."

I remembered suddenly how neatly he'd combed his hair, the night he came up to Hal's to talk to me. He wasn't who I'd thought he was, an overzealous, dedicated cop. I'd liked that Nance, even as I'd fought him.

"The window," I said. "Was it you who shot through the window?" I asked, not because I really wondered in this little town, but to keep him going.

"That was a different deal. I thought Danny might be on to me 'cause of Chip. I figured Chip had told him all about it, not named names, but Danny might try to figure things out—I just wanted to discourage him a little. Maybe you'd do the same, considering what was at stake. Do what I did, to protect yourself."

"With just the right circumstances, maybe not your kind of circumstances, but with my own," Hal said, "I would. We're brothers, Nance, you know that?"

"Naw." Nance looked skeptical. "Don't give me that. You don't know until you've been there."

"I've been there," said Hal. "Once you're there, you never come back completely. You're lost, Nance, but there's still time to do something, to try to make up for things in some way."

"She was a pretty girl." Nance's face was suddenly pained and vulnerable. "The world goes 'round those pretty girls and gives them what they want, for a while. You don't ever want to hurt them. You just want to keep them nice and safe, but they don't understand that. They push you away. They don't know what's out there, when you're not protecting them anymore. Sooner or later it all turns on them and swallows them up."

"I'm going to walk towards you, Nance," Hal said. "Chloe's going to cover me. You're going to hand me that gun or Chloe will shoot you."

"Not unless you're feeling suicidal," said Nance. "You feeling suicidal, man?"

"I told you I was," said Hal, and walked straight toward him.

I knew Nance would shoot him and I knew why Hal was doing it. There was one bullet in my gun. I squeezed the trigger. I heard the shot.

Not one shot but two, no, three shots—one that I'd fired at Nance and the one Nance fired at Hal. Had Nance fired twice? I was confused. I saw Nance fall, but somehow it didn't seem connected to me. Nothing made sense. Nance was under a lot of stress, obviously. It had all been too much for him and now he'd fainted.

All these things came into sharp focus simultaneously, as if I had acquired some special vision, even though what I was looking at was Hal, lying on the ground.

And right there a picture swam into my mind of Logan, grinning at me and saying, *Just remember, you're feeling emotional, don't shoot.* I felt a surge of protective love for Logan. It was really pretty funny and I appreciated the humor of it. Logan. Nance fainting.

Hal.

I hadn't had to fire the gun, but I had, and where had the bullet gone? I started to laugh and laugh. I would laugh forever, never stop. I'd always been told I had a good sense of humor.

Someone came up behind me and said, "You got any ideas about the police academy, Chloe, you better forget them. I think that shot you fired off killed a goddamn yucca plant."

Brody. And behind him, Aaron, eyes big and scared, seeing too much behind his grown-up glasses. "We called the EMTs," Aaron said.

"You shot Nance, Brody," I said accusingly.

I knelt, held Hal's hand, and Aaron held mine. Aaron held my hand tightly as if he'd finally found someone strong enough to protect him, until a man came over and coaxed him away. The red lights from a police car and an EMT truck circled, flashing red on us over and over.

On the other side of Hal a medic knelt, inserting an endotracheal tube in his throat to clear the airway, where Nance's bullet had hit. The sight of blood makes me nauseous and my knees get weak, but I still held his hand, fighting the nausea.

More EMT people were with Nance, who lay on the ground in his blood-colored shirt. It was beginning to enter my mind now that he hadn't fainted after all. My bullet had hit a yucca plant, but Brody's had hit Nance, maybe killed him.

Brody was over talking to the police. I found out later Brody had been a snitch, they call it, persuaded to be by Internal Affairs, investigating Nance. That was how he'd gotten off easy on the drug deal. Aaron had seen Nance sneaking up and had called Brody. I'd told him to call Brody that first time we met, if he couldn't reach me. Brody called the police. But I wasn't thinking now about Logan or possible new loves. I was taking my leave of an old one.

I didn't look at Hal's throat, the tube. The bullet had severed major blood vessels; mind and body were separating and he was choking to death in his own blood. I watched the light go out of his eyes, felt the life leave him.

"No one will know, Hal," I said. "I promise."

I kept on repeating this under my breath until Ruth and Annie, wielding clipboards and referrals to competent counselors, came over and got me to let go of Hal so the EMTs could carry him away.

chapter thirty-three

HAL WAS BURIED IN CALIFORNIA NEXT TO my brother James—they'd bought plots side by side back when James was very ill—but a memorial service was held for Hal in a little chapel close to the Windward House. Danny and I sat side by side in a pew, as one by one dying young men spoke of Hal and his generosity, his kindness, his willingness to listen and be there for them even if it took all night and into the morning.

Danny and I held hands throughout the service, me in my usual black, Danny in his own uniform, black Levi's and white shirt buttoned to the neck. He looked pale but better. After the memorial we stood by the chapel door like family and shook hands with everyone.

The day before, I'd learned that Hal had left Danny a few thousand dollars and me the house in Dudley.

"You got yourself a house," Danny said, as we drove back to Dudley. "That's pretty amazing. Are you going to sell it?"

"Maybe I'll try living here," I said. "I talked to Ruth and Annie at the Victim Witness Program, I might take their training. What about you, now that you're rich?"

"You ever heard of Karmê Chöling?"

"Of course. It's a Buddhist colony in Vermont. I visited James there."

"I might go there, become a Buddhist."

"Really," I said. There was a pause. "Right away?" I said.

"No. I want to stick around Dudley for a little bit. That Michelle . . . ?"

"Aaron's mom?"

"Yeah," said Danny. "I've always liked her. I'd like to get to know her a little better."

"Danny." I made my voice very patient. "She's an alcoholic."

"She doesn't have to be, it's a choice." His voice rose, turned fervent. "She's had bad luck, got involved with jerks, you know."

Not for me to talk him out of this, I thought, *not my business.* We drove on for a while through the desert landscape, that landscape I had seen less than two weeks ago for the first time. Here and there shrubs and trees blazed yellow in the red dirt. We were two people who had both lost someone we loved so recently, but at least we still had each other.

"I still can't figure out . . . ," I said, after a while.

"What?"

"Roger O'Leary. I was sure he had something to do with all this."

"Chloe," Danny said, "he's a creep, that's all. Sometimes a Roger O'Leary is just a Roger O'Leary."

I began to laugh. Soon Danny joined in. We laughed and laughed all the rest of the way back to Dudley.